MÉXICO20

NEW VOICES, OLD TRADITIONS

PUSHKIN PRESS
LONDON

Co-edition: Pushkin Press / Consejo Nacional para la Cultura y las Artes
Dirección General de Publicaciones

D.R. © 2015
Pushkin Press
71–75 Shelton Street, London WC2H 9JQ
www.pushkinpress.com

D.R. © 2015
Consejo Nacional para la Cultura y las Artes
Dirección General de Publicaciones
Avenida Paseo de la Reforma 175, Col. Cuauhtémoc
C.P. 06500, México, D.F.
www.conaculta.gob.mx

HAY FESTIVAL

imagine the world

México20: New Voices, Old Traditions first published in 2015

001

ISBN 978 1 782271 34 5

Set in Monotype Baskerville by Tetragon, London

Impreso en el Reino Unido / Printed in Great Britain by CPI Group (UK)

www.pushkinpress.com

CONTENTS

FOREWORD

Stepping into a party or onto a battlefield, we first scan the crowd for friends. On the battlefield the test of rapport is truth. At a party we have the privilege of choice and adventure, and seek out peers and confidants of equal temperature.

Step into the current day and the place feels like both a party and a battlefield; and I can't help noticing that we scan the crowd more intently than before.

I'm invited to write here because whichever of the two our time mostly is, it's also a homogeneous backdrop against which real literature grows more energizing, sparkling out—and from which it behoves us to look beyond our setting for new ideas, invention and beauty. By real literature I mean writing that knowingly splashes through this last honest forum, uninfluenced and for its own sake: that is, art that doesn't hide itself. In this it's not from a sense of personal connection that I look first to Mexico, nor for the rapport Mexico and the UK have long shared—after all, they are fellow veterans of empire and conquest, as well as parallel harbours of radical thought—but rather I look to it because its literature takes and wins risks that all writing should, but which our markets by their nature are killing. The pieces that follow are by twenty of Mexico's outstanding writers under forty, as selected by three of its most celebrated authors: Juan Villoro, Guadalupe Nettel and Cristina Rivera Garza. This debut *México20* anthology needs no introduction save to say: hold on to your hat, but do note as you read: the Mexican book market differs from ours, if not necessarily in ways we could recreate—still, from somewhere in the extent of that difference, together with the odds facing new voices, an exceptional level of art emerges. Before you dive in, all I can do is set our scene: it's the first quarter of the twenty-first century. A battle and a party are under way as this book finds your hands. The battle grows harsher, the party gets wilder, and we watch from the foot of a vertical curve of change. Looking around we're reminded that as far back as 1930 writers like Walter Lippmann foretold the collapse of the nation state as a viable model of human organization. In his own words, writing between last century's world wars: "The inexorable pressure of the machines man has invented, of the liberties he has achieved, and of the methods by which he gets his living compel him to forge unity out of the anarchy of separate states." Today we can see for ourselves that our borders didn't contain us for long, we can breach them at light speed.

So I say all that remains is to scan this crowd for friends. For someone of our same time watching things unfold from a different point on the spectrum. For comrades, peers and confidants of equal rapport and adventure.

And *voilà*: here are a damn good few.

D.B.C. PIERRE

JUDGE'S INTRODUCTION

A collection of texts is not always, or not necessarily, a machine designed to produce the past—the confirmation of one or several careers when we turn to look back. Nor need it be the opposite kind of machine—a future generator, whirring into motion as predictions and bets are made. It's better perhaps to conceive of that same collection as a way of raising windows, from which it's possible to see—to catch a glimpse of—some of the diverse ways in which certain writers have decided to approach their work in the here and now. In the fiction-reality that characterizes the collective imagination of our times, can a collection of texts participate in what the Argentinian critic Josefina Ludmer called—in reference to her concept of post-autonomous literatures, in which reality is fiction and fiction is reality—the production of the present? Why not? Rather than the creation of a literary corpus or the delineation of strict national borders, this collection is porous and varied. It is founded on the strength and strangeness of the texts themselves: the way in which they question our reading habits and guide our eye to unexpected sites along today's bloody neoliberal panorama. It's worth noting here that, although a good number of these authors hold fast to what we recognize as fiction—novels or stories with characters and plots that bring about an "unfolding of meaning over time"—many others look to transgress established notions, juxtaposing forms and mixing up devices in texts that are almost impossible to classify. It's clear, too, that although Spanish is the dominant language, we're in multilingual territory—and the texts written in a combination of (at least) two languages might just as well be understood as original works in translation. The very notion of territory, in particular any territory described as national, calls for extensive revision in an era of both forced and sought migrations. Perhaps, as John Berger suggested of Turkish poet Nâzım Hikmet's work, "the here of [these texts] is elsewhere"; perhaps these written works rely, from the outset, on "readers who [are] further and further away", on that other language towards which they move.

To bring together twenty narrative texts written by authors under the age of forty at the time of selection, to be translated into English: this was the job in hand, entrusted to three of us—all professional readers, yes, but with markedly different reading practices. And, of course, twenty texts cannot be plucked from a pile without conversations, rereadings, differences, debates, disgruntlements, more readings, and, finally, agreements. It must be said that having access from the outset to PDFs of all of the texts under consideration afforded a conversation as rich in textual nuance as in empirical examples. It's normal, advisable even, to start any search by defining its field of interest. It's also true that, once the search has begun, the definition of the field, and the field itself, will undergo a constant process of transformation. Narrative is, after all, a living practice—not a lesson set in stone. If we acknowledge that every aesthetic decision inevitably implies an ethics, we must also accept that what is being played out in these authors' different ways of narrating are different ways of being in the world and of constructing that fiction-reality currently dominated by a state in crisis and a galvanized civil society.

Some of the texts in this anthology have enjoyed the dynamic support of transnational publishing groups—from Mondadori to Planeta, as well as Alfaguara, Anagrama or Tusquets, to mention but five—and their support has helped shape a group of well-known authors, recognized within the national—and in some cases international—arena. Other texts here were first published by indie publishers—Sexto Piso and Almadía are two of the most established; Ditoria is a more recent example—and you will also find authors whose first publications came to be thanks to the resources of state publishers, such as Tierra Adentro. And perhaps this shows us that in the full throes of the globalization of the publishing industry, there is still room—there are still points of entry—for glocal reconsiderations, in some cases even with the assistance of the state, which, not for lack of trying, still hasn't entirely relinquished its responsibility in matters of cultural production.

What is clear from this selection is that there are Mexican authors who write from abroad (Eduardo Ruiz Sosa, Brenda Lozano, Valeria Luiselli), and authors whose Spanish is the product of a constant rubbing-up against other languages: Zapotec, an indigenous language from the south-east of Mexico (Pergentino José) or Venetian (Eduardo Montagner), for example. Some of the texts take leaps of faith with narratives that blend fiction or autofiction with literary criticism (Juan Pablo Anaya, Verónica Gerber Bicecci), or journalism and literature (Fernanda Melchor). There are authors here rooted in Mexico's centres of cultural production, in both Mexico City and Guadalajara, but there are also those who have opted to write from less hegemonic positions (Antonio Ramos Revillas, Carlos Manuel Velázquez, Fernanda Melchor, Luis Felipe Lomelí). The argument that this is a collection of texts (and not necessarily authors) is also supported by the inclusion of a chapter from Gerardo Arana's posthumous novel. Indeed, it's less important to whom the text belongs than who makes it their own from the experience of another language and from another perspective of fiction-reality, which, shaking off the old passage from Spain to Latin America (or vice versa), is now established from south to north, or north to south, passing—and imperatively so—through the process of translation. Anthologies should not confirm any kind of hierarchy, but rather contain—returning to Berger—a space, ample space, and with this cargo on board set out across the ocean. The crossing, then, lies ahead of us. If we're lucky, this will be a voyage—which is to say, a conversation.

CRISTINA RIVERA-GARZA
Translated by Sophie Hughes

LOVE SONG FOR AN ANDROID

JUAN PABLO ANAYA

One Sunday, to help ease the wretched wait for Monday morning, my parents decided we would go to the cinema. While my mother was keen to escape our emerging residential district in the north of Mexico City—with its empty plots, shanty towns and social-housing blocks—my father was tired. There was no time to pick a film: our destination was decided, it didn't matter what was on. The Futurama was the neighbourhood giant and the penultimate screening of the night lived up to its name. A dystopia set in Los Angeles in 2019 became the scene of the first stirrings of my sexual life. As the days passed I realized I couldn't get those images out of my head. I thought then that love was something like this.

—I—

On the screen Lieutenant Deckard is about to be killed by one of the replicants he is searching for, when Rachael—another replicant model—shoots the techno-organism of her own species to save his life. Cut. We're in Deckard's apartment. Rachael's there too. She knows this is the hunter's home and she's one of the hunted. But he's in her debt, so she tells him her plan and asks him a question. It's about disappearing, running away. "What if I go north? Disappear. Would you come after me?" The debt establishes a contract between them. "No, I wouldn't. But somebody would."

With this truce in place, Rachael stays at Deckard's apartment. The last time she was there, the lieutenant set out to show that her memories were lies, to point out the falseness of her photographs and prove that her recollections were implants: a prosthesis of other people's stories that had shaped her personality. Convinced by now that she's a product of biogenetic engineering, it's her turn to ask the question: "Did you ever take that empathy test yourself?" This is like asking: "How can you be so sure you're not just one more product of that corporation which makes human copies with artificial emotions?" A saxophone plays a slow phrase, sinuously, softly. A synthesizer offers a bed of harmonies; the music sounds like neon lights, the protocols for a romantic encounter. Lieutenant Deckard says nothing. He sits back in his armchair, drinking whiskey, a pensive look in his eyes.

Deckard is asleep, but the saxophone repeats the same phrase. Rachael is sitting at the piano, where the lieutenant's family photos are obsessively on show. She plays the piano, he wakes up. "I dreamt music," he says. But he might as easily have said: "I dreamt I was also a machine," or: "I dreamt I was falling in love with an android whose accidental perfection was the exact copy of a human being." Now they're both awake, Rachael takes up the doubt game again. She says she remembers taking piano lessons, but how to be sure after discovering that this "know-how" we think of as such an important part of ourselves is not a lesson learnt by processing the data gathered by our own senses, but merely the functional result of an implant? If Rachael thinks she knows something, or has felt something, she is always left doubting who really lived it: her or the supposed owner of her memories.

In the middle of this dilemma, the romantic protocol accelerates. A kiss sitting at the piano. Rachael tries to leave the apartment. Deckard won't let her and pushes her roughly against the wall. The beautiful android responds with stunning clarity: "I can't rely on my memories." Her last word is interrupted by the passionate lieutenant, who starts to carry out a type of programming exercise:

"Say 'Kiss me'."

"Kiss me…"

"I want you."

"I want you."

"Again."

"I want you. Put your hands on me…"

At that point, my mother—who hadn't come to terms with the idea that I was already a teenager—went to cover my eyes. Still, the images never left me.

Ten years later, in 1992, *Blade Runner* was re-edited in line with the director's original instructions. While Deckard's lesson to Rachael was clearly successful, it seemed just as fragile. This new version revealed that the detective also possessed a type of "know-how" resulting from implanted memories. We discover this at the end of the film when Lieutenant Gaff leaves an origami unicorn outside his door. The same unicorn he day-dreamed about on a daily basis in this new version of the film. The same unicorn that ambushed the sunny dreams of many other replicants.

Over the years, this scene has now and then come back to haunt me. Little by little, a host of questions began to take shape in my head. What would it be like to copulate based on the knowledge formed by other people's memories? How would you weave back together that abstract pattern of propositions and habits? How could you find in a prosthesis—and perhaps all of us are prostheses—the possibility of fornicating passionately?

—2—

The Nexus 6-model androids that star in the film *Blade Runner* were created in the image of human beings, but implanted with someone else's memories. Their experiences are therefore always seen through the eyes of a stranger they confuse with themselves. It's a situation that makes them incapable of living and, perhaps, also of writing their own story. A newspaper column I came across a few years after seeing the film, entitled 'A Theory of Replicancy', underlines this last point. I hardly understood it at the time. Not long ago I searched for the title online and saw it had been published in a book. Now I understand that this "theory of replicancy" interpreted the dystopian landscape of the film as a metaphor for the devastation of peripheral countries, which would be inhabited only by "copies". According to the short article, in geopolitical terms this condition would be characterized by a system of corporations (located in various centres of power), which, through the flow of merchandise and the symbolic conquest of the collective imagination, would generate an international proletariat with a system of interchangeable values. This diatribe reread the film as an unconscious or veiled metaphor for the power relationships between the centre and the periphery, transforming its human copies into the heroes of this "liberation theory".

As I write these lines, this reading feels somewhat shortsighted, as it attempts to categorize the birth of a new species as a simple metaphorical representation of reality. It dismisses the two central pledges entrusted to us by this science-fiction story to help us imagine a point in the future: the possibility of being an orphan without nostalgia, and a well-founded sense of suspicion towards our own counterfeit memories.

Any father who procreates using artificial insemination can

generate a peculiar sense of absence, an orphan-like state. In the case of these humanoids, the man behind these actions, methods and knowledge is the high priest of biomechanics, who lives at the top of the pyramid-shaped tower belonging to the corporation that shares his name: Dr Tyrell. If a pyramid embodies the archetype of the world as a mountain and the mountain as the giver of life, the Tyrell Corporation building represents the dawn of a historic moment when the dream of machines has finally been realized, with the continuous production of human copies destined to carry out the lowest tasks in the division of labour. Children of a father incapable of engendering unique beings in his own image and likeness, the replicants cannot be considered individuals, as their experiences, knowledge and even the meanings of their memories were not generated naturally through their own bodies. This is the background to the ontological drama that sets the film's actions in motion.

Descartes' argument "I think, therefore I am" has caused these beings with superhuman levels of intelligence to question the limits and possibilities of their own identities. Meanwhile, the dangers implied by the Tyrell Corporation's slogan "more human than human" have been reduced, as the replicants' tragic flaw is their limited lifespan: just four years. With so little time, and in the knowledge that their memories are simply the haze of someone else's existence, these androids have organized an uprising to demand just a little more time from their creator. Enough to let them have a past, to build a new set of memories and thereby conquer their own identities: something that Descartes' theory has not been able to satisfy.

In response to his creatures' request, Tyrell simply argues that all living beings are condemned to a finite lifespan and that once the wheels are set in motion it is impossible to alter the ageing process of an organic system, unless this ends immediately in death. Faced with this argument, Roy Batty, the leader of the insurrection, carries out a cold, furious act of revenge: he kisses his impotent father, takes his face in both hands, digs his thumbs into his eyes and twists his head until he hears his neck crack.

There is a contrast between this android's attitude towards his creator and his behaviour to Lieutenant Deckard, the man who is hunting him and has "retired" the rest of his companions. With his father dead and the revolution overthrown, Roy has the look of a wounded animal enjoying his last moments of life by letting loose his most hostile instincts. The roles are reversed: the hunter becomes the hunted. During this chase, Deckard is unable to jump across the gap between two buildings and is left hanging from a ledge. What comes next is essentially a scene that could never have happened with Tyrell. Unlike the doctor, Deckard is no god of biomechanics: he's a simple warrior fighting on an equal footing. And so, Roy saves Deckard just as he's about to fall, perhaps because he recognizes the impersonal signs of a life spent dicing with death. You might argue that the experience of recognizing the limits of his own lifespan has led this techno-organism to show pity for all living things. But the concept of *pity*, when applied to a machine that has obliterated its own father and whose final lease of life is fuelled by a burning desire for revenge, doesn't ring true. The last time I saw the film I noticed that Deckard never begs for mercy. In fact, he spits at the android, which is what sends him falling into the abyss. It seems, then, that the reason Roy grabs his arm just in time is rather a sense of admiration for the type of life demonstrated by the lieutenant: a life lived beyond the needs of the individual. As if by dicing with death he provides a glimpse of the pure experience of the living, liberated from all its accidents.

The orphan-like state of these "living" beings can be seen in their unstable position within the natural order. One of Rachael's memories, which Lieutenant Deckard sets out to expose as an implant, describes a cruel scene of matricide. According to Rachael, when she was little girl she had a disturbing recurring dream. In a bush outside her window, a spider had woven the silk web that would be its children's home. When they were born, they ate their mother. This implant-memory seems to install the original unity myth of a phallic mother in the minds of the Nexus 6-models, in which any desire could be satisfied, and whose primitive body they became emancipated from through an act of violence. It is precisely this narrative of separation that marks them with a longing for a sense of unity with nature, a source of fulfilment, *once upon a time*, sacrificed in the name of a sinful freedom. But neither Rachael nor any of the other replicants has an original mother. Like them, she is simply a product of technology. Without this primordial connection, the replicants have no place within the order of creation to guarantee their identity as a species. Their ontology excludes them from such a longing.

Children of a techno-scientific bureaucracy, bastards of historical circumstance, the contract that ties these techno-organisms to any authority figure, that would legitimize the meaning of their memories, is not guaranteed by any foundation beyond the instrumental rationality of the living, realized by human inventiveness on a sophisticated production line. As Donna Haraway has said, you can see why these bastard children have no qualms in being unfaithful to their origins. Their parents, after all, are not essential.

The other pledge passed down to us by this story involves the Nexus 6 androids' complex sensibility structure. This is what allows them to perceive and experience the world around them on the basis of false memories and what tethers them to their simulated personalities. A cruel trick that means they are still capable of establishing some relationship with the future. While all the characters in the film deal with this situation in different ways, only Rachael gives us a glimpse of the limits of such a condition. It's true that she only appears in the background, as part of the love story experienced by a hired android assassin. Yet in this unnatural alliance between the hunter and the victim, between a man confident of belonging to the human race and his robot lover, they are the first to step beyond the conflict between species that the plot seems to present. Little by little, over the course of the film, Rachael discovers herself to be a perfect, synthetic doll. The watershed moment happens when she performs, through the act of coitus, an impersonal melody brought to the stage by her implanted memories with the precision of a robotic mime.

Rachael first met Deckard when he made her take the empathy test: a questionnaire aimed at evaluating her emotional responses to scenarios with varying levels of drama by observing the dilation of her pupils. This test was designed to prove whether the subject under examination came from the ranks of the production lines or whether he or she could claim to be unique. On that occasion Rachael asked Deckard the following question: "Have you ever retired a human by mistake?" Another question echoes clearly between the lines: "What is the difference between a replicant and a human?" The film suggests that identity is founded on a relatively fragile quality: memory. The hypothesis that gives Deckard's test meaning is that human experiences create a singular set of memories over the course of time. This creates a type of fold in our being, different for each individual, which helps us curb the unlimited flow of images over time, establishing a brief interval where we can interpret any new event based on what has gone before. In other words, those yesterdays frozen in our memory enable us to approach and measure any new eventuality, activating a particular emotional response. Each individual, then, shapes a unique point of view. The experiences folded into his or her memory transform that person into a singular expression of reality.

Blade Runner's replicants almost reach this level of individuation. In fact, Roy's elegiac monologue in his last moments of life affects us so deeply precisely because it alludes to the value that mortals place on the memory folded into our bodies, which will be lost forever after his death:

> "I have seen things you people wouldn't believe. Attack ships on fire off the shoulder of Orion. I watched C-beams glitter in the dark near the Tannhäuser Gate. All those moments will be lost in time, like tears in rain. Time to die."

Listening to this speech, I can't help asking myself what will die with me when I die. Will my love for Rachael die? Is that why I'm writing these lines? The sense of optimism with which the rebel leader describes the wonder of his own experiences contrasts starkly with the level of distrust that the android's phrase "I can't rely on my memories" shows towards any record from the past.

Rachael's scepticism echoes one of the first replicant theories ever put forward. In that thesis, Bertrand Russell argued that it is impossible to refute logically the hypothesis that the world was created five minutes ago with a population that "remembers" a completely imaginary past. Anything that seems to date back a little further, to the depths of time, could be an elaborate tableau put together by a corporation in the mind of a group of robots. The mechanism of these staged scenarios could be similar to that of writing horoscopes, in which the voice of destiny expresses itself through the random selection of groups of phrases from among a bank of thousands. In the same way, it is possible to imagine a company dedicated to mixing—with the intensity of an adventure novel and the continuity of a *Bildungsroman*—photo albums, film and TV images, as well as some more subjective shots (sometimes a little blurred), to generate real industrial personalities. A model that is no longer the copy of a human being: the Nexus 7 android. This simple idea forces us to distance ourselves from any hasty elegy and undermines the concept of the individual that gives us goosebumps when we hear the rebel android's speech. In the end, with a memory like the one just described, his sense of self would be nothing more than a random pastiche.

—3—

> *The tune had been haunting London for weeks past. It was one of countless similar songs published for the benefit of the proles by a subsection of the Music Department. The words of these songs were composed without any human intervention whatever on an instrument known as a versificator.*
>
> GEORGE ORWELL

Being born into an atmosphere of collective dreams finally leads us to personify them, making our organisms ever more subtly organized. Little by little, an efficient body is formed over the course of our daily routines. With increasing levels of skill, we control our sphincters, our blushing faces and the length of our laughter, deftly managing our nervousness to hide or overcome it. In this sense, fiction sometimes does "the living" a favour, creating characters that go beyond any typology defined by a group of sociologists. Immersing myself in another possible world has helped me dislodge a certain character who was beginning to put down roots inside my body. That's not to say that the process of invention carries out some kind of exorcism. It's just that sometimes it can discover a wellspring where stereotypes become transformed. In search of that stream, I decided to write about Rachael and others of her species.

In 1984, two years after *Blade Runner* first appeared at the box office, a radio station was airing an apocalyptic promo that evoked the landscape of the film, but with an all-too-familiar setting: "Out of the rear-view mirror we see the Petróleos Mexicanos gas plant going up in flames." The closing line was: "We are the dystopia Orwell imagined." Various characteristics of the 1984 I lived through were similar to Orwell's Oceania, but the one that stands out most for me is the industrial production of a certain media *cool*ture. I remember how long it took my mother—just a few years after arriving in the city—to digest that extreme saturation of images, advertisements and sentimental soap operas, where the bad sister fought with the good sister over the same man—a crying shame, in my mother's opinion. In fact, our media landscape was not unlike the one described in the novel:

> There was a whole chain of separate departments dealing with proletarian literature, music, drama and entertainment generally. Here were produced rubbishy newspapers containing almost nothing except sport, crime and astrology, sensational five-cent novelettes, films oozing with sex, and sentimental songs which were composed entirely by mechanical means on a special kind of kaleidoscope known as a versificator.

I don't know if the radio advert was referring to this type of industrial production. However, the dystopia I'm interested in is perfectly summed up by the image of the versificator: an efficient device that produces stereotypes in precisely the right way to stir the audience's feelings. In the symmetry of the images it reproduced, this kaleidoscope vocalized precisely those forms of ready-made subjectivity that I eagerly began to take on myself. The world I saw around me became embedded in my body, always through the use of that versificator. I grew up with it and, like a backdrop to my life, it plays a relentless soundtrack that accompanies every moment of my days.

The implanted memory that shaped the feelings of *Blade Runner*'s most sophisticated replicants can be seen as an analogy for our own experience. The daily intake of TV series, breakfast cereals, songs, porn magazines and a long etcetera forms a complex framework of values and discourses that has shaped us more than any national myths, the catechism or the Boy Scout code of conduct. This implanted memory could be said to define our existence just as it did in the case of the replicants.

Acknowledging our relationship with the characters in the film allows us to distance ourselves from our own habits: a chance to accept our experiences as a series of events to which our possible reactions have been predetermined by an implant-memory. This is the first bond we share with the androids of the film: a set of feelings shaped by a memory that has formed our habits and left us with a type of enigma: a ghost in the machine. The anima that drives the machine forward. Our second link to the androids is their implanted personalities, which cause the past we remember to lose all authenticity. We then catch a glimpse of a system built around time-bound robots, always on the brink of reinterpreting nobody's story (their implanted memory) based on the chance events that come their way.

Rachael becomes the protagonist of the first true post-replicant act. This consists of picking herself apart to observe her own mechanical processes, finding a personal strategy to allow her to experience life again. The phrase "I can't rely on my memories" is the starting point for methodically observing the habits that make up who we are. Our habits don't "shape" the spongy substance that makes up our organisms. Instead our body is formed as an organism through the daily exercise of that memory in which our habits put down roots.

As the author of these lines, I take every possible opportunity to investigate how my own sexual or erotic behaviour is shaped, firstly, by a set of romantic ideals, almost all of them based on the dramas found in hair-metal ballads, with a rebel who lives the passion and suffers the misfortune of finally "opening up his heart". After these clichés have achieved their desired effects, we can see how the beginning, middle and climax of my sexual experiences have been adapted to fit the natural progression, in the eyes of any porn consumer, from soft to hard core. In short, I invite you to imagine the substance of your genitals and the rest of your body made up of water, protein, blood, tissue, romantic ballads and cheap porn… *And give me something to believe in, yeah!*

If there is some kind of enigma to be unravelled, it can be found precisely in what, for a long time, has seemed to demand no questions. We breathe air so naturally that we don't even notice it. The same thing happens with the habits passed on to us by memory. A post-replicant act doesn't seek to denounce the falseness of our implanted memories, or try to achieve some kind of ontological promotion (such as the one sought by Roy's rebellion) by arbitrarily distinguishing between the real memories and the silicon ones. On the contrary, it aims to reuse and reorganize those implants. We can think of our set of memories as the collection of pieces that make up a jigsaw puzzle. The image that appears when we bring the different pieces together is what defines our identity. The legacy of this set of memories makes up the "know-how" of our habits. With the phrase "I can't rely on my memories", Rachael blurs the outline of the image shown on her jigsaw puzzle, offering us the possibility of a free collection of impersonal pieces and fragments that we can reshape and complete whenever the present requires a new set of memories in order to build an experience.

Knowing my body is shaped by an implanted memory has led me to conclude that, like Rachael, I need a strategy so I can experience again. So I can think again.

—4—

In nineteen-eighty-always, ah what times we had.

PAULO LEMINSKI

It's the year 2009. For someone born almost four decades earlier, there's something futuristic about this date. A few days ago I peeled the plastic cover off a new DVD that someone had given me the previous Christmas and that claims to be *Blade Runner*'s "definitive edition". I watched the film again. The differences between this version and the 1996 "Director's Cut" are minimal: a few complementary scenes, clearer images and a shade of blue that tints the whole film with the blurry quality of neon light. With these new tones, I relived my old love for Rachael. However, this time I knew there was nothing to remember. Questioning my memories to discover who I was now and how I had changed since that day in 1982 when I first saw the film was a cliché that would contradict the lesson those images had drilled into my body. Instead I decided to explore a different question: how can I make myself a stranger to my own memories?

Neurologists make a distinction between long-term and short-term memory. Long-term memory always relates to questions about who I am and what knowledge I have. It's encyclopaedic and invites us to remember a long story that began in our childhoods. On the other hand, while short-term memory is based on long-term memory, it includes oblivion as part of its dynamic. It selects from a series of preconceived ideas and weaves them together with elements from the world of experience in a form of code-capture process. This mechanism allows us to act again, or write again, despite our own underdevelopment, and is always motivated by the constant movement of our desire. Short-term memory is not about constantly creating a *tabula rasa*, a clean slate to overturn the traps set for us by our implant-memories. This would make perception impossible, and would make the journey of writing an impossible process. Instead it always takes the implanted memory as its starting point, and weaves in and out of it, intermingling and celebrating its infinite variations in each new union with the world.

The post-replicant act I saw in Rachael takes place in the gap between my short- and long-term memory. In this interval I can build the foundation for a post-replicant practice, by following this new code of conduct:

1. I will avoid letting my experiences stagnate in a closed group that claims to give me certainties about my identity.
2. I will accept the present as a constant roll of the dice. Any piece of information might help me reshape what I see as "knowledge".
3. I will prefer an eloquent lie to a handful of sterile truths. I will scorn anything that attempts to instruct me without increasing my vital force.
4. I will transform my memory into a mutant animal, an open group, always on the brink of expansion, conquest and code capture.

5. I will populate my memories with other people's ghosts. I will turn them into flesh and blood by using them to give sense to my actions, just as if I'd once lived them myself.
6. I will ingest any type of story and fragment of junk information, with the hunger of a bulimic girl afraid of such calorific content settling in her body.
7. I will process data on a superficial level. Within the minutiae of my short-term memory, any piece of junk information could reappear and assert itself as a meaningful fragment that demands to be included in my long-term memory group.
8. I will therefore reset what I consider to be my "knowledge" whenever chance hands me a media-based epiphany: the kind that causes some fragment of junk to appear on the surface of my memory.

With great fanfare and with no apocalypse, I hope these strategies will help me access a universe of staged scenes, where everything starts unassumingly at the touch of a "play" button—although it seems that button is always being pressed by someone else. Having dismissed the possibility of feeling nostalgia, these are the only love songs I can sing to my favourite android.

Translated by Catherine Mansfield
From the essay collection *Kant y los extraterrestres*

METH Z

GERARDO ARANA

METH Z

The stone was rolled away

MARK 16:4

Pegaso Zorokin had fallen in love and decided to quit drugs. He didn't think it was a great idea himself. He had promised his girlfriend. Everyone took drugs at school. There was no reason why taking drugs should be a bad thing. Pegaso was thinking aloud, collapsed on the couch. Meth had barely left any scars on his face. Pegaso Zorokin did not look bad for twenty-two. Before going out to see María Eugenia he dyed his hair blue and burst out laughing. He looked at himself in his light box and shaved himself with a knife. He looked so much like her. So much like his wife, his little blue bird. They looked so much like each other. There was just one problem with María Eugenia. She did not like him taking drugs. Pegaso looked at his reflection scornfully. He cut himself several times on the wrists and made a vertical cut in his left eye.

There was no reason for María Eugenia to find out. The young man lit the rock in his clockpipe. The hands spun furiously. He held the smoke between his teeth. He looked at himself in the mirror until his chest lit up. The pipe remained hanging in the middle of his bedroom. He thought about turning time backwards. About not lighting the pipe. A volcanic pulse stopped him. Too late, Zorokin, the world had finally transformed.

Time travelled backwards.

Pegaso put on his zinc boots and started the car. The wizard thought he looked very handsome when he drove. Pegaso Zorokin had messed up again. It was not easy to give up drugs. Zorokin had been high all his life. When they taught him how to shoot up Pegaso had been only nine years old. He made drugs in a lab flask. At the age of twelve Zorokin had been given a prize for inventing Meth Z. Three of his classmates had died while on it. It was important to give up drugs. It was important to stop making drugs. María Eugenia was worth it. Why was it so difficult for Zorokin to understand? Now the rock was liquefying his mind. The wizard felt alive. Zorokin skilfully drove his black Volvo. He put some Can on the stereo and put his foot down. He had just arrived at María's house when he saw himself in the rear-view mirror. Pegaso was nervous. His eyes were blue and there were scales between his fingers. María Eugenia would realize. He had broken his promise. Before he went up to María's flat he opened his case, found some scissors and cut off his eyelids. He put magnets behind his ears and lit a cigarette. He had to lie to María. He looked at himself in the mirror again. What a dick. He had cut his eyelids off. He had gone back on the rock. His girlfriend was going to get pissed off. Pegaso was furious. He didn't want María Eugenia to see him like this. The kid started the Volvo up again and crashed it into a bridge. He climbed out of the blazing car and went into town to buy some glasses.

The kid walked all down the Paseo de los Insurgentes and stopped in the Parque Hundido. It was only three days back that he'd promised he wouldn't take any more drugs. The rock had made its way to him. How to explain it. The wizard destroyed a marble statue in a rage. It was a statue of General Vicente Guerrero. When the rebel shattered a copper sword fell to the floor. Zorokin picked it up. His fists were bleeding. He grasped it and tried to melt it. Do my will, Zorokin screamed sleepily. And a burning magma ran between his fingers. A police patrol stopped in front of the park. Zorokin leapt down the steps. His fists shone silver. The sword had melted. He touched the officer's chest and made him burn. The bullets in his cartridge belt exploded. Zorokin started to cry. He had done it again. At least it hadn't been so bad this time. The last time it had been a government helicopter. Young people committed murder in his country. Young people took drugs in his country. Poor Zorokin the wild wizard hooked on the rock. Pegaso Zorokin sat down and sent time backwards. This time he succeeded. He managed to turn back time. The officer is alive. The statue of General Guerrero pulls itself together, the sword goes back to its place. Zorokin reaches the plaza. The officer approaches again.

"I need to look in your bag, sir," he said bluntly.

Pegaso Zorokin opened his bag. There was nothing in it apart from cosmetics and a book by Boris Vian.

"It's my books from university," Zorokin said and started to cry.

"Be careful," the officer said.

Pegaso nodded. How stupid it had been of him to send time backwards. He should have let the policeman die. Absorb his thalamus and wildly make his corpse disappear. Zorokin went into a Sanborns department store, drank an americano and bought some Armani sunglasses. He crossed the city on foot. María Eugenia would realize. María Eugenia knew everything. The thought drove Zorokin crazy. Mexico City bewitched him. Things, and the passing of time, seduced him. María Eugenia would know. She also had been a drug addict. Pegaso himself had made her drugs when they were children together. María Eugenia was clean now. It had been years since María Eugenia had allowed any substances into her body. María now ate only pears and almonds. He had sworn that he wouldn't get high again. He had broken his promise after three days.

Pegaso Zorokin turned up at María Eugenia's door wearing dark glasses. Pegaso made love to her for the first time and when they woke up they found a diamond floating above the bed. Pegaso asked if he could keep it. Meth Z, his favourite drug, became more powerful in conjunction with the crystal. María Eugenia took off his glasses and burst into tears.

"You smoked a rock again," she said solemnly.

"I won't do it again," the wizard replied.

Pegaso felt repulsed and tried to turn time backwards again. Zorokin had no strength. The kid, his eyes filled with tears, began to disappear. María sat on the divan. Pegaso turned his back on her. The diamond was calling to him strongly. He lit a cigarette and floated off the floor. Zorokin said a paternoster and sank down again to embrace María. María put the diamond into her reliquary. The reliquary was made of magma in suspended animation. Only she knew how to open it. Zorokin had put his glasses back on. He was sweating. He felt anxious. His teeth had clamped down so hard that he had bitten off his tongue. The filter of his Camel was covered in blood. María came close to him to clean his chest.

"Please, Pegaso, go," she said, in tears.

"Give me the reliquary!" Zorokin said, bathed in blood. María put it into his hands.

"Open it!" the wizard shouted, baring his fangs.

With his right hand he grabbed hold of María Eugenia's throat and started to strangle her. Zorokin was crying. He only had three teeth, and hundreds of pins stuck into his palate. His tongue jumped out of his mouth. It was full of little holes. María Eugenia put her fingers into the burning box. Her hand flamed with blood. Her eyes grew bigger. Her hand became bone as she reached into the box. The blue ligaments snapped free of her flesh. María Eugenia took the diamond out. Pegaso opened the spoon that he kept in his wrist and put the diamond on the bowl. The diamond blazed red-hot. She knew how Pegaso felt. Her left hand was ruined.

Pegaso slept, the spoon was ruined. Pegaso's eyelids grew back. The wounds from the meth were cured. His teeth went back into place.

"You are right, Zorokin, drug addicts are a lot like saints. Drug addicts are people who want to become God," María Eugenia said and kissed his forehead.

Later the woman took the stone away. The resurrected man carried on sleeping.

María found her tortoise and broke it into a thousand pieces. Then the book began.

BROKEN SHELL

La destruction fut ma Béatrice

MALLARMÉ

Señor Zorokin, the narrator and conjuror of the abyss, before starting a story crushed a tortoise against the walls of his room. Destruction is a way of bringing life close to death. Señor Zorokin's was an interesting creative process.

The crime, abominable; his stories, we know well, works of genius. Narratives filled with action and future, irresponsibility and confidence.

How could it be otherwise? Señor Zorokin, before he ever became a narrator, was a specialist in destruction. Destruction is narration in reverse. There is always a work of art hidden within its own destruction. In order to find it you need to be brave and humble. Humble above all. There's not much more to say about his method. There is nothing more terrible than a creature discovered dead in its own bedroom. A priest crashes into something and his temple, his skeletons become a work in progress. A black work, a new story. Yes, the process is horrible. In only a few moments, as bedroom and inhabitant are mixed together, an organism is created that is a transmutation of flesh, splinters and explosion. If there is a novelist around, then the event will not go unnoticed.

Every literary text, as well we know, presupposes a way of building relations with the world.

*

A few weeks ago, under the crown of an elm, among scratchy grass and golden apples, a horrible tortoise appeared before me. On its shell was written in thick black pen: Zorokin 1987. I hurried to my room, holding the tortoise in both hands, then crushed it with a hammer and sat down next to its corpse to think. I lit some meth in the creature's ruined shell. I breathed in the blue smoke and started to talk to myself, as if I were a machine, a machine for making smoke and words.

I thought of lots of things, grouped them together and gave them a meaning. The book had begun.

LIGHT BOX

This is my symbol, the word machine.

MARÍA EUGENIA

Dr Zorokin, in love with Steiner's phenomenological Christology and following a method based on intuitive architecture, called the machine Jerusalem. His creative process really was interesting. The doctor gave up all his other plans a week after having started his invention running. He said that he knew his machine by heart.

Human murmurs were audible in one of the machine's periscopes. Weak little phrases that didn't mean very much. He heard them by accident as he was dusting his invention. Hundreds of spiderwebs flooded the mechanism like foam.

Dr Zorokin had dedicated so much time to building the machine that I imagine he ended up by expecting great things of it. It was then that I began to suspect that Dr Zorokin was in fact deceiving himself, waiting for an accident or a revelation. Such things have happened in the past. Dr Zorokin refused to accept that it was a long time since the human race had passed through the age of discovery. His stubbornness was the only force that kept him hoping.

I think that Dr Zorokin was trying to invent something from nothing, like the great inventors in the Salvat encyclopaedias do. When he told me the purpose of his invention, I tried to explain the difference between creation and invention. As I was speaking he cut me off and said:

"María Eugenia, Jerusalem is the invention machine, you can see I'm busy."

He smiled in a mad way, bit a pencil and concentrated on loosening a screw with a fork.

A machine to make more inventions, how ridiculous. The risk in following intuition as your methodology is that failure can be extremely disheartening because it is your hopes and not some calculated scientific procedure that is at stake.

I can't be hard on him. This Jerusalem project has kept him in his right mind for quite some time. A creative mind is a healthy mind, I repeated as I watched him spend the whole afternoon hanging pendulums in different positions. Come on, María, I said to myself, let your husband go mad; let him have a happy childhood.

As he developed his invention I was working on a novel. I couldn't find a solution to the book. The book became more and more like his machine, and that terrified me. The machine distracted me: with that instrument out there I found it very difficult to write. Disorder is extremely tempting, and the problem was that novels demand a certain degree of organization, a certain amount of empathy with the processes of life. Novels, I have always believed, are force fields.

Minefields, Beckett would correct us.

Jerusalem, disordered in its parts and its aims, seemed to me once its shape had finally been delimited to resemble a rhinoceros turning its back on me. A rhinoceros sitting in the middle of our flat. The rhinoceros was accompanied by lots of breastplates and shields, and what I had in my room was actually a knight killed by the weight of his armour.

Ever since the doctor had started work I had felt obliged to keep the windows shut. I was scared that a cloud could ruin his invention. Sometimes I'm unsure if Dr Zorokin is a scientist, a poet, a child or simply an idiot.

An idiotic scientist who finds in poetry a way to recover his childhood.

One day Dr Zorokin woke me at three o'clock in the morning. He had finished the machine. He wanted me to be present at the first demonstration. It was the first time that Jerusalem had been put to work.

Jerusalem, an invention for inventing inventions.

He went over to the bookcase, took a book and placed it in one of the machine's black slots. The book was one of my favourites. I thought that this machine was, or would be, a guillotine. He took a sheriff's badge out of his pocket and gave it to the machine as well, then he came to me (I was crying by this point) and took from me the star-spangled scarf I held to my breast. He folded it carefully and put it into another of the loading stations.

"Darling, I want you to know that I'm very fond of that book."

The doctor pulled the trigger on a repurposed harpoon. He pressed three buttons. He pressed a piano pedal, breathed on a pendulum, and a cloud of sawdust puffed up into the room.

"I really liked that book by Beckett."

Jerusalem acted up. There was smoke and sparks and an awful dull noise, and a sheaf of papers appeared in one of the printer trays. Although most of the pages were black, you could make out a few words.

Just a few words.

Dr Zorokin picked up the pages from the floor, looked at them without much interest and began to bewail his fate, saying that he had made a machine to write poems. The doctor shut himself away in his room. Then I started my book.

ANARCHOSENTIMENTALISM

Let's see. One man tells another man a story. The man who tells the story leaves clues so that he may be discovered. His presence is visible in the way he describes his surroundings, the way that, in what he describes, he discovers meaning, relations and the place the story occupies in the world. It is interesting to find ourselves as we tell stories. Stories, and stories about stories. In the end, we are no more than the stories that we are told. The story we tell. It is interesting to study a man just as he is about to tell a story. Here is a man, this is what all stories tell us. Here is the man who was thought and who thought this story.

I studied psychology because I thought that the most important thing that a man could understand was man himself. I was wrong.

During my time at university, when I went to my classes, it was clear that I was fooling myself. Madness was beautiful to me. Bipolar frequency was the structure of a short story. The past—a novel. I knew that I would be a bad psychologist when I found myself counting the beats in the confessions of desperate adolescents.

"My parents never understand." Tetrameter.

"Sometimes I think I want to kill myself." Pentameter.

You can look through my files; the notes I made on my patients' writings divide them into syllables and stanzas. During my time as a student I edited the material I gathered in the therapy sessions and took it to a poetry workshop run by an effeminate man who, worried about my own health, tried to drug me and get me into his bed.

My undergraduate thesis was a study of the personality of one of Dostoevsky's characters. I think I don't need to say any more about myself. That is the problem, but it's my problem and not the problem of this novel. Every literary text, as well we know, presupposes a way of building relations with the world. This is a novel and I am aware that novels require a conflict. Let's recapitulate. The problem of this novel is that I am a psychologist and use literature as a methodology. Let's order the novel. Let's get our thoughts in order. The problem is that for a week now, aware of how dangerous the method is, I have asked one of my patients to bring me her texts. The problem is that it is María Eugenia whom I have asked. A problem big enough for a novel, a book of essays or a story. When characters are ideas and the structure of the novel is inspired by the personality of a delinquent, everything points towards disaster. María Eugenia was my experiment. María Eugenia was my novel.

María Eugenia hated me because she had to get up every Saturday morning to come in for a consultation. Her father waited for her, reading the newspaper in a black Volvo. I knew a lot of things about María Eugenia but I did not know that she wrote. María Eugenia had black thoughts and was determined to carry them through. I knew this before she ever came into my office. María Eugenia once fled her home in order to destroy herself. She wanted to cross the whole of North America, smoking a cigarette at every gas station. She didn't even get out of Mexico City. She said things in order to scare me, to make me despair and refuse to treat her any more. This teenager did not like me. The girl wanted to intimidate me. I had an extremely strong desire to fuck her. She was like black light. A rebel angel. A beautiful, strange and wicked angel. Her parents said that she was a delinquent. Her father made her come to therapy. Her ex-boyfriend, a Serbo-Croatian student, had been found guilty of breaking the windows of a branch of HSBC. She loved him. She called him Pegaso Zorokin. María Eugenia wore a star-spangled scarf. She always had a yellow pencil with her. She said she was addicted to catastrophe. Nick Cave she found irresistible. German cinema enchanted her. She believed in ghosts. She thought that ghosts were hunting us. She had had three boyfriends. One tried to kill himself. Another had tried to strangle her. The third one had taught her how: María Eugenia, although I am sure she would have hesitated in the final instance, knew how to kill. María Eugenia thought that we all had a right to drugs and to choose our own death. María Eugenia did not believe in God. This adolescent thought that man had come to earth to destroy that idea. Nothing was going to stop her. She was nineteen years old. She did not smoke. She was terrified of cancer. She knew Schumann's *Album für die Jugend*. One day she stole her father's revolver and shut herself in her room for three days. An unhappy D.F. rat. An angel of the underground. An exiled creature. Once her parents caught her kissing a girl. They hadn't taken their clothes off yet. She liked *Dragon Ball Z*. Her most intense memory was of a morning when she went with her father to the theatre. It was a production where her father was playing the Devil. She had had a tortoise since she was a little girl. She thought that it was a bit retarded but she loved it anyway. That day in the theatre her father looked at himself in the mirror for more than ninety minutes. He had to play the Devil and he knew that the Devil lived within him. María decided to fall in love with him. She said this to frighten me; she said lots of things to frighten me. María knew that if she wanted something strongly enough then she would get it. She admired suicides and didn't think that angels paused behind us to think. As well as having uneven teeth, she confessed that she liked the sense of mental emptiness generated by taking shots of compressed air. She was fascinated by science fiction. She had taken part in an orgy. She had tried Meth Z, which was by her account the most dangerous drug on earth. Her boyfriend had prepared it for her in an Azcapotzalco basement. María cut up her jeans with a razor and knew that it is never to late to have a happy childhood. María was studying literature and knew her favourite ideas off by heart. Also, María Eugenia wrote. Fiction. Tales. I was so thrilled by the idea that María Eugenia wrote. As soon as she had told me she wrote I could not stop myself from asking her to bring her stories with her next time. Her texts, more than documentation for the therapy, would serve as the corpus for my experiments. María Eugenia, the next Saturday, arrived with a yellow folder. Her stories were inside it. She asked me to read them. I couldn't wait, given such a signal, and so I opened the yellow folder and set myself to read the first story. I read not only the first, but also the second and the third. No one said anything for a quarter of an hour. I read each of her stories three times. They were her thoughts. Thoughts which made the disastrous attempt to impose limits to and design on time in the world. She called them stories. Then I realized that her stories could be read as essays, but that they had unavoidably to be commented upon as if they were poems. Tunnels where it is impossible to see beyond the tunnel itself. I concentrated on the final story, written, I am sure, with phrases stolen from other books. The story was about a novelist, a writer of cowboy stories who decides, after reading Samuel Beckett, to abandon his work and instead compose deep thoughts. I kept reading until I found a black page at the end of the folder. I didn't say anything, there was nothing I could say, I just saw her biting her fingernails and thought: this is the first time I have ever met a real writer. I wanted to ask her things, the kind of thing you ask writers, but she, on edge, confused my questions, spoke to me about love, about history and about a group that she really enjoyed. I listened to her, chewing on a pencil, as if wanting the pencil to be one that she herself a long time before had bitten. The pencil I would have to use to start writing my book.

AN EDITOR DOWN ON HIS LUCK

Samuel Beckett must have felt pretty lonely while he was writing.

PEGASO ZOROKIN

And the villain just didn't appear. For a moment he thought that it would be the goose-boy, but no, there were only apple cores in the zinc bucket he was carrying. The blacksmith, although he had a suspicious walk, had forgotten his iron mallet. The eyebrowless violinist opens his case at the table. It contains nothing but scores and breath mints. More disillusioned with every moment, he realized that the possibilities were running out one by one. The possibility of a murderer. The possibility of a crime. And, above all, the possibility of seeing Pegaso Zorokin coming through a perilous adventure.

It's the calm before the murder, he thought, trying to explain to himself why Silver City was so quiet. He was sure that at any moment a *bandido* would appear with his rifle hidden beneath his black cape. Even so, the situation was starting to worry him.

The prisoners preferred sleeping a siesta to digging a tunnel to escape from the police station. The guillotine was blunt. There was not a single trunk filled with explosives in the mayor's cart. The Indians stayed in their camps. The pumas did not go hunting. The duels over card games resolved themselves without serious incident. The fog was not thick enough to be considered a threat. There were no cave-ins that might affect the mine's nervous system. The bone collectors carved little calcium-rich miniatures. The Mexicans drank in moderation. The whores seemed calm and not a single cow had got loose.

Evil has its silent ways, he said to himself as he lit a cigarette. In the games room of the hotel an air of tranquillity blew all suspicion away.

At any moment the lid of the piano would blow into a thousand pieces, he thought desperately. But the piano remained unsplintered.

At any moment a stampede of buffalo would rush through the hotel windows. But that afternoon the buffalo, indifferently grazing, did not seem interested in acts of vandalism.

"What the hell is happening in Silver City?" the editor finally said out loud in desperation.

He could not believe it. He bit a pencil and read to himself another chunk of the speech of Pegaso Zorokin, his intrepid protagonist:

> My question, ah, yes, yes, I had a question, I can still think of it, sometimes I see it, but it passes, lighter than the air, I know it well, I have followed it at night. Sometimes I ask myself about the night.

A cowboy speaking like some character out of Dostoevsky and the editor uncapping his fountain pen. Not a desirable situation for a professional with strict editorial deadlines.

Pegaso Zorokin, the handsome cowboy, had nothing to do for the first time in years. The outlaw now drank vodka, spoke about his insomnia and criticized educated societies. After exiguous description, the character had spent the last thirty pages in a monologue. The other characters listened to him in sadness and despair.

The editor, fairly confused by now, took the bundle of papers and went out to read them out loud to his secretary, who looked at him without really knowing what to say.

> If I've made it this far, Pegaso Zorokin said to them, to the point where I can tell my story, where I am allowed to tell a story and to say that this is my story, the only thing I want is the certainty that nothing will change as I live it and tell it. This, my friends, is the only way I have to be sure that my friends and I were happy. Then I'll feel well. We'll feel fine, won't we? He asked María Eugenia, who looked at him a little scared. Anyhow, my friends, the sad outlaw continued, I'm here and that's something; here you are, for ever, you'll never change, I would never dare change you…

The editor had a headache and he went back to his office without waiting for his secretary to say anything, sat down in his chair and let the papers rest, hanging between his legs. He found a cigarette in one of his boxes and opened the manuscript again.

> Is it possible to think and act at the same time? Pegaso Zorokin asked himself. Can you live a thought? Can you write a novel while travelling? Narrative or death, action or conscience. My God. That is what Pegaso Zorokin said just as he shut the hotel door, for a woman kissed his hand and looked over the abandoned tennis court.

This was what Pegaso Zorokin was like now, the cowboy who in his good days had crossed the whole of North America, smoking a cigarette at every gas station and having a good fuck in every motel.

It was a real shame.

The cowboy had got caught up in a rarefied plot. More than an adventure it was a nightmare, the polar regions had entered the story, from the Middle East to the Gulag. Substituting speed of action for the abyss of conscience.

When characters are ideas and the structure of the novel is inspired by the personality of a delinquent, everything points towards disaster. A book to shred in the black guillotine.

And even so, with the same determination with which Pegaso Zorokin closed the door, the confused editor flicked through a couple of pages, looking for the last line of the novel, scared that the cowboy, one of the most lucrative literary characters in the South American market, was going to kill himself.

> María Eugenia, time is fleeting my friend, you and my mother can keep the rights to my crimes, there will be someone who wants to make a movie, the cowboy said, crushing the star-spangled scarf that he carried in his breast pocket. María Eugenia! he said, pointing a pistol at her. I love you and so do all the rest, they really do. A sandy gust of wind blew off his hat. Pegaso Zorokin, with the pistol in his hand and his heart in his chest, forgot about his life. "What is this? Since when?" Pegaso Zorokin shouted and shot his pistol into a blue and terrible sky.

"What is all this?" the shocked editor asked himself in a panic. He took his overcoat and went out to look for María Eugenia, the famous author of cowboy tales.

He shouldn't have lent her that book by Beckett. María Eugenia should never have started reading it.

Translated by James Womack
From the novel *Meth Z*

THE BIRDCAGE

NICOLÁS CABRAL

"Shall I give him some?"

"Not yet."

There they are, sitting at a long table, in the middle of the hangar, clearly lit by the spotlights, while the cage, rusted all over, sits completely still, suspended from one of the rafters, holding something, someone, lying motionless, in silence, naked on the concrete floor.

"Shall I make him sing?"

"…"

On the surface of the table, which is narrow but long, sits, at all times, a heap of files, files rarely consulted but which are, nonetheless, looked at keenly by the two individuals who are talking and, at the same time, chewing food, peacefully, taking long pauses, producing low-pitched bodily sounds that echo on the walls of the hangar.

"They said he sings. I want him to sing."

"He sings, but he'll do it later."

There is, it's worth noting, at one corner of the table, or desk, a lone, black button that can be reached from the position which one of the individuals occupies, stiffly, while the other, lost in thought, chews his food, drinks and, from time to time, belches, which produces reverberations at the outer limit of the hangar, whose roof whistles softly, from time to time, because of the wind, which is blowing outside.

"They said he sings when you push the button."

"When you push the button he howls, he doesn't sing."

"I'd like to hear him sing."

"You will. In the meantime shut up."

In the cage the occupant moves, a little, perhaps on account of the heat, which, in this factory, is becoming oppressive, as demonstrated by the sweating of the two individuals, who are chewing, and who are sometimes mopping their brows with handkerchiefs while they watch, with interest, the gentle swaying movements which the birdcage, as they call it, has started to make.

"I want him to sing!"

"Shut up, or I'll use the club on you."

The person in the cage, who is naked, as we've said, seems to draw himself up, slowly, but drowsily, he hardly lifts his head, he looks for something, finds it, a pencil and paper, picks them up, unhurriedly, and looks, with a frown, at the things he has in his hands, only to put them straight back down in front of him and, incomprehensibly, to lay his head down again, on the concrete floor, although this time he does not close his eyes.

"Give me more food."

"Take my plate, eat what's left."

"Shall I give him some?"

"Not yet."

And so the individual takes the leftovers, wolfs them down, quickly, desperately, as though he hadn't eaten a thing for days, while his superior, silent and imperturbable, wipes, with a paper napkin, his lips, and belches, this time discreetly, finally to settle his gaze on the files, which are perfectly stacked, without realizing that, while he's been distracted, the caged man, who is about to sing, has stood up in his suspended cell:

> woe to them that conquer with armies
> and whose only right is their power

The guards, in their surprise, turn towards the, as they would have it, birdcage, where the singer, who has stood up, as we've said, can be observed, his member and testicles hanging in plain view, his hands firmly holding the paper, from which he has perhaps read the above-quoted lines.

"He's singing!"

"Press the button! It's clearly stated in the manual."

The cadet obeys, and so an electric shock, applied to one of his big toes, where a cable is attached, effects, with a great crash, the collapse of the singer, who, once toppled, shakes the hangar with a deafening scream, a scream which, as it spreads throughout the factory, causes the guard to tremble, as he steps away, with a fright, from the device, placing his hand on his chest, perhaps in regret.

"Don't be a coward, the regulations are clear: if he sings, he gets a shock."

Broken, sweating, the prisoner recovers the piece of paper, which had fallen from his hands, puts it in front of him, reads, for a few seconds, until lighting on the phrase he was looking for—or that is how it seems, as his gaze is fixed there, on the text, although it is soon directed towards the guards—and, when it seems he's about to say something, he sinks into a terrifying silence and covers his legs with the sheet he has with him.

"Good job too, else I'll come up there and give it to you with the club!"

"Shall I give him some?"

"No, pass him the bowl."

The subordinate, with a clumsy movement, gets up from his seat and, walking in the direction of the cage, stops at an industrial container, looks inside it and picks up an object, which they've called a *bowl*, with which he scoops, as though it were a spade, a series of balls of food, which he sniffs curiously, before, having made a movement towards them suggesting he really did want to try one, approaching the suspended metal enclosure and, without further ado, depositing what he has carried there in the opposite corner to the one occupied by the singer, who is gazing, absently, into the middle distance.

"He's not eating."

"He will."

Let's talk, if only briefly, about the cage: its dimensions, which are not great, allow the singer, when he so decides, to stand up, his head a little bowed, his bare feet on the—we've said it already—concrete floor, or sometimes on the sheet, his head brushing the roof, which is of steel, the material from which the bars are also made, bars which, being hard, although rusty—we've said that too—limit the space, which is always lit by a small, low-wattage bulb.

"Can I try what's in the container?"

"Take one piece, no more."

"Mmm…"

The individual, who has remained standing, next to the birdcage, as they call it, as we've already said, reaches his hand into the container, takes out a ball of food, puts the whole thing in his mouth at once, chews, calls out something incoherent, swallows, then goes back to his seat, looks, gratefully, at the sergeant, sits down and, in an access of enthusiasm, lets out a resounding fart.

"That's not bad."

"I shouldn't think it is."

The hours pass and, almost without the guards' realizing it, the daylight begins to fade, creating something of a spectacle: in the middle of the dark hangar, the cage, whose light bulb is always on, becomes a glowing lamp, with, visible in its interior, a pale-coloured shape whose features are less than precise, as though it had been created with thick brushstrokes, brushstrokes which have, nonetheless, outlined a naked body, now standing up.

"Will he sing?"

"We're about to find out."

A vague tune emerges, it would seem, from the mouth of the singer, while the two men look at each other, disconcerted, and, not knowing what to do, become lost in a tortuous debate, one which is obviously indecipherable, until an inhuman sound brings them back down to earth, makes them turn towards the cage, where they register, with some terror, an open mouth, demarcated by the whiteness of the teeth, a mouth whose interior, which is profoundly dark, seems to absorb the surrounding light, while emitting a sound of such magnitude that, within a few moments, it is reverberating against the walls of the hangar.

"Press the button!"

"But he didn't sing..."

"Press it, you imbecile!"

The cadet obeys without further hesitation, reaches his arm out and, almost as though he were letting it fall there, places his hand on the black button, which immediately produces the shock, bringing about the collapse of the singer, who now howls, while his living quarters sway back and forth, owing to the impact of the body on the floor, and new sounds are produced when the bowl, as they call it, as we've already mentioned, falls, shortly before the tin can, into which the prisoner, with great difficulty, deposits his excrement, falls too, scattering its contents.

"You'll have to clean that up. Get him a new can."

"Why me?"

"Because that's what the manual says."

"The manual mentions me?"

"Do it or I'll use the club on you."

With a look of distaste, although without delay, the subordinate walks, slowly, murmuring something unintelligible, towards one of the walls of the hangar, where, beneath a tap discernible from a distance only with difficulty, sits, like a piece in a museum, a tub which, in its interior, holds a brush, a sachet of cleaning fluid, some gloves and, at the bottom, a small, narrow, translucent plastic container which attracts the attention of its future user, who, grumbling as he goes, takes it out along with the rest of the contents, before filling the tub, without thinking much about it, halfway to the top with water, with which he will carry out, and he knows it, the most unpleasant task of the day.

"You sure that's what the manual says?!"

"Hurry up or you'll clean it with your tongue, you fool!"

The guard, lamenting his position as a subordinate, comes back with the tub and the implements, which, with the exception of the sachet of cleaning fluid, are floating in the water, walks towards his seat and, shortly before reaching it, and after showing his commanding officer, by way of a wince, the displeasure caused to him by the task, changes direction, heads for the hovering cell, advancing with regular steps and stopping, decisively, at the point where, owing to events already related, the tin can and its contents lie spilt, obliging him to roll up his sleeves, put on the gloves, put some cleaning fluid into the little container, fill it with water and…

"Good evening, we've come to relieve you!"

The sergeant looks, in surprise, towards the entrance, at the end of the hangar, where two colleagues of theirs, immaculately uniformed, close the door, walk towards the desk, exchange remarks amongst themselves, arrive at his position, stop, several yards from the sergeant's seat, look at him intently, as though expecting him to make a comment, then smile, perhaps a little hypocritically.

"As you can see from the time, you should be getting back to the barracks."

"We'll look after the singer."

"Presumably you were expecting us."

"Although it doesn't seem you're quite ready to leave."

To one side of the cage, or the birdcage, as they call it, which we've said already, the cadet, with the plastic container, full of water and soap, in one hand, and the brush, with its metal bristles, in the other, looks on as the scene at the command post unfolds, watches the unmoving neck of his superior, who, it seems, is saying something to the crisp, elegant new arrivals, who remain standing, waiting for them, the cadet and his commanding officer, to leave the hangar.

"Nobody informed me of this relief."

"That's odd. But it makes no difference: call your subordinate away, we'll take over your posts."

"Shall I ask him to abandon the task in hand?"

"That's right, your shift is over."

The guard looks, with some unease, towards the soldier, who, his shirtsleeves rolled up, is keeping perfectly still, waiting for a signal, a word that will tell him, at long last, whether or not he should continue, while thinking, no doubt, that he is a lucky man, trusting that, by an extraordinary coincidence, the shit will stay on the floor, waiting for the other guy, the less fortunate one, the one charged with cleaning up the—and this is what he calls them in his head—faeces of the singer.

"Shall I leave the order incomplete?"

"Affirmative."

With a smile, the cadet takes off, with some difficulty, the rubber gloves, then, without further ado, throws them down next to the tub full of bubbling water which, in a moment of silence, at least for its abortive user, produces an effervescent sound, a sound which, a moment later, is drowned out by the voices rising from several yards away, becoming louder as the soldier slowly approaches the desk.

"Very good then, sergeant: your subordinate will have to continue with the task already under way."

"In what does it consist, sergeant?"

"In cleaning up the excrement of the singer, as the can accidentally fell from the birdcage, sergeant."

"Should a new one be put up there, sergeant?"

"That's right. You'll find them in the place stated in the manual, sergeant."

The incoming cadet maintains, with difficulty, a blank expression, while thinking, not without disgust, of his next duty, a duty which, before leaving the barracks, he had not anticipated, not even in his darkest imaginings, but which he will now, unavoidably, have to carry out, pretending that it is nothing more than another of the day's assignments.

"Proceed with the task, private."

"Yes, sergeant."

While heading towards the appropriate position, the subordinate looks over at the—as they would have it, we've said so a number of times already, who knows how many by now—birdcage, from whose interior there seems to emanate, to judge from its movement, some activity, on the part of none other than the singer, who, from a stooped position, moves to a vertical one and, as his head reaches the ceiling, lifts a piece of paper, looks at it and, with a bold, steady, even brutal voice, reads:

> If the hoar frost grip thy tent
> Thou wilt give thanks when night is spent.

The four guards, quite taken aback, a few of them passing each other next to the—yes, we've already said it—the so-called birdcage, the others across from it, to one side of the desk, look at each other, their eyes wide, waiting for some signal, some comprehensible, executable signal that will allow one of them to carry out the task which is, pitilessly and in crystal-clear terms, stated in the manual, a manual which, day after day, night after night, passes from each pair to the next, so that in that way, without any doubt, without the slightest hesitation, the watch over the singer in the—yes, we've already said it, we'll say it again—in the so-called birdcage, can be carried out according to requirements, as the sergeant being relieved thinks to himself while alerting his opposite number:

"The button must be pushed!"

"But who should do it?!"

"Your subordinate, obviously!"

"Private, press the button, on the table!"

The young soldier, startled, takes in the order and, once he has understood it, runs, with a fraught look, towards the desk, trying to locate, from a distance, the position of the button, which, a few yards further ahead, appears in front of his eyes, like a black jewel, alone on the table's surface, and shining, as though asking to be touched, pressed, a desire rapidly fulfilled by the private, who, when he hears the shock being administered, violently, behind him, turns and observes, in its final stages, the collapse of the singer, who lets out a bestial roar, a troubled sound that seems to spread itself through the air, as though it were a toxic gas, making the sheets that cover the hangar vibrate.

"Very good, officers, you've acted according to procedure. It's time for us to leave."

"Thank you for your help, sergeant."

The officer—that is, the one from the watch that is now over—signals to his subordinate, with a gesture, that it's time to leave, a signal which the cadet, at first distracted, acknowledges with satisfaction, as can be seen in the steps he now takes, rapid but not without their clumsiness and which, unobstructed, allow him to catch up with his superior, who is already close to the door of the hangar, where, without a shadow of a doubt, a notable drop in temperature can be felt, from a warm to quite a chill one, one that later may even be freezing.

"Private, continue with the cleaning."

"Yes, sergeant."

When his body turns, in the direction of the suspended cell, known among the soldiers—perhaps we've mentioned it already—as the birdcage, a look of resigned irritation can be seen, without much effort, on the face of the cadet, who walks, with steady paces, towards the point where the can rests, perfectly still, flanked by two pieces of excrement which, without hesitation, he picks up, having put the gloves on, and which he places, adeptly, in the tub, the tub which, a few minutes later, he empties into the mouth of a stinking drain at the edge of the compound.

"Clean up the food, private!"

"Yes, sergeant!"

Effortlessly, the soldier takes off the gloves, places them on a rail, returns to the cage area, looks out the bowl, puts the balls of food back inside it, looks at the edge of the floor of the cell—which is made of concrete, we've probably mentioned that before—reaches up and firmly places the container in a corner, before bringing his hand back down, giving a satisfied smile, and walking in the direction of the desk to observe his superior leafing through the manual, sinking into his seat, and reading aloud something incomprehensible.

"Shall I give him some?"

"Not yet."

Translated by Ollie Brock
From the short-story collection *Las Moradas*

EMPTY SET

VERÓNICA GERBER BICECCI

To my brother Ale, the other half of the empty set

The dossier of my love life is a collection of beginnings. A definitively unfinished landscape that extends amid flooded excavations, exposed foundations and ruined structures; an inner necropolis that has remained under construction for as long as I can remember. When you become a collector of initiations, you are also able to appreciate, with almost scientific precision, how little the endings vary. I am particularly prone to quitting. But in fact there isn't much difference, all my relationships end much the same. The different sets intersect in more or less similar ways, and the only thing that changes is the point of view you happen to have: quitting is voluntary, mutual consent is the least usual option, and abandonment is more like something imposed.

I have a talent for beginnings. I like that part. But the emergency exit is always at hand, and so it is relatively easily for me to take a blind leap when things don't feel right. I flee into the unknown at the slightest provocation. That's why I don't want preambles this time, I'll try to skip the beginning, I have too many already. I am tired of prologues, and I could only start off with any conviction from that denouement, that rupture which changed everything in the first place, which turned me into a deserter, a compiler of hopelessly abbreviated relationships.

One fine day, without warning, I awoke at the ending. I still hadn't got up when, from the doorway, just before leaving to teach a class, Tordo(T) said to me:

You're not the person you used to be.

I spent the rest of the day trying to figure out what he meant by that, and I couldn't get out of bed. When did I stop being the person I was?

It all sounded very strange, suspicious even.

I thought he might be having a midlife crisis. But no. I soon realized that when someone says to you: "You're not the person you used to be," what they actually mean is: "I'm in love with someone else."

He broke me. Tordo(T) broke me.

Almost overnight, I had to pack all my clothes in a suitcase, pick out a few books, write a farewell letter no one had asked for, call a taxi and return to the only place where I could go: Mum(M)'s apartment.

I had tried to forget that place on the third floor. Its blocked drains, disposable plates and glasses, the sink on the roof terrace where we occasionally rinsed the pots and pans, the fused electrical appliances and the tin bathtub to which my Brother(B) and I became accustomed as if we were living in another century. I had ceased to think about its inevitable resemblance to a palaeontology lab: the thick shroud of dust; the assortment of skeletons that had been plants, stuck in their pots; the balls of fluff adhering to one another, forming furry bolsters in the corners; the smears of grease on the kitchen walls and ceiling; the grey patina on the windows formed by countless layers of dried rain; and the strange varieties of mould growing in forgotten containers in the fridge.

We never called a plumber, although we could have asked Dad, and we didn't hire anyone to clean, nor did we clean anything ourselves because (we were convinced) she must have left some trace.

We did nothing.

The house remained suspended in time. Exactly as it was the day we stopped seeing Mum(M).

I went to my room and crawled under my faithful old Humpty-Dumpty duvet. I quickly discovered that abrupt ending had caused things to go back to the beginning, to some beginning. Or at least to where they had been a while ago, before Tordo(T). I knew because I opened my eyes in the middle of the night and heard her walking down the corridor; she was talking to herself in that strange, furious language I was never able to decipher. My body got up automatically, I peered out of the door to my room and all I could see was the bluish light from the computer screen illuminating the corridor. But she wasn't there.

I could always find my Brother(B) in the study late at night. He suffered from insomnia. I think staying awake was his way of waiting for Mum(M). He set up a makeshift Internet connection with a telephone cable and Dad's passwords from the university; he only went online in the middle of the night for fear someone might catch him duplicating the username. I would wake up with a start; I didn't want to wait for her, but I had become such a light sleeper that I could leap out of bed at the slightest sound. Although I never asked him, I'm sure my Brother(B) could hear her, too. I followed the light, and found him sitting there, surfing, it was like I'd never left, like I'd never lived at Tordo(T)'s place. Nothing had changed.

You're back, said my Brother(B).

There was no need to tell him anything. Defeat is wordless.

RANGMEBOO

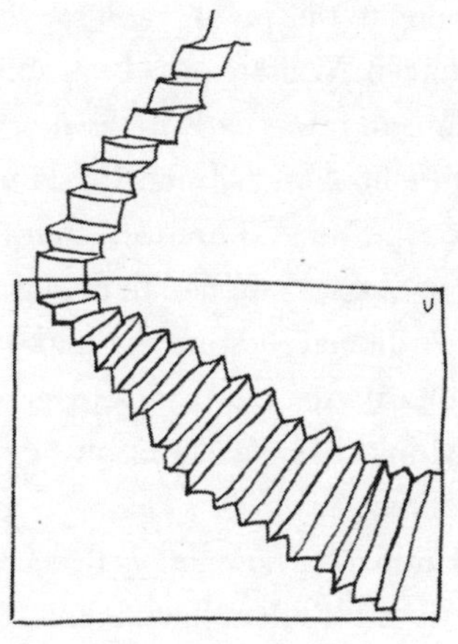

How did we get here, to this point? It all started two days before my birthday no. fifteen. Winter 1995. I am still fourteen and my Brother(B) is seventeen. It was early in the morning, we were getting ready to go to school and Mum(M) said no. She said it was best we stay at home. She said not to switch the TV on, not to switch anything on. She said we had to be quiet.

I never did turn fifteen, despite the dark-chocolate cake we had ordered for a party that never took place. Her interminable absence (that of Mum(M)) stole all our birthdays away, it messed up the passage of time.

There is no identifiable cause, only effects. Correction: only a frontier in space–time, turbulent fluctuations, fitful. Fit full.

Only a succession of meandering paths without meaning. A set that slowly empties. Jumbled fragments. Correction: smithereens.

I repeat: winter 1995.

Mum(M) starts talking about the trees in the park. She says she can see faces in the bark. That all those faces are looking at the house. That all those faces are looking at us.

She orders us to stop watering the plants.

"If anything should happen to me," Mum(M) says.

Like what? my Brother(B) and I reply as one.

...

And then we no longer understand what she is saying.

Or is it that she can't hear us?

What are you saying, Mum(M)?

That's how she starts to fade.

And in the end we could no longer see her.

8/8/76

Marisa,

I've decided to change your name. In my diaries you're called Lina.

I've never written to anyone the words I write to you. They all refer to unobtainable things, except for the mention of your green shoes (which might not even be true), although I can't forget the way you trod on me.

If this were only a word game, I'd carry on playing until the end.

Your (I had written "yours" but I scratched out the "s", never mind),

S.

We behaved as if everything were normal, and yet no one entered the house.

A bunker.

A time capsule where everything remains in a state of perpetual neglect.

Soon afterwards, my Brother(B) went to university and I started in the sixth form. It took Dad several years to realize Mum(M) wasn't there. Sometimes I'm not completely sure he understood, they hadn't spoken since the divorce (or perhaps he's much better than we are at pretending nothing has happened). Dad is a methodical man and scarcely notices anything outside his routine. He calls us once a week, on Wednesdays at 2.45 p.m., because on that particular day he has a few more minutes to spare, and we go to his house for lunch every Sunday. But I guess he suspected something because he always had a brown envelope prepared, with enough money to cover all the bills and he never, ever, ever asked about Mum(M); partly because they were no longer on speaking terms and partly because his current girlfriend was always there frowning and wishing my Mum(M), my Brother (B) and I didn't exist.

Not that we were illusionists, we didn't even come to any agreement, and the act of invisibility happened naturally. It was enough not to say anything. It's easy to let others fill in the gaps. A sufficiently ambiguous gesture can transform someone else's monologue into an imaginary conversation. Silence is a variable which is constantly mutating so that the other has to decide whether it's a yes, a no or another response.

And in any case: how can you hide something which isn't there?

It's amazing, too, how little it takes for everyone to believe your life is no different from anyone else's. In the beginning people asked us a few questions, but, in fact, no one wanted to know the answers. Then they simply stopped caring and, even if they had asked, we no longer had answers. No one remembered they hadn't seen Mum(M) for a long time. Forgetting occurs without remorse, whereas memory demands payment. It confirms absence. Rather than of a pair of conjurors, we were like those two mischievous brothers in Andersen's tale, who, passing themselves off as tailors, weave an invisible suit of clothes for the emperor. We made them believe that Mum(M) was there, although even we couldn't see her; she had crossed a frontier which neither my Brother(B) nor I knew how to cross. We made them believe our everyday life was no different from that of any other divorced family. Fortunately, the bunker aroused no suspicions. Moreover, it was a place where for years not a single person crossed the threshold. The space Mum(M) ought to have occupied was empty, she had left us part of a hole, and the rest was outside the visible Universe(U), in an unknown place.

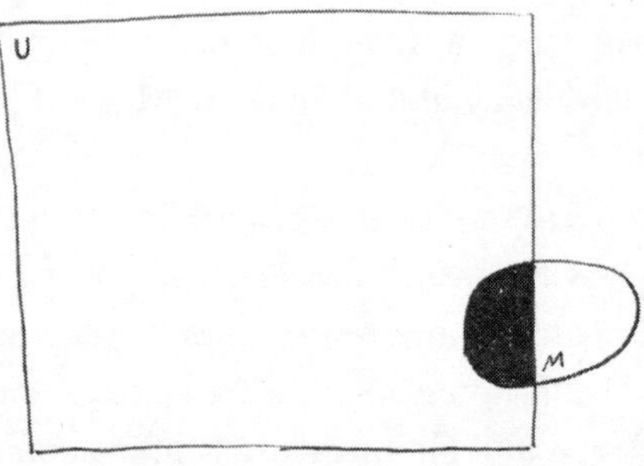

Sneezing and watery eyed. When they asked me the reason for my trip at immigration I couldn't speak. I had spent the last ten hours thinking I might have bought Alonso(A) a ticket for a different flight. But I hadn't. I considered sitting in the airport in Buenos Aires for a whole week until my Brother(B) arrived, and taking another plane or a coach with him to Cordoba. I could get up every now and then to buy juice and a sandwich, reserve my place while I went to the toilet. A week wasn't long.

But after staring at the floor for a few hours I decided to go into a travel agency where there was this poster:

GLACIERS AND THE WORLD'S END

FIVE DAYS AND FOUR NIGHTS

ALL-INCLUSIVE

Why not? Afterwards, I'd take the bus to Cordoba and arrive at Grandma's(G) house the same day as my Brother(B), with no money in my pockets.

Locks appeared on all the doors in the apartment. The windows were covered with black canvas. And so we were protected from who knows what.

Have you seen Mum(M)?

No. Have you?

I lean over the toilet bowl. I wonder whether the swirling water flushed her down. No.

Did she go out?

No.

From the outside, the bunker is solid, unassailable. Inside it's becoming increasingly unstable and unpredictable. I thought I saw her yesterday, I tell my Brother(B)... But I am mistaken. We don't know where she is.

So when is the last time you saw her?

I don't know? And you?

I don't know.

I know.

Where?

We were in the dining room.

When?

You had a bowl of cereal.

That could have been any day.

Mum(M) walked over to her chair.

Ah, yes, with a cup of milky coffee.

She took a mouthful instead of a sip and burnt herself.

No, that was a different day.

It was the same day.
The day she spat out her coffee?
Yes, it sprayed over the tablecloth, it's still there.
Did she say anything?
She gesticulated. Or maybe she shouted.
No, she dropped the mug!
Was it the blue mug?
No, the mug they gave her a couple of years ago.
Ah, the one that says: STILL PERFECT AFTER 40?
Yes, that one.
I wonder where they bought it?
I don't know. But there's a curse on it.
On the mug?
Yes.
Did we go to school in the end that day or not?
I don't think so.
What happened to the mug?

OBSERVATION SHEET III

LOCATION: roof terrace towards the sky
DATE: 1st October 2003
LIGHT POLLUTION (1–10): 7, evening
OBJECT: cloud
CONSTELLATION: AeroMéxico
SIZE: Boeing 747
LOCAL TIME: 18.30
DIRECTION: unknown
EQUIPMENT: telescope
FILTER: no
OBSERVATION:

NOTES

For a while I was obsessed with aeroplanes. They seemed like the perfect symbol of my family history. Aeroplanes had separated us, and, occasionally, they brought us together again. They are also the nearest thing to a time machine. When I land in Argentina, where my Grandma(G) lives, I always feel as if I am in another time or in a previous life, which I can scarcely remember.

According to my Brother(B) we had turned into a couple of professional *suspicionists*. We had great difficulty believing that events didn't always have a dark side, a shadowy space which we couldn't see, and which, despite being empty, always had some other meaning. People often say things aren't black and white; I'm not so sure. Black and white are nothing more than problems of light, of the wholeness or the absence of light. Black is emptiness and white is fullness, or at least that's what I learnt at art school. No matter, the point is that the things we are unable to see aren't hidden in the mixtures of grey, or in the white or in the black, but rather in the thin line separating those two wholenesses. A place we can't even imagine, a horizon of no return. It is at the edges where everything becomes invisible. There are things, I'm sure, that can't be told with words. There are things that only occur between the black and the white, and very few can see them. Something similar happened to Mum(M): an optical illusion, an inexplicable enigma of matter. And to Tordo(T) as well, although in his case, recreating the sequence was relatively easy.

The last thing he said to me was:

Something broke, I don't know exactly what, but we can't be together any more.

He didn't know what had broken?

But I needed to find out.

And so I ran through the sequence of events again and again, I cut out minutes here and there, and I ended up realizing what was obvious: we are always doing a drawing we can't see the whole of. We only have a side, an edge of our own story, and the rest is hidden. It isn't worth recounting the details of the break-up, but the process was more or less the following:

Once upon a time there was an intersection IT:

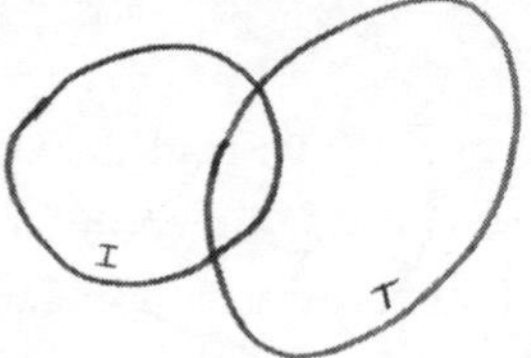

Suddenly, in the intersection IT an empty space appears:

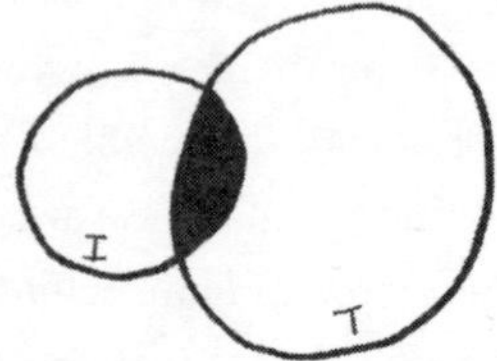

In fact, this space is indicative of the intersection TH which I is unable to see:

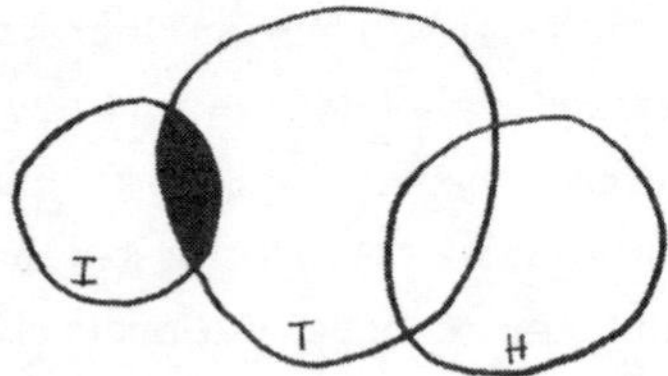

And so T moves away with H and I is left with the hole:

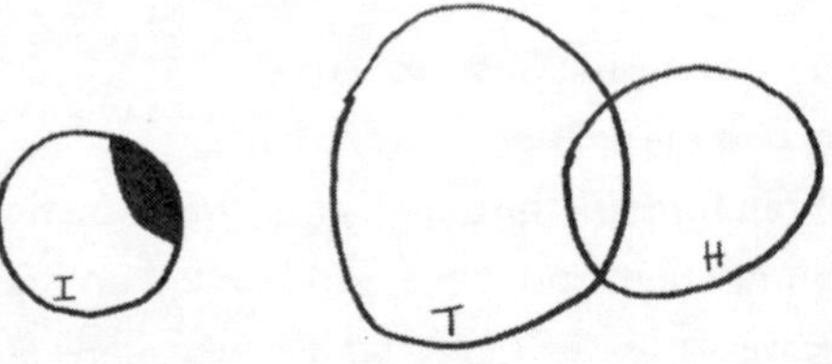

I am I, Tordo is T and H is Her.

Conclusion: I was the only one broken, and I'm not sure whether I am still carrying the hole around or whether a piece of me is missing:

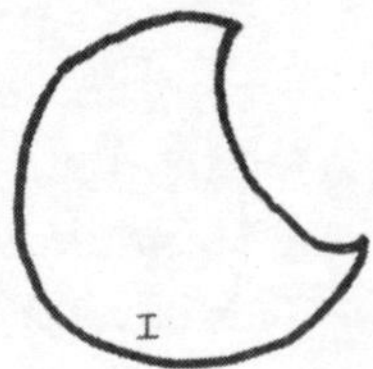

A long and lonely period awaited me in the old bunker. My Brother(B) went to live with his girlfriend the same week I came back. I helped him move some boxes of books and records, two suitcases of clothes and his pillow. We made a couple of journeys on foot, his new apartment was a few blocks away. In the bunker there were chests and cupboards crammed with useless objects (and coated with dust, as if Popocatépetl's smoke hole had spewed out all its ash there) but he didn't want to take any of them. Seven years had passed and we were still trying to keep the spell going. Although we were no longer very clear exactly what it consisted of. My first night alone, I heard Mum(M) talking in the living room again. The light from the computer no longer illuminated the corridor, and so I felt my way along the walls. Nobody. I went back to bed.

I had to start doing something, anything.

Either that or go crazy.

After careful deliberation, I decided that out of all the problems in Mum(M)'s apartment the most worrying was the damp seeping through the main wall in the living room, because it meant that one side of the bunker was crumbling. The wall was bulging and the paint had formed blisters which you could pop with your fingers. The outside was forcing the inside to give way. I didn't want the bunker to suck me in for ever, and yet, after all this time, I couldn't let the system collapse either. I got up the next day determined to solve the problem; I found the number of a timber yard in the yellow pages and ordered three sheets of three-ply plywood (each measuring 122 cm x 244 cm and a centimetre thick) to cover and strengthen the wall. The sheets arrived very quickly and floated in through the balcony because they wouldn't fit through the door. I created a workspace on the living-room floor, in the middle of all the furniture. I spent several days sanding, filling in holes and resanding imperfections until they were completely smooth. On top of the film of dust on the furniture a layer of sawdust settled. When I finished, I stood looking at them as I might a blank canvas, although the surface wasn't completely empty. The veins in the wood made a pattern. Some veins were wider than my little finger, others much narrower. I traced one that was the exact same width as my forefinger. There wasn't much to think about, I just had to fill a given shape without spilling over the edges; it was the leisurely pursuit of a pensioner, but one that required almost Zen-like levels of concentration that could help me to kill time. I had some black and white paint, two "non-colours" and their possible combinations.

Mum(M) used to call Dad "Lito", affectionately. I once heard her say that was his revolutionary name. Then Dad said he had never been a revolutionary and didn't have a secret name, he simply handed out leaflets in factories. In my family, everyone contradicts one another until in the end all that's left are holes. Worse: no one wants to talk about the holes. In primary school I understood that my "nuclear family" lives in Mexico, and the idea seemed right because I imagined an explosion scattering us all around the globe. That bomb, in our case, is called dictatorship. And the explosion, exile. Mum(M) also declared that dad was blacklisted and then, infuriated, she said everyone was blacklisted. That was all. What we heard reached us in a jumbled way, a load of random anecdotes which in my head were nothing but pure chaos.

18th October

Solona,

m'I, ngninpla na dne fo arye pirt ot Natigenar.

d'I keli uoy ot meco. Tahw od uoy yas?

V

He didn't reply.

Tordo(T) is an artist, but he would like to have been a writer. He invented a new name for me every day, as if he were trying out characters. And occasionally he would search for similarities between me and the actresses in the films we saw together; he always found something, some detail. I, on the other hand, wanted to be an artist, and yet I thought about almost everything in words. My fellow art-school students said that this was extremely odd.

Tordo(T) turned up for our only date showing off the tattoo he'd just had done at a famous studio; I didn't know the place, and hadn't even heard of it, but I said nothing. He peeled back the gauze rather arrogantly, his shoulder was still swollen and streaked with dried blood. It was a view from above of him halfway across a tightrope. He'd had a tattoo done of himself! That should have been the signal for me to run a mile. I didn't. I thought his tautological gesture brilliant. Later on, of course, I changed my mind. In any case, I was implicated in the metaphor of him walking on a tightrope at the same time as we started seeing each other; but more disturbing was the idea of two Tordo(T)s occupying the same body. His tattoo could have been an omen and I failed to see it: he did of course end up splitting into two. I don't know, possibly I was attracted to the idea of waiting for him at one end of the rope, hoping he would choose to walk towards me… Obviously I wasn't seeing things clearly because eventually he went off in the other direction.

Two Universes(U).

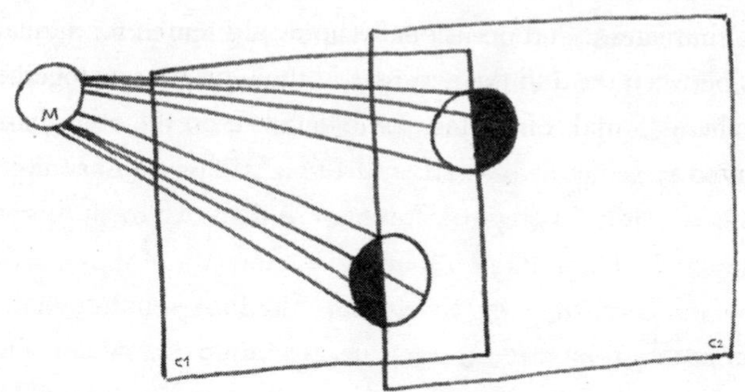

Or, rather, two countries:

Argentina(C1)

Mexico(C2)

And Mum(M)

Perhaps if we could learn to be in two places at once.

Mum(M) found a way of staying right in the middle, in a place where no one could find her.

In order to forget someone you have to become extremely methodical. Heartbreak is a kind of illness that can only be fought against with routine. I didn't know that, my survival instinct discovered it. And so I started finding things to do, and following a schedule. All morning I would lie on my front on the big sheet of wood tracing the pattern of a vein with a paintbrush dipped in black, white or grey paint. No more than two or three veins a day. If I tried to paint a fourth my hand would start shaking and I'd go over the edge. Sometimes I had to use a three-haired paintbrush, sometimes a small decorating brush. Above all, it was an exercise in patience.

As I painted, I remembered my sculpture teacher from my first year at La Esmeralda art school. He was Japanese. Despite living in Mexico for twenty-five years he spoke Spanish as if he had just arrived, meaning he hardly spoke any Spanish. His main concern in sculpture was that we understand the life cycle. For our first class, he took us on the underground to buy four hens at La Merced market. In a kind of pagan baptism we decided to name them Klein, Fontana, Manzoni and Beuys. They lived in an enormous cage in the studio for the whole term. Twice a week we would take them for a walk through the school courtyards; there was a rota for feeding them on the blackboard, and some people, I don't really understand how, actually grew fond of them. At the end of term, Mifusama Suhomi arrived with a huge cooking pot and a mound of charcoal and told us we had to kill them.

There was a profound silence. He wrung their necks himself and then we plucked them. He cooked a soup which we all had to eat in order to complete the cycle. Rife—Death—Rife, he said. I've never tasted anything like it since. I don't know whether he was a good artist or not, but he certainly had a flair for cooking. And although his Spanish was poor, he used words precisely, the way a sensei would. Two were more than adequate to convey something as elemental and complex as that things begin, then end, then begin again.

His teaching methods were very odd: he showed us what plaster is and how it is made instead of how to use it to make moulds and casts. And where marble comes from instead of giving us a hammer and chisel. It was the same with wood: to may pwywood (trwee gylate ensai big penceawl chal-pener) woo shawing fratten en big shee. In his class I discovered that the veins in wood reveal in great detail the adventures of a specific period in the life of a tree. I liked to believe this, that each vein in my sheets of plywood was telling me a different story so that I didn't have to think about my own. The area between each vein corresponds to a ring on the tree trunk, and each ring corresponds, roughly, to a year in the life of the tree. Then I discovered there is a science that studies this. Dendrochronology can calculate the age of a tree by counting the radial growth of the rings inside its trunk from the centre outwards. I would have liked to be a dendrochronologist. But you can't see the age of a tree in my plywood sheets. The big, gyrating pencil sharpener slices the trunk at an angle. Cutting on the diagonal shuffles everything: in each shaving there are different, random moments in the tree's life, not a linear chronology, much less a concentric one.

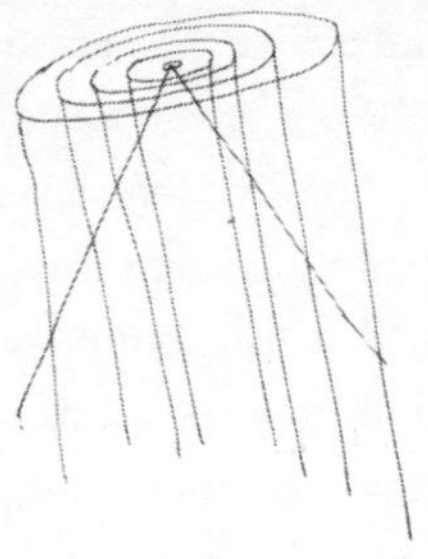

Mifusama Suhomi gave us each a pencil and a sharpener. Then, after several attempts, he told us: shawing pelfec, nao you. It was cone-shaped. Something very similar to this is what is then flattened into layers to produce plywood. In the bunker I had three sheets of wood in which time was shuffled and layered. I wish that was possible: to shuffle time. I'd like to invent a science that investigates the way plywood shuffles time. It would be good to move around the moment when some things happen, to put endings at the beginning, for example. Or the past in a future far enough away to ensure we never reach the moment when we have to confront it. I spent the morning in this kind of speculation.

Translated by Lorenza Garcia
From *Conjunto Vacío*

RED ANTS

PERGENTINO JOSÉ

Mao cha nzo go? I say—*Does anyone live in this house?* but the red ants pay me no mind.* They're busy with their work. I come down the stairs inside the entranceway, taking my shoes off so as not to make any noise. There's a woman with a fan:

"The people here cast no shadows," she says, "and their footsteps make no sound."

She's right, there's no sound at all. I put my shoes back on. The house is awash with warm air. Someone comes over—a man in a soldier's uniform. What am I doing here, he wants to know.

"I'm looking for Georgina," I say.

"You have to give me more than that," he says.

"She hasn't been home in two days, her daughter's beside herself."

"Go on," the official says, making a note in a dog-eared logbook. He murmurs something I don't catch.

"Looking for Georgina, is that it?" he says, sneering at me now. "We've had a lot of problems with the illness this year, more than ever. Come this way, if you'd be so kind."

He holds out a card, green in colour and bearing a photograph of Georgina's face.

"I hadn't expected to find a photo of her here," I say.

"I don't know what you mean," says the official. "It must be your memory. This is just a card, it has a green background but otherwise it's blank."

---

* The original is in both Spanish and Zapotec, the latter being one of seventy or so indigenous languages spoken in Mexico.

The sound of a violin drifts in my direction. A little way off there's a courtyard with chairs and ferns and spiny reeds. The music builds, like the winds of a great hurricane.

"Excuse me," says the official. "Would it frighten you if I asked you to come underground? Down these stairs?"

"Not at all," I say.

The violin fades.

"Be careful as you go down. Mind telling me her name again?"

Now we've stopped in front of an old computer. The official types, and my words appear on the screen: Georgina Navarro, she hasn't been home in two days, her daughter's beside herself. Georgina's picture also appears.

The child called out for her mother all night long.

Lo nzind ntio xnii laxio, ya kuand na nza, I said. "We'll go looking for her when it's morning."

There was no one else to comfort the child. She cried, she wanted her mother.

"Don't cry," I said. *Ngont nta la.*

There's groundwater all around now, and the sound of crows, and voices, hundreds of echoing voices.

"I was worried you'd find me," says Georgina. "Why are you always trying to find me?"

I don't know what to say.

She crouches down and picks a stone up out of a puddle. "Sometimes you get frightened, sometimes you talk to people about your fears… I told you to wait for me at the entrance with the ants."

"Your daughter's worried, she's been crying and asking after you."

"Lubia. Where is she? I haven't seen her in days."

"She was right by the building, she'd have known if you were in here."

Georgina falls quiet for a moment.

"A mist came in during the afternoon," she says. "Lubia and I were coming through the coffee plantation, we had plastic bags for umbrellas. You couldn't see more than a few feet ahead of you, and when I turned around Lubia wasn't there. I retraced my steps, the birds were going crazy in the rain, but Lubia was nowhere to be seen… We'd been picking coffee since morning, the rain hadn't stopped us. When the leaves get wet in the country around there, the gnats fly up, pretty soon you feel like you're going to explode with the itching. We'd stayed in spite of the rain—the plantation owner had given us the plastic bags—but when it started turning dark, then we were going to leave. And Lubia was tired, she was worn out—so much so that I'd made a nest in the underscrub earlier on, clearing away the wet leaves so she could nestle down for a while. My body was starting to vibrate from the itching. Señor Ezequiel had let us have that part of the plantation to ourselves, so I could go out picking with my girl and not have to worry. I gave her a little basket of her own. 'She's walking now, so she must be eating, yes?' the owner said. 'So she must be strong enough to pick too.' 'Yes, Señor Ezequiel,' I said.

"On our way home, I had the half-full sack of coffee on my back. I thought Lubia was walking behind me as usual, but, next thing I knew, she wasn't. There was only the sound of the birds. I dropped the sack and came back along the path. I carried on until what light there was, in all that mist, started to fade. The fireflies came out from among the the drenched plants, and crane flies came out in place of the gnats. I shouted and shouted for Lubia in the plantation, but nothing. I walked on alone, and the birds continued making their racket and the rain continued dripping on me through the trees. Soon night really had fallen. I carried on shouting for Lubia. I went back to Don Ezequiel's house to tell him. The old man was warming himself by the wood-burner.

'That's kids for you,' he said. 'She'll be out there somewhere playing.' 'No, Señor, that can't be. I looked and looked, I looked until it was really dark.'"

Now I interrupt:

"All this about Lubia," I say. "But what about me?"

Georgina drops her head. She turns and walks, unhurriedly, back along the underground paths. The graceful violins begin again. As though Georgina's answer were contained in them. In the distance I can see the courtyard with the chairs, the ferns and reeds, and the red ants, still busy. So busy, nothing else registers.

Translated by Thomas Bunstead

THE LEG WAS OUR ALTAR

LAIA JUFRESA

A couple of years ago I joined a public swimming pool. Since it was more expensive to use it either very early in the day or in the evening, for a few months I would wake up each morning at 10.45 a.m., and by eleven I'd already be three streets away from the house, squeezing my head into a swimming cap, pulling a pair of goggles over my eyes, then jumping in and letting industrial volumes of chlorine wake me up: splash!

By mid-morning, of course, the majority of the human race, or at least its productive portion, is hard at work. So while laws were being discussed and conflicts aggravated, I trod water. Around the time office workers start to think about their lunch, I'd be bobbing up and down on my pull buoy. Millions of children would soak up their daily doses of information, while I drew breath every one, two, three strokes. As the world's cogs oiled the progress of who knows what ambitions, around in circles I went: splash, slurp, gasp, and I wasn't alone: a gaggle of little old ladies swam along with me.

This mature company I kept turned out to be not only pleasant but also, and above all, good for my self-esteem. Even with my lacklustre front crawl I managed to double, sometimes even triple the speed of my fellow bathers, and, compared to theirs, my flabby muscles seemed positively strong.

One of the old women would put aside her prosthetic before getting into the water. She always left it in the same corner, in line with the edge of the pool. The leg was made of hard plastic and painted an ochre colour which was slightly chipped at the knee, almost entirely worn away at the ankle. There was something of a religious icon about it; something in its position, or in the brief ritual that went on before it was laid out in its place. Until well gone midday, the old, the crippled and the unemployed paid holy reverence to swimming while, settled on its altarpiece of Venetian tiles and almost despite itself, that svelte limb glowed with a special, inert aura. The leg was our altar.

A great fat woman also frequented the swimming pool, though not on her own initiative. The moment her daughter disappeared into the waiting room with a magazine, she would sit herself down on the steps by the edge of the pool, swish her feet, soak her pins and chit-chat; or, to be precise, dish out inopportune pieces of advice. To every temple its preacher. "The strength should come from here," she would explain to the others, who couldn't have located the spot she pointed to—somewhere between her love handles—even if they'd tried. But the fat woman knew exactly what she was talking about, because, as she never tired of reminding us, thirty kilos ago she had been a professional swimmer.

Among the old girls I had my favourite. She was the most silvery-haired and the only one who genuinely swam. She was beautiful, and boasted the palest pair of eyes I've ever seen. Not clear in colour, but rather swathed: as if someone had tied an infinitesimal white cloth around each of her pupils. We swam keeping pace with one another, and rested together. During our breaks we would lift our goggles onto our foreheads, and as she spoke to me—more often than not about her grandchildren—I would let myself wander across the curvature of her milky eyes. She didn't seem to mind. We shared nice little chats in which she talked, I nodded, and her cataracts reflected the wisdom held by that fraction of the human race that celebrates pauses. To me, this woman was our prophet.

There were two men at the pool. The first was a foreigner. I've never been able to tell the age of Asian people, but this fella was pretty old. In any case, he had a small, compact body and something of a resigned warrior about him. He swam alone. In fact, you could tell from how he carried himself and from his countenance when outside of the water that, beyond the sliding doors of our temple, he must have been alone. Or perhaps not, perhaps a wife waited for him at home with a freshly squeezed juice, for which he'd thank her with no more than a dip of his head. Who knows, because we never talked to him. He spoke Spanish, that's for certain, because when he re-emerged from the changing rooms dressed to leave, a local newspaper would be poking out from under his armpit. The fat woman called him "the Chinaman", but the receptionist, ever watchful from the front desk, spoke to him using "master". The truth is that his swims far surpassed our quick dips, as much as we tried to style them out. I liked hanging off the side of the pool to watch him; his slow fluency transported me to a cherry blossom-filled park where tiny old people danced to the still, mute music of their t'ai chi classes.

Secretly, we all envied him, the Chinese master; we envied him his rigour, and if our little community had initiated some kind of crusade, some competition with a neighbouring club, for example, he would have been our man—our elected representative. But there was no such thing as competition at the pool. Our mid-morning was that of a cat laid out in the sun.

Outside the water, overseeing the proceedings on the other side of the leg, was the instructor. He was a scrawny man who played the trumpet. By the time I turned up at the pool, the worst hours of his day had come and gone. You could tell because the whiteboard would be full of notes he'd made in colourful marker pens for the early-bird crew, whose regimes were far more complicated than my ten laps of backstroke, fourteen of crawl. I kept up the exact same routine over all those months, which is why I'm able to say just how much my style and flexibility improved.

The instructor made the most of the sleepy session—ours—to practise his finger work, and in my memory the sound of the trumpets became inextricable from the smell of chlorine. I often asked myself where the trumpet came from. Not the instrument itself: the hobby. He also ran, I think, because his T-shirts were usually emblazoned with the anniversary of some or other marathon. But his most peculiar trait was the Olympic prowess with which he ignored the fat woman. He didn't instruct or correct her; but worse than that, he wouldn't actually talk to or even look at her, and not once did he ask her to vacate the stairs, despite the fact that the rest of us were forced to get in and out via the kiddies' pool. The ease with which they mutually disregarded one another hinted at a much longer history between them. The fat woman insisted on dishing out her own advice, usually completely contrary to his; but since she didn't exist to him, not a word of it went in. In contrast, each morning the instructor would give the fat woman's daughter a friendly kiss and hug hello and goodbye. This ongoing comedy of the absurd was one of the best things about the pool for me. It was also, along with the rest of the ritual, doomed to end.

One morning, a new woman turned up at the pool and, carrying her shoes in her hand, made a beeline for the instructor. The receptionist glared at her from the front desk, her arms crossed. When I had first gone along to enquire about joining the pool, the receptionist insisted I look at it from the outside, because, as a sign on the sliding door clearly stated, OUTDOOR SHOEWEAR HERIN NOT TO BE WORN FROM THIS POINT.

I hung off one side of the pool to watch the woman. She was young and svelte and this made me twitchy from the word go. It was clear that if she joined the pool she would knock me off my young-lady podium in two seconds flat. And yet, when I heard her talking to the instructor, who went on fingering the notes of the trumpet behind his back—either out of nervousness or because he didn't want to lose a minute's practice—I heard her say that she didn't know how to swim. I relaxed. If she didn't know how to swim, we weren't going to have any problems. What's more, a bit of new blood would do us good. Perhaps this woman, who looked about my age, would be someone I could talk to in the changing rooms, or share a protein shake with after our work-out—for example. I could pass on some of my backstroke and front crawl expertise without her forgetting it all five minutes later, as the others did. At the behest of the instructor, my other pool mates had to keep an abacus by the edge of the pool, along with their bottle of water. But every day someone would forget to bring theirs or neglect to slide the little balls across at the end of each lap.

I remember how that evening I took the precaution of shaving, so as to make a good impression on my new swimming buddy the following day. But the young woman didn't show up that morning. Nor the next one, or the one after that. I spent a week waiting, thinking that she'd join at the beginning of the next month, given that the receptionist point-blank refused to divide the paying month into anything smaller than a fortnight. But while the new month came, the woman didn't. Without her, the atmosphere at the pool began to darken. If the public pool wasn't good enough for her, why should it be for me? At the same time I recognized that this obsessive comparing myself with a complete stranger was pointless, and, more than anything, diminished my concentration. I resolved to go on swimming until I got over it. But I didn't get over it, and then everything took a nosedive for the worse.

A couple of weeks later I found the receptionist with our user cards littered across her desk and a snazzy new computer in front of her. I was outraged when she explained that she was logging the information. The cards were no more than a few, flimsy rectangles, printed with light blue stripes and typewritten, with a punched hole for every fortnight we had paid. But on mine, my name was misspelt and I'd never corrected it because I was really rather fond of having a different name at the swimming pool, like the ones devotees are given at ashrams and which usually have some grandiose meaning. As I anticipated, the receptionist's logging inspired a nasty orthographic elan. Once I'd been stripped of my secret identity, my trips to the pool became a torture. Soon after, my body started to crave more sleep, and even through I never skipped a session, I began to turn up a little bit later every day. The instructor was clearly unimpressed with me. The fat woman said I needed rest.

In an attempt to recover my enthusiasm, I bought myself a bright-green swimsuit: a complete one-eighty from my old black costume. The first day I wore it, my favourite old lady watched as I jumped in and swam towards her, as I did every morning. But when I reached her side she said, "Hello there! Are you new?" I wasn't about to lie to her and, in any case, most likely she would have recognized my voice, so I hurriedly confessed my name and swam off. But neither the backstroke nor the front crawl could rid me of the disillusionment of being to our prophet no more than a piece of clothing, interchangeable by definition.

The final straw came the day the manager of the pool, whom I'd never seen before, showed up in person to do her annual inspection and decreed that the leg couldn't stay where it was. She explained to its owner that it was going to get wet and that she was loath to take responsibility. But as I left that day I heard her telling the receptionist that the leg had "given her the heebie-jeebies" and that it lent "the wrong impression" about the business. Superstitious nitwit.

From then on, once the instructor had helped the leg's owner into the water, he would carefully stow her prosthesis between the floats. From that position, rigid and horizontal, the leg produced the same sense of reverence a fallen sequoia might inspire. But I could never get used to the new regime and I fell out of love with the ceremony. All at once, the old women seemed like a drag, the Chinaman pretentious and the instructor immature. One day, I took advantage of a pain in my shoulder to miss a week, then another, and then I never went back. What's more, my loss of faith extended to the neighbourhood, until everything about the area produced in me an unbearable malaise and I ended up moving. Not long after, I got a job and thus joined the world's productive portion: splash!

With my new salary I could afford the early-morning classes, but at that time of the day people don't believe in anything.

Translated by Sophie Hughes
From the short-story collection *El esquinista*

RUBBED OUT

LUIS FELIPE LOMELÍ

All history present in that visage, the child the father of the man.

CORMAC MCCARTHY
Blood Meridian

—1—

He can smell him. He knows he is there because he can smell him and his odour fills the night, drowns it. El Güero could not say exactly what his father smells of, but he knows it is his smell. His alone. And he feels as though he's been hit across the base of his skull with a length of pipe and somebody is binding his arms with wire, tighter and tighter, making the veins stand out, cutting into his skin, which is sunburnt after two weeks' grind on the building site for the first pay packet of his life. At the age of thirteen. And he earned it. He put up with not getting paid the first week. There was nothing the second week either, because last Saturday the foreman José Isabel had trotted out the same old story: he was on probation. Just to see if El Güero would get fed up and take off. But he didn't. That's why he got his reward on Monday and ran up to the rooftop of the half-finished building, hammer and chisel in his blistered hands, to look out over the city that would be his.

And he felt happy on the way home on the bus, thinking about what he'd do with the money, as if the last freckles of childhood had suddenly been wiped away: he'd buy himself a mobile phone, get his hair cut like the big boys, or start gathering the materials to build another room, back there.

Back there where his father should not be.

Where he never is.

The bastard must have parked his eco-taxi in Altavista—the snobby neighbourhood next door—to avoid the local kids doing it any damage. That's how come I didn't see it, he thinks. And he takes a deep breath. He clenches his fists without realizing it. The television flickers on the living-room wall like the reflection of a fire. But you can't hear it. El Güero can't hear anything. Maybe his sister's watching it with the sound off, not wanting to make any noise—or wanting to hear the noises their father is making in the bedroom. El Güero hesitates. He can't get up the nerve to go in or lean through the flowery curtain to see whether the person watching TV is his sister. He clenches his fists still tighter, fitting his fingernails into the open blisters, and drums the little roll of banknotes against the fabric of his trousers. He should go in. He's standing in the middle of the street and that's not a safe place to be: the Calcos are already drinking up the hill. He should go in and tell his father to go back where he came from. He should go in and tell him there's already a man in the house. El Güero taps his wages. He should go in and tell him he's not welcome there. El Güero does the sums. He should go in and say to his mother *You be quiet, I'm not talking to you*, because she's bound to get between them. Tell him, there's already a man here. And stay tough. Take what he doles out and stay tough. El Güero does the sums. He steps towards the pavement. The glow of the television broadcasts its fire on the wall. The flowers on the yellow curtain smoulder. His father's smell blazes in a slick of diesel, engine oil. El Güero takes another step and the smell of his father clogs his nose, sears his eyes. It blinds him. His father's smell chars the walls of the house, flares up, sets fire to the pavement and the street, the copper wire cutting into his arms turns red. El Güero chokes. He scrapes his fingernails across the ridge of stars burning inside each hand. And he chokes, all fucked up.

Fucking hell.

—2—

Monterrey is full of ghosts. It's a creeping bush with glittering ghosts. El Güero has also thought of it as a web. And he has imagined hundreds of spiders spinning their goo out across the desert, laying it softly over the dust, skirting round the giants of mountains to form a city everyone calls *La Sultana del Norte.*

Another night, also hunkered down in the square up where the antenna used to be, on one of the peaks of the Sierra Ventana, he imagined that Monterrey was made of the same substance as suns.

But today it is a bush full of ghosts.

Glittering.

And he opened up the bag of Resistol and got stuck in, while the ghosts came and went through the bush: fireflies with the voices of his ancestors.

—3—

"Did your old man turn up?"

Fede eyes him from the edge of the park. He can read him. They have been mates since they were just kids, so long that they don't even know when it started. Which is why he doesn't go straight over, but waits until El Güero nods before approaching him.

In the distance, but not all that far off, they hear bangs: far enough away not to worry about them, but close enough to know who is doing the shooting.

Fede walks over and El Güero passes the bag. It's the Dragons and the Calcos who are firing. That's what they do: start drinking on their corners and sure enough some waster always pulls out a piece. And the other side answer back. And so they calmly settle down to firing off rounds, from time to time and from one beer to the next, killing themselves laughing because they're so hammered they couldn't hit the bullseye in their wildest dreams. Or they could *only* do it in their dreams. The metal shutter of the kindergarten the Calcos sit outside is all pitted with holes. Strictly speaking, the Calcos don't sit on a corner but on the kindergarten steps at the dead end of the street. But that is their corner.

Tony's gone too far, Fede says, and tells El Güero that Tony went down on his bike and was cruising round Doña Esperanza's street when he clocked Koyi off in a world of his own, walking past the tortilla place, like he was on his own turf, cap on, looking really out of it, and Fede says Tony said, "Hand it over, man, you're off your patch." And he pedalled after him and caught up and, as soon as he had him in range, reached out and nicked the cap. See ya, arsehole, Fede says he said, and Fede tells El Güero they're all out on the prowl now and want to do Tony in.

"He's in deep with the big boys, he even got me to get him this," Fede says and nonchalantly pulls out a little Taurus .357. And El Güero realizes that was what all the lead-up was about, so he could show off his toy. Fede's always been like that.

"Don't you want to try it out?"

"Nah, what if it stirs up the Dragons?"

Down below, the city is still a bush full of ghosts. But one phrase keeps going round in El Güero's head: *in deep with the big boys*. He is sitting over the Tethys Sea and the ghosts glimmer in the depths. He stands up. He stands up on the concrete bench that juts out over the mountainside. He stands facing into the teeth of the wind and asks,

"Are you going back to yours?"

"I can't today," Fede replies.

El Güero looks at the ghosts and down the street to where his house is, where his father is. Fede has the revolver in his hands.

"I can."

—4—

Lina watches him with her cat eyes, from up on the roof, beneath the empty washing line. She watches him and she's been watching him before, before she joined the Boxercitas, since before she came to the neighbourhood.

And long before that.

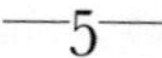

—5—

You go down the hill. You summon up the courage and go down. You have to face him. He's your father. You walk down the hill and don't look at Lina who is watching you from her rooftop. You don't hear the last thing Fede shouts to you. You don't hear the shots. You go down. You think of your father: with your bare hands, it's got to be with your bare hands. You have decided this, even though you've always considered him an immense man, tall and broad. He can knock you down with a single blow because he started work in the brick factory when he was younger than you: that's why he is an animal. And he is enormous. It is impossible to bring him down. You think: it's just that it *has been* impossible. You clench your fists and feel the blisters burn all the way up your arms to the nape of your neck. You walk downhill over the pot-holed concrete, ridged so that cars don't skid. You close your eyes. You cannot see. You do not feel the air. The night smells of nothing, tastes of nothing. You don't hear the yell from one of the Calcos when a bullet grazes his shoulder and he squeals like a stuck pig. The others laugh. But you don't hear them. You don't see Lina. You see nothing at all. Just your father. Get there and tell him to go back where he came from, and not to come back, never to come back. You've done the sums and you already know the dough's not going to stretch, your wages won't be enough for you all, but nevertheless you will stand there and tell him to his face—everything you want to say, everything you have to say. And it is this: that he never come back.

Fede's right: Tony's in deep with the big boys. But he's in deep shit, just for the sake of a cap. If you're going to do something, you've got to really go for it, right? You've got to show who you are. You know you don't get anywhere by beating up kids. You know the real thing lies in bringing down giants. So that they cannot crush you any more. So that what happened when they made you and your sister Leidi sell wooden snakes doesn't happen again. Never again. Because you know what you're made of, right? A stray bullet hits a black water tank behind you. You don't hear it. The liquid starts to gush out. To be a giant you have to confront other giants, you know this.

Your house is one block away.

—6—

El Güero realizes it before he gets there, he notices: no smell. He creeps in so as not to disturb his mother or Leidi, and definitely not little Cabrito, because if he starts crying then of course he'll wake everyone else up. And he always wakes up bawling.

His bastard of a father isn't there; he did not stay the night. There's just a whiff of him still clinging to the walls, burning off.

El Güero relaxes his muscles.

Exhales.

Turns off the television.

Leidi is asleep on the couch in the front room with her arms round Cabrito. She sleeps there sometimes, since the baby was born. There isn't another bedroom. El Güero goes over and covers them both with the blanket Absalón's wife—his aunt Eduviges—knitted them: little squares of coloured yarn. He looks at the squares and then at the faces of his siblings. Nothing has happened. When they're asleep, it's like nothing has happened.

El Güero walks into the bathroom and puts gentian violet on his blisters. He looks at himself in the medicine-cabinet mirror: his slick fair hair, cut short, and the few freckles that refuse to fade. He looks at himself: he knows he is the worst electrician's mate in the city and he knows he is alone.

But he feels like he can bring down giants.

Translated by Anna Milsom
From the novel *Indio borrado*

A VOIDANCE

BRENDA LOZANO

5

No one wants to look at themselves.

This is why—luckily—the other exists.

6

From that day on, the day Grandfather cut salt out of his diet, I started to get on with him really well. I talked to the gastroenterologist like never before. After that day, we began to see each other more and more. That day was a re-encounter and an encounter. But I'll go back to what happened next with Grandfather later on. I've made it clear that I talk about him easily, without being asked. And I talk easily, too, about José. I'll talk now about how it started with José.

Two months go by since we buried Grandfather. I settle into the apartment he so generously left me. I take books out of cardboard boxes. I unstick the pale brown tape from the boxes. I have nothing. I have no bed, I have no furniture, but I have so many books. The boxes seem bottomless. The number of books, like any large number, is vulgar. I hold back. I'm not going to fuel the vulgarity by taking more books from their boxes; I want them to fulfil some modest function. They shall have a function: I select thick books to make a bed with. In my room I arrange my grandfather's collection of classics that now will be a bed. I can already hear him muttering. (This is what you do with my library? The library I left to you, which I put together over sixty years, is going to be your bed, fruit of my loins?) I pat the padded installation of books, my bed, as if I were a salesman trying to convince a customer.

The telephone rings. I haven't answered it for two months. I have a brilliant idea: I answer. A friend invites me to a party at his house. I have an ordinary idea: I slip out of my apartment. I see a few people I know and I see, above all, people I don't. One vodka is all it takes for me to speak out against ambition, against luxury. One vodka and one person I don't know is all it takes for me to say that ambition is born out of failure, that money is the source of ugliness. My friend turns up, he asks me how I've been these past two months. I don't change the subject. How contemptible, how vulgar are those who seek luxury. Luxury furniture, for instance, for an apartment. Books, arranged a certain way, can be the most comfortable bed. But there, on the chair opposite, is he. He, who I don't know, and who looks as if he's listening to my speech on the utility of books. He, sitting down, a tequila in his hand. Sitting without saying a word. We exchange a glance. I envy the mute. I salute their silence and I fall silent. I fall silent, I think of the furniture I'll build with books. I think: you'd be surprised, Grandfather, at the utility of the Graeco-Latins. Who am I kidding? I think of him, sitting down, drinking tequila.

Another vodka gives me the courage of a Greek hero to go and sit next to him. I have the necessary valour to concoct an entire mythology, but I produce a phrase that would settle for his attention. My phrase and I fail. My phrase: a little straw horse, a minuscule horse, which was trying to be monumental to reach him. He barely looks at me, drains his tequila, gets up, goes to the kitchen. I listen to the old man. (A whole century and its thinkers to build a city, but all it takes is a minute to destroy it.) I sink into silence. He comes back, comes back with more tequila. He sits down next to me.

We exchange a few words. I'd like to say something more but I don't. My victorious shyness. I want to talk more to him but I'm embarrassed. I don't know what to say. I leave now, wordlessly, as I arrived. On the way home, I dismantle the illusion of company. I dismantle (oh for an AK-47) the couples in the street. The stupid illusion of company. Illusion and stupidity are synonyms. Company and I are antonyms. I enter my building, crashing into the door: a frustrated bullet. I go into my apartment. I fall asleep on top of Plato, Hesiod, Aeschylus, Euripides and Terence. Socrates, who didn't write so much as his name, is my pillow.

I wake up, it looks as though the books have multiplied. It looks as if Emilio Nassar, to amuse himself, has brought more books while I slept. I miss him. I flick through his books. I pick through his books as if between the pages I might find some note in the margin that would tell me everything's going to be OK. But in his books, as in life, there are no notes in the margin.

The doorbell rings. I don't believe it but it's him. He says he's called José, that we met yesterday. I open the door, he's carrying a book. He hands it to me, I've hardly taken it before he explains. He explains that he wants to contribute to the making of the furniture in my apartment. He apologizes for having looked up my address, for arriving unexpectedly. I, who the previous night would have built a kingdom to exchange it for a horse, say that I was about to go out, that he's in luck. I ask him in, he accepts.

We talk. Down goes the sun, the sun goes down. I ask him to stay for dinner. I order a takeaway. Young people talk and we are young people. We chat but, I suspect, we want to do what two young people do in apartments. Two young people in an apartment go to bed with one another. This is why apartments and young people exist. But no, I talk about Grandfather, he talks about his mother, a professor of literature at the National University who died some years ago. Grandfather studied medicine at the National University and I take classes in the Faculty of Arts. I take some beers from the fridge. I make a toast to the National University and, privately, I make a toast to our alma mater leading us to bed before long. How can I put it? I like José, I like him so much I'm afraid of getting near him.

With this enthusiasm I could pack up the books again in a minute. It would be no small thing, but before I try he says he has to go, he has to edit a text for the supplement. I find out he works for the cultural supplement of a newspaper. Before he leaves I say wait a minute, I go to my room. I want to swap the book he bought me for another. I pick a book from Grandfather's library, that is, from a corner of my bed. I consider various dedications; it takes me fifteen minutes to finally pick one. To José, from someone who always runs away and who will get out of this one, too. I cross it out—a great big lie. To José, from someone who wants to go to bed with him very soon. I cross it out—a great big truth. To José, who with this day justifies everything since the Big Bang. I cross it out, bang—a lie. My attempts to dedicate a book to him crumble on top of me. To José, with love. I give him the book.

José reads my dedication and hugs me. In silence he hugs me. He hugs me and I hug him. I hug him and he kisses me. He kisses me, I kiss him, we kiss each other. We kiss each other, we drop to the floor. We kiss each other on the floor. We kiss, we touch, we kiss.

You'd be surprised, Grandfather, at how much life is like those low-rent novels you used to insult so much. You'd be surprised at how much the months I spent with José are like those novels you hated so much. But am I writing to my grandfather? Who am I writing to? I'm addressing him, Grandfather, and I'm addressing him, José, because this is the only way I have of addressing myself. Maybe because words are what's left for someone who lets another go. Because we let someone go so as to remember them, just as we go so as to be remembered. Perhaps because we love so that we are loved, just as we abandon others so that they might abandon us.

7

When I am here I want to be there.

8

Grandfather has been calling me every day for a week. A week after I start seeing him again, he asks if he's ever told me about his first love. He's told me so many times about the schoolteacher who taught him how to read that I've lost count. The story of his first love isn't new, but it is new that he repeats it and that I pay attention.

Grandfather used to take every opportunity, he really did, to emphasize his lengthy history, to emphasize how much time he had spent in Mexico City. On the way to the restaurant where he would tell me once again of his first love, any park we saw was enough to set him off talking about his distant past. (My father was a hard, steely man. So hard, so strict that he never hugged me. But, my God, the day he taught me to ride a bike, in a park exactly like the one we've just gone past, I cornered my father in an alley. I was a kid, Emilia. I fell off quite a few times, I fell hard, right off the bike. My father picked me up off the ground, furious. He dusted off my short trousers, patted me roughly a couple of times, retrieved my bicycle and we began again. As if I hadn't learnt anything, as soon as I took my feet off the ground I fell off again. He picked me up and I clung to him. I hugged him against his will. My father did not throw in the towel: he was going to teach me to ride a bike because he wanted to observe the results of his teachings. I didn't throw in my own towel, either: I would fall over a thousand times to prove to him I would do what I wanted. After all, nothing was going to happen if I hugged him. But that was the one day I showed him that I would do what I wanted in that way. I was a kid, but I wasn't a fool.)

Grandfather's past was a sensitive button; you could press it without realizing. And he, without realizing, multiplied the buttons that lit up his past. To put it another way: when near him you were like a bull in a china shop, and it was impossible to dodge the plates. It was impossible, too, to stem the sermons Grandfather gave, which began way back in ancient civilizations. And so you had to move very carefully.

Once, for instance, I accompanied him when he went to give a lecture at the National University. Emilio Nassar had developed a technique for determining serum bilirubin and had to give a talk on it. But he didn't talk about this, and demonstrated his nonconformist views on classical medical knowledge. (Those ancient French roots!) He criticized fashionable ideas. (We must go back to Thucydides: it is men, not walls, who make a hospital.) Needless to say, he did not touch upon the topic that was the reason for his lecture. Grandfather could well have begun like this: I've been asked to talk about a technique for determining serum bilirubin, but I'm going to talk about myself. And this is what he did. He talked about his experience, his career as a gastroenterologist. Grandfather went off on a tangent. Contrary to what might be expected, this trait of his gave him an unwonted authority. During the talk I understood nothing about medicine, just as I've never understood anything about medicine, but this time I did understand that this doctor had a digestive system that allowed him to be led by whatever digressions he felt like. He wanted to make it clear that he'd do whatever the hell he wanted.

After the applause, Grandfather stepped down off the podium. Óscar and I were waiting for him. A few of the doctors came over to him. He said hello to all of them, he knew them all. On the way back to the car, Óscar asked him what it had been like to be back in the university. We knew that Grandfather would find any excuse to launch himself back to his time in the faculty, no matter what set him off. He spoke about the department, about the professors who were there in his day, about the first class he and Óscar took together. It was easy to bring the mustiest old tales from his life up to the surface.

Let's go back to the car as we drive to the place he wants to take me to talk about his first love. He wants to take me to a restaurant because, he says, he has something important to show me. He says it's crucial we go to this restaurant because this place used to be something different. This restaurant was the boys' school he went to. He wants to take me, a week after we meet again, to the place he studied as a boy.

We're on our way to the city centre, after he's talked at length about his father, after he's talked at length about the parks, a litany on buildings. These buildings here and those ones there remind him of his childhood. He talks about how much an apartment cost back then, when he lived there with his mother (a beauty of Spanish origin) and his father (a Mexican of Lebanese origin). (You wouldn't believe how much my father paid for the apartment on Calle 5 de Mayo, on the corner of Motolinía, where we used to live.) He talks about credit terms, about the splendid views every apartment used to have. He tells me how well these buildings have been built, how they resist the passage of time, earthquakes; of how spacious the lounges are, how light the bedrooms. As if he was trying to sell me an apartment from his past.

We get to the restaurant. We get to the boys' school that doesn't exist any more. Grandfather asks me to come up to the first floor with him. Up to this point, you might say that everything was defined by his punctual instalments of nostalgia. But everything else, what happened on the first floor, was enough to give Grandfather over to the care of a nurse.

On the first floor of the restaurant, he points out a space between two tables attached to the wall. That was where the schoolteacher who taught him how to read used to sit. And so here we are, on the first floor of a restaurant in the city centre that sixty or so years ago was his classroom. I look at the space between the tables, I look at Grandfather, I look at the space in between the tables and I look again at Grandfather. He says: "Take note: this is where your dear grandfather had lessons." I try to imagine, I try to imagine him. I try to make the tables disappear, make the people disappear. I try to imagine the classroom, a little boy sitting opposite us who is my grandfather and who might have smiled just as he's doing now.

Using words, Grandfather recreates his old classroom. He says that the schoolteacher, the schoolteacher who taught him how to read, was very fond of him, that the love of his teacher was the certificate for his time at school. He talks of his teacher, his beautiful teacher who, as he tells it, smiled like no one else. (It's hard to be the author of a woman's smile. It is easier to devote one's life to the study of gastro-intestinal diseases than to understand why a woman smiles.)

He talks and talks. He learnt to read thanks to her, for her. He walks irritably over to a corner, bashing into everyone who gets in his way so he can get to where he wants. This, he says, was where the bookcase was. Grandfather acts. He looks for invisible books on an invisible bookcase. He examines the titles one by one. Those books that aren't there, they unleash the same thing as Proust's madeleine does. The difference between Proust and Grandfather is that Grandfather spares himself the seven books and saves time by wolfing down the madeleine. I learn, the families in the room learn of the books schoolboys used to read decades ago. His greed aside, we learn how the boys used to sit. Grandfather moves chairs, moves tables, moves a woman, pushes a waiter out of the way to show me a piece of his past. Dr Nassar runs through the surnames of his classmates out loud. No one in the restaurant understands him. No one here understands him and I do still less.

He raises walls, pulls down others, with words. He moves the waiters and the chairs that obstruct his past. There are witnesses to his madness. But I cannot ignore the sparkle of his movements. To say the sparkle of his movements is a saying and it's saying it wrong. But saying it like this, it looks like the way he sparkles when he talks of his past. He shares his past, not only with those present and with me, he shares it with himself. He is generous with himself. Maybe this way, by telling us about his past he sees, he sees once more that his passage through life has been magnificent. You only have to look at him now, stretching out an arm to figure out where the blackboard was with its five white pieces of chalk. But that's enough. That's enough, Grandfather, I'm going downstairs to a table for two. That's enough, let's go, stop it. A miracle: Grandfather does what I say. He, domestic dictator, doctor of doctors who whenever I ask him to do something always mutters, What, the tail wagging the dog? He does what I say, a miracle.

He walks slowly down the stairs. As if talking about his past had crafted him a heavy cloak, the heavy cloak of a king proud of his kingdom. We sit down. I order something to eat, he doesn't order anything. He says that a week ago, after learning of the dangers of salt, he decided to go on a diet. You really won't eat anything, Grandfather? We fight, he wins. He orders a *café con leche*. A *café con leche* with so many specifications he may as well go to the kitchen and make it himself. With this kind of milk, without sugar, in this particular kind of cup, on that particular kind of saucer. Grandfather is headstrong, stubborn. It's impossible. It's impossible to contradict him. When he likes and how he likes. The waiter had better not get it wrong. I tell the waiter that Grandfather won't go to his grave because he's worried that at his funeral they won't serve the *café con leche* as he likes it. Grandfather finds this funny, he laughs. He finds it really funny, his hoarse laugh rings out. He tells the waiter that nowadays you can't carry anyone out of their house feet first without making sure there'll be proper coffee served at the wake. The waiter leaves. Grandfather switches between laughs and a few irrational wishes for his funeral.

So it goes. The day of the funeral I could hear Grandfather's voice. His voice saying things more or less like the things he said to me on the day he took me to see his classroom on the first floor of a restaurant. I heard his voice at the wake: Who are these young upstarts? Is that your grandmother's latest grandchild with that grey paediatrician? Why are there so many people at my wake? Who invited every single member of Mexico's middle class? Emilia, tell Óscar that the black suit he's wearing is an exact replica of the one I've got on. I'm wearing my black suit, Emilia—do I look just as handsome as ever? Tell Óscar not to even think about pouring himself a cup of coffee. It's the worst coffee anyone's ever made. Watery, instant stuff. I'd rather lick the pavement than drink that coffee, but thankfully I'm already in the coffin. What kind of funeral parlour serves powdered milk?

When Óscar told me that Grandfather had died all I could think of was a black suit, the black suit Grandfather had by the side of his bed, laid out on the rocking chair, the night that he died. I spent hours thinking about that black suit. At the wake I listened to his complaints the whole time. On the way to the cemetery it was all I could do to comprehend why time didn't stop, why the day didn't cloud over, why the streets didn't empty.

Why doesn't time freeze, at the very least, when you're on your way to a cemetery?

Stuck in traffic, I watched as a man changed the billboard at a cinema. A man in blue overalls, a man with his back to us, changing the title of a film. Looking at the man changing the title of a film as if nothing had happened. Changing the acrylic letters one by one as if nothing had changed. Grandfather's voice came back: another crime against literature. Another modern film for narrow minds. When will people read instead of prostrating themselves in front of such vulgar rubbish for two hours? I went in the nick of time, Emilia, you hear me—films like that, trash like that, do not belong to my time.

At the funeral, Grandfather continues: Tell those guys, the four insufferable bores carrying my casket, that I'm wobbling. What's wrong with them? Whose idea was it to have two dwarves and two giants carrying my coffin? And on the subject of the coffin, Emi, you'll never guess what it cost me. It's as good a piece of work as any of my research into invasive amoebiasis. The coffin and I are the same. Your grandmother looks pretty, she looks so pretty in black. Black looks as good on her as it ever did, but it's a shame she's standing next to that grey man. Grey never suited your grandmother. You can tell your uncle right away he'd better not dare read something out of a self-help book to send his father off. Tell him I'll switch funerals, I'll switch to the one next door if he dares read something he picked himself. I've still got time to change families. Although I would ask you to save me the effort since your grandmother looks so beautiful.

It was all wrong: birth, death, life, sleep, solitude, company. Everything was out of place, everything was the wrong way round. Nothing right, everything wrong. I didn't understand anything. Grandfather's funeral was like a film set, a bad film set, the worst. I half expected the curtain to fall and for Grandfather to stand up and come and watch a movie with me. As long as everything was still like this, after the death of my father, after the death of my grandfather, as long as time continued on its course with men changing billboards at the cinema without the city crumbling and the sounds ceasing, I would refuse to believe that anything was going well, that things were happening for the sake of something better.

I looked at Grandfather as he descended. He was descending into the grave. Slowly he went, and I wondered if it were true I'd never see him again. If it were true that this was how you said goodbye to someone.

The telephone rang like never before and like never before I stayed quiet. Days of silence, days of deafness, days of reading. I didn't want to answer the phone, I didn't want to hear any more condolences. Until one day, two months after his funeral, I decided to move to the apartment Grandfather gave me and rent out the one my father left to me.

Two months later I moved. I left everything, I took books, only boxes of books. Something became clear in this move, something became clear as I carried the boxes. Although my father died when I was a little girl, although Grandfather went on the Sunday he wanted to go, it would never be that clear to what point they had gone. And the not knowing where they were, whether here or there, was the only thing that was clear.

To not know where your loved ones are is to not know where you are. That's precisely where I was, floating in nothingness, avoiding everything in a void. I didn't know if I was here or there, I didn't know if they were here or there. And it's not like I know now, either, it's not like I could point myself out on a map. And after meeting José, breaking it off with him, I'm growing further and further from the possibility of pointing myself out on a map.

9

The fear of doing the same thing twice.

The fear of doing the same thing twice.

Translated by Rosalind Harvey
From the novel *Todo nada*

BECAUSE NIGHT HAS FALLEN AND THE BARBARIANS HAVE NOT COME

VALERIA LUISELLI

"Everyone has a theory but there's no explanation," says Mom, pointing at the headline of today's paper. Strewn over the table are three coffees and a large bowl full of sliced papaya. There's an ashtray, a lighter and the newspaper—all my brother's. There's a copy of Cavafy's poems, which Mom is reading, and a Yellow Pages open to VULCANIZERS, which I'm leafing through in search of telephone numbers.

We got a flat tyre 281 kilometres before Acapulco and about a hundred kilometres after the tollbooth. We were lucky it happened near the diner—a Soviet-style establishment called Siberia Dos, with long metal tables waited on by women who had identical hairstyles. After a quick lunch, my brother and I replaced the burst tyre with the spare. But we still had to find a vulcanizer and a proper tyre, because the spare turned out to be too small and the car was now unbalanced, huffing along as if it had a set of mismatched legs, one shorter than the other. "Like a crippled earwig," my mother said. I didn't really understand that.

In the crippled car, my brother driving gingerly on the undersize spare, we asked her, "Why have you got Maná's first album in the glove compartment, Ma? Why do you even own a Maná CD, Ma?"

"What's it to you?" she said from the back, and she was right: what's it to us? We made an effort and listened, strenuously, respectfully, to the first track, and the second. When the fifth track came on—to be exact, when Fher Olvera sang the ridiculous lines "*Un tambor sonó muy Africano / Es el pumpin pumpin de tu corazón*"—Mom doubled up with laughter. She offered to change the CD, and passed up a Leonard Cohen album the three of us have always liked well enough. I can't remember the first time Mom sat in the back seat like that, while we rode in the front—of course, I don't mean that metaphorically.

The house is perched on the edge of a cliff over two hundred metres high. At the foot of the cliff, the sea stretches out like a tombless cemetery until it touches Japan. We've come here because Mom wants to give my brother and me some news. In fact, she gave us the news while we were changing the flat tyre outside the Soviet diner, so we don't really understand why she's giving it to us again. The news is that Mom has a boyfriend. Having heard this, we could have just driven back to the city after we'd changed the tyre.

The last time she made an announcement like this was when she told us our father was going to go live with Sara, and she was going to go live in a bungalow in Malinalco for a while, maybe a year or two, with her silent-meditation group. That was Christmas 1999, and the news was given to us, for reasons I cannot remember, on the roof of our building. That same Christmas, after dinner, my brother and I went back up to the roof to smoke a joint, and tried to do mute meditations ourselves. But both of us kept getting distracted by little things, little thoughts, little bugs.

Luckily for us, Mom's mute-meditation group broke up around the New Year, before the great pilgrimage to Malinalco, and she stayed with us until we each got married and had children of our own. Then she was left alone in a house that was too big and too silent.

As soon as we arrived in Acapulco, I put my backpack in the end room—there's a narrow hallway with four bedrooms that each look out onto the garden—and went to the patio at the corner of the house, from which you can see the sea. The house belongs to my mother's sister, Celia, who married an architect and has no children. I was sure that, standing solemnly before the wide, wild sea, I'd come up with an idea. A wild idea, clever and broad, that would justify this slightly absurd journey our mother had obliged us to come along on. An idea I could say out loud during dinner to make my brother laugh and my mom feel uncomfortable.

The other part of the news was that Mom's boyfriend had gone blind and then become a Sufi, in that order. Blind, thirteen years ago; and Sufi, twelve years ago. Before that he was a Basque pelota player.

"He's meeting us in Acapulco tomorrow night, and will spend the weekend with the three of us," Mom said yesterday, as we were getting into the lopsided car.

My brother started the motor, and I rooted around for CDs in the glove compartment.

"He's coming by bus because he doesn't drive," she added, for clarification.

Neither my brother nor I knew what a Basque pelota player was. My mother must have suspected this, because she embarked on a detailed explanation of the sport. My brother didn't ask questions about pelota playing, Sufism, or anything else. He's a polite, respectful person who almost never asks personal questions. I do, sometimes, but on this occasion I emulated him and kept my mouth shut. Deep down, though, I wanted to ask how the Basque pelota player had gone blind, and if his blindness was related to having been a pelota player or if his Sufism was related to his blindness. Instead, I just sipped my coffee in silence, letting it scorch my tongue with each sip. Basque pelota can be played with a racket, with a wooden bat or with your hands, my mother said. That was when we put on the Maná CD.

For dinner we had cereal, the three of us standing, watching each other eat. No one said anything except "Pass the milk" and "Here's a bigger spoon" and, later, "Goodnight". Before going to bed, I walked to the patio overlooking the cliff again, and tried calling my husband and the kids, but there was no answer.

Mom has a boyfriend and she's doing OK. I fell asleep embracing this one thought, the fan laboriously slicing through the heavy night air.

At breakfast the next morning—cereal again—I break the silence and say, "*Vulcanizer* comes from Vulcan, the Roman god of fire." I repeat the name, "Vulcan", almost in a whisper. I say it to the window, beyond which the sea stretches out towards Japan, but really I say it to my brother. "*Vulcanizer* comes from Vulcan."

He says, "Hmm," and goes on reading the newspaper. The headline reads: FIVE DECAPITATED BODIES FOUND IN TRUNK OF CAR: HEADS MISSING.

Must we say so much? So directly? Say things to the window—that's what our father used to do when he was giving us an order. He'd say things to the window, never straight to us, knowing that the child to whom the command was directed would answer promptly. We never said "Hmm" to our father. We always said, "Right, OK."

Mom comes in from the kitchen carrying a tray with three cups of coffee and a bowl of papaya. She sets them down on the table and, pointing at my brother's newspaper, says, "Everyone has a theory."

My brother has three children. I've got a daughter and two stepsons who affectionately—or, rather, sometimes affectionately, sometimes not—call me "Refrigerador". When the six children, my brother's and mine, get together, they form a perfect tribe.

A noisy bunch, more self-confident and full of life than we two were as children—we were always a bit quiet, not melancholy but perhaps saturnine, which is almost the same thing but not exactly. We were always observing the adults around us. Now we observe the children around us. In that liminal place, I think, my brother and I learnt to feel more at ease, maybe even happy. Now, without our kids here, we have no one to observe but our mother. We don't really know how to look at each other.

After breakfast, Mom washes the dishes, my brother goes to the market to buy an octopus for lunch, and I sit on the patio overlooking the sea, dialling numbers for vulcanizers. I also call my husband, to see how everyone is doing back in the city, but he doesn't answer the phone, so I leave a message. Everything fine here, missing you all. My mother has a new boyfriend. He's very nice—an athletic, spiritual man. Give the baby a kiss from me, on the nose, and give the boys a hug from Refrigerador.

Looking out at the sea beyond the cliff, a theory springs to mind: that's where they throw the heads.

Mom comes in while I'm having a bath and sits on the toilet seat, her pee cascading noisily into the water in the bowl. I think of that Pablo Neruda poem where he listens to his lover pee. She tells me that she's learning Braille. She has been reading a bilingual edition of Cavafy's poems with her boyfriend. The edition is in Braille and—she hesitates—in "normal". I ask her to pass me a towel. I wonder if she has had a bath with her boyfriend yet.

"What's your boyfriend like, Ma? Is he good-looking?"

"Well, he looks a bit like Slavoj Žižek," she says, "but blind."

"Slavoj Žižek?"

"Yes," she says, "the one on YouTube."

It's difficult to imagine how fathers and mothers make love, be it with each other or with someone else. There was a moment, during my first years of college, when everyone used to emulate the protagonist of *Hopscotch*, who always has sex on the floor and then smokes a cigarette. Then, a few years later, they all started emulating the protagonist in *The Savage Detectives*, who masturbates his partner by giving her little slaps on the clitoris. I wonder what my daughter will make of all that, twenty years from now, when she reads my copies of the novels I underlined here and there. Sex is always generational. From a certain point of view—especially from above—it's a bit ridiculous. My brother's generation fucked like the couple in *9 ½ Weeks*. I'll never know what books and films my parents' generation decided to emulate. But it horrifies me to imagine Žižek fornicating with my mother.

At lunchtime, we sit down to a meal of octopus ceviche my brother has made. Mom talks insistently about the need to change the tyre before her boyfriend arrives that night, and how the two of us must make sure to check the size of the new one. Then she digresses. She explains that Sufi whirling dervishes might be emulating the movement of planets, rather than the gyration of tyres. During her digression, I think of all the possible holiday activities that are useful for killing time with family members: poker, Risk, Monopoly, chess, Pictionary. They all require the faculty of sight. We have to find a game where no one needs to see the pieces.

While we do the dishes, my brother asks me if I feel jealous of Mom's new boyfriend. He washes, I dry. "No, I'm not the least bit jealous," I say without hesitation. But I spend the rest of the time we're shuffling dishes around thinking about it. I ask him if he knows any games we can play with Mom's boyfriend.

"Perhaps poker dice," he says after a pause, because you can feel the dents in the dice. But as soon as we begin trying to refine the details, Mom comes into the kitchen and we both fall silent. No, I'm not jealous, I think again when we've finished the dishes. I want to say that what I feel is the exact opposite of jealousy, but I'm not sure what such a thing would be called, or whether it exists.

My brother and I leave the house to go to Variety Vulcanizers, whose owner I've spoken to in order to explain our problem. They've assured me that they have the exact size tyre we need. When we get into the car and switch on the ignition, Leonard Cohen's 'I'm Your Man' comes on. It sounds abnormally loud. I turn off the radio. My brother says, "You know, *vulcanizer* doesn't come from Vulcan."

"Yes it does," I say, and he turns the music back on.

The city of Acapulco is like a military parade, armed forces everywhere—the army, the navy, judicial, federal and state police. The most frightening ones are the navy: Mexican sailors dressed like American ones.

Once we get to the vulcanizer's, the problem is quickly—but not effectively—solved. The tyre they have is a bit bigger than our other three.

"It's better to have it be bigger than smaller," argues the vulcanizer. He raps out: "The bigger the better, like the more the merrier." He also offers us a marijuana *tostón* as a bonus. This last part of the deal convinces my brother.

"We can gradually replace the other three tyres with larger ones," he says.

"Do you still smoke pot?" I ask my brother as we walk towards the cash register, making our way between tyres, odd bits of trash, tubes and a bone from a chicken wing.

"No, you?"

"No."

After he has paid for the tyre, the lady at the cash register hands my brother a business card, on which is printed a small figure. She explains to both of us that it's Vulcan, the Roman god of fire.

"See?" I say. "I told you."

"Told me what?"

"Nothing. Never mind."

Back at the house, Mom is standing at the mirror, getting ready. The sun will set soon, and she's going to drive to the bus station. The ex-pelota-playing Sufi boyfriend must be less than fifty kilometres away. It's the first time in ten years that Mom's had a boyfriend. She looks beautiful. I tell her she looks good. She says, "Well, he won't be able see me anyway."

I'm not sure whether to laugh, but she does, and then I do too, a little. I fasten her necklace for her.

We never ever forgive our parents anything, though they almost always forgive us everything. But, at the same time, we admire them much more than they ever manage to admire us. Perhaps admiration is just an acknowledgement we offer to those people we find unfathomable. And for all that time passes, as we become adults and raise walls and families and acquire careers, we're never unfathomable to them.

My brother and I play poker dice at the dining-room table while waiting for Mom to come back. He takes out the *tostón* and I make a joint, carefully emptying a cigarette and surgically removing the filter.

"Do you think they throw all those heads into the sea?" I ask.

"Don't go having a bad trip before we smoke."

"Right, OK."

We smoke like beginners, with exaggerated gestures, emulating old expressions. Our present-day faces are much sterner than they were before.

"Four queens," he says.

I don't pick up the cup, even though I know he's lying. Then I look at the dice and see that there is, in fact, only a pair of queens. I pick them up and throw again, and lose, and lose again. Just like that.

The love we feel for older siblings—who are also in some way unfathomable—is also disproportionate. But we don't make them pay for our inability to fathom them, as we do with our parents. We adore them, full stop. Or if we don't adore them at every moment, we at least still love them a lot.

Mom comes back at around 10.30 p.m. The pelota player doesn't come in with her. We wait for a moment in silence, thinking that perhaps a blind person needs a bit more time to get out of the car, that he'll soon appear in the doorway with his white stick in hand. But no one appears, no stick peeks into sight. I know from the look on her face that no one's going to come. She puts her handbag down heavily on the table and sits with us.

"Are you guys stoned?"

"No," my brother says.

"A little," I say.

"Can I have some?"

My brother extracts the remaining half of the spliff from the box of cigarettes on the table, lights it and passes it over to her.

She takes a long drag and, holding in the smoke, asks us, "Did you guys get the wrong kind of tyre?"

"No," I reply.

"Yes, sorry," my brother says.

She lets the smoke out with a faint smile. My brother picks up the poker-dice cup and says, "Four aces and a queen." Mom intercepts the cup. She raises it, sets the four aces aside, and then shakes the cup with its single die before slamming it down on the table. Sneaking a look inside the cup, she says, "OK, I win. End of the game."

She suggests another game: she reads to us in Braille, and we listen.

"That's not a game, Ma," says my brother.

"Shut up and listen," she scolds, feigning authority, and looking not at him but towards the window to her right.

While she's taking the heavy book out of her handbag, she tells us the rules: she reads aloud, skipping words, and we have to guess the words that are missing. That's all.

"That's all?"

"Yes, that's all."

She reads:

> Waiting for the *Something.*
> What are we waiting for, *something* in the forum?
> The *something* are due here today.
> Why isn't anything happening in the *something*?
> Why do the *something* sit there without *something*?

She reads the entire poem this way, while we look at her, perplexed, not knowing if she has lost it, or if we just don't understand her game.

"You two have no sense of humour and no poetry culture," she says, and takes the joint from the ashtray.

"So where's the pelota player?" my brother asks.

"I'm not too sure," she answers, holding in the smoke. "What's your theory?"

"Cold feet?" I suggest.

"I think he's here in the house," she tells us. "We just can't see him."

"Don't be creepy, Ma," I tell her.

"I'm not. It's just a theory. We're all entitled to a theory."

"He probably got lost," my brother says.

"He got on the wrong bus," I add.

My mother is the only person I know who laughs with her entire body and isn't deformed by the physical effects of laughter. Most people acquire something monstrous in mid-cackle. Something monstrous and something demented. The voice expands and breaks, the eyes disappear, bodies sway like wounded *piñatas*. I once had a boyfriend, neither handsome nor ugly, whose face used to take on a porcine quality when he laughed—his nostrils flapping furiously, his face pink and swollen, his eyes two tiny, expressionless marbles, fixed on infinity, like eyes open underwater, or like the eyes of the beheaded.

Nothing like that happens to Mom—she looks beautiful every time.

Translated by Christina MacSweeney

LIGHTS IN THE SKY

FERNANDA MELCHOR

1. At the start of the Nineties, Playa del Muerto, or Dead Man's Beach, was no more than a strip of greyish sand located in Boca del Río, seat of the municipal government, neighbouring the port of Veracruz. Its scorching dunes were scrubby and full of thorns that trapped the rotten branches and plastic bottles the river dragged down from the mountains when the waters rose. It wasn't a very crowded or even a particularly pretty beach (if any beach in this part of the Gulf of Mexico can be called pretty) and there were times—especially at high tide or during storms—when the beach disappeared and not even the breakwaters could stop the waves invading the highway linking the two cities.

The locals avoided it. Every year, dozens of intrepid bathers, especially visitors from Mexico City, met their deaths in its treacherous waters. "No swimming", said the notices erected a few metres from the water. "Danger suddan pools" warned a skull crudely hand-painted in red. The powerful undertow that propelled the waters of the estuary towards Antón Lizardo Point—home to the Heroic Naval Military School—littered the beach with pits, concavities that produced erratic currents in which it was easy to drown.

2. I was nine when I saw the lights, glowing like fireflies against the black canvas of the beach. The only other witness was Julio, my brother, who was six months short of his seventh birthday. We were busy destroying the home of a blue crab, poking about in

the sand with a stick, when a brief flash made us look up at the sky. Five glittering lights seemed to emerge from the depths of the sea, floating for a few seconds above our heads, then retreating inland towards the estuary.

"See that?" said Julio, pointing towards the horizon.

"Of course I did. I'm not blind."

"But what is it?"

"It's a spaceship," I told him.

But none of the grown-ups paid us any attention when we dashed back to the bonfire, not even our parents. Sitting away from the flames, from all the others, they were arguing so heatedly that they didn't even want to listen to us.

3. A few weeks earlier an exceptional occurrence had taken place: Thursday the 11th of July was the date of what would become known as the longest total solar eclipse of the twentieth century. That afternoon, Mexico had its eyes fixed on the heavens, impatiently awaiting the miracle that would turn the sun into a ring of fire and the moon into a shadow. The eclipse wouldn't be visible from Veracruz, but what did that matter when we had the TV, the screen tirelessly repeating the same static shot of the sky and the image of the crowds waiting for the eclipse to happen, congregated in town squares, standing on flat roofs and central reservations, taking care not to look directly at the brightest star, as they had been warned by the news.

In Mexico City, south of the ring road, Guillermo Arreguín was using a video camera to film the sky from the comfort of his balcony. He wasn't interested so much in the climax of the eclipse but in the planets and stars that, so he had read, would shine more brightly thanks to the forced twilight. When it was completely dark, Arreguín panned the camera from one side of the balcony to the other several times. It was during one of these movements that he was able to record, high above the buildings, a "shining object".

Arreguín's video made the *24 horas* newscast that very night. A couple of days later, an article in *La Prensa* newspaper described the filmed object as "solid", "metallic" and surrounded by "silver rings". But the word "extraterrestrial" wouldn't make its triumphant appearance until Friday, 19th July, in a broadcast of the debate programme *What Do You Think?* devoted entirely to a discussion of the supposed presence of aliens on planet Earth. During the transmission—which went on live for a record time of eleven hours and ten minutes, such was the audience's interest—the presenter Nino Canún gave the floor to an individual called Maussán, a ufologist (so he called himself) by trade, who claimed to be in possession of fifteen additional recordings of the strange object, all of them made by different people, in different cities, on the day of the eclipse. Maussán assured viewers that the videos had been subject to tests that proved that the "object" filmed was indeed an extraterrestrial craft, and made the most of his successful appearance on the show to announce the next broadcast of his documentary *The Sixth Sun*, in which he would reveal the secrets behind those mysterious sightings.

And so began Mexico's UFO Wave.

That summer I learnt everything there was to know about the subject: little grey men, "abductions", the plot of *Men in Black*, the connection between extraterrestrials and the construction of the Great Pyramid in Egypt and the crop circles found in English fields. All that fascinating knowledge was imparted to me via two sources: the TV (or rather, the collection of videos by Mr Maussán, for which my brother and I whinged until we got them) and the kilos of comics I devoured every week. I basically spent every afternoon lying on my stomach, my eyes skipping from the screen of the idiot box to the colourful pages of my comics.

As far as comics were concerned, I was insufferably clueless: I liked *Archie*, *Little Lulu*, *The Adventures of Donald Duck* and I didn't deviate from those. But there was one publication on display at the news-stand that attracted me like a moth to a flame: the weekly *Journal of the Unusual*, a veritable encyclopaedia of human morbidity represented in poor-quality, doctored photos, a prayer book to the macabre and frightening. I can still remember some of those cherished "reports": the giant, man-eating, flying manta ray from the Fiji islands; the primary-school teacher who had a third eye at the base of her skull, with which she could spy on her pupils' misdemeanours; the shadow of a hanged Judas in one of the Virgin Mary's eyes, miraculously painted on St Juan Diego's cape; and, of course, the alien autopsy carried out in Roswell, New Mexico, among others.

Thanks to these edifying reads I had been able to grasp, over the course of that summer when I was nine, that the strange light I saw at Playa del Muerto in the company of my brother could be none other than an interplanetary spaceship, crewed by little grey and extremely wise beings who had managed to challenge the laws of physics. Perhaps they came to warn us about some imminent cataclysm that would destroy planet Earth, now that the end of the millennium was just around the corner and people carried on immersed in their stupid wars that killed people and drenched the poor pelicans with oil. Maybe they were looking for someone to understand them, a person to whom they could bequeath their science and their secrets. Perhaps they felt alone, I thought, roaming the cosmos in their crafts of plasma and silicon, searching, always searching for a friendlier planet, another world, other homes, new friends in distant galaxies.

4. After the sighting we witnessed at the beach, Julio and I took the firm decision to continue monitoring the sky. Perhaps we'd

be taken more seriously if we managed to record some kind of proof.

The problem was that Dad refused to lend us his video camera.

"How can you be so idiotic and believe in that stuff?" he would say when he saw us with our noses glued to the television, trying to decipher the mysterious signs left by flying saucers on the Nazca plains.

Dad couldn't stand Maussán. The ufologist's greying beard and sad eyes put him in a bad mood and he couldn't bear the sound of his voice, especially if he had to listen to his stories replaying through the screen all evening. He even reached the point of threatening to hide the VCR.

"Can't you see he looks like a stoner?"

Poor Dad, he just didn't understand. We felt sorry for him. But Mum was different. She and a friend took us back to Playa del Muerto one night, so that we could see the UFO again.

That night there was a full moon and the water was so still, out beyond the silvery reflection of the heavenly body, that it seemed an enormous mirror. But everything had changed since the last time we were there, in mid-July: now the place was packed with cars and people. Dozens of adolescent bodies were sprawled over the stones of the breakwaters and crowded round bonfires lit with dry brush. Their cars filled the sandy plaza, parked so close to the shore that the salt water wet the tyres. The belches, the beeps, the strains of the latest hit by Soda Stereo drowned out the murmur of the wind. Lovers, draping amorously over the soft tops of their cars, shielded their faces from the camera flashes. I watched with horror as television crews set up tripods to film the festivities. I saw fat women destroying the dunes with their clumsy stumbles. I saw little brats pointing fingers sticky with ice cream at the sky, asking out loud: "Mummy, what time is the UFO coming?"

"This is lame," said Julio after a while and, without offering further explanation, ran off to play tag with some other boys who were there. I thought there was no more cowardly way to give up on a cause.

After what seemed like hours of peering vainly into the blackness of the sky, I began to feel sleepy. I returned to my mother and curled up on her lap. Her breath smelt of wine, her fingers of tobacco. She was chatting to her friend about the UFO; about some lights—white and red—that they were able to see in the distance, but I no longer had the energy to keep my eyes open.

"All this commotion for a dealer's plane," said Mum.

"It's an excuse for a party, at any rate," joked her friend.

5. The first reports of the detection of irregular aeronautical activity over the towns of the Sotavento region (mainly Veracruz, Boca del Río, Alvarado and Tlalixcoyan) date from 1989. The inhabitants of this wild landscape, ranchers and rural labourers, were already used to the presence of nocturnal lights. The eldest referred to them as "witches"; the better-informed, light aircraft. They even knew the place where those lights came down: a gap in the verminous scrubland used by the army as a natural landing strip. It was known as Viper Ranch.

On that natural flatland surrounded by swamps, it wasn't unusual for the residents of Tlalixcoyan to notice the presence of soldiers. The Viper strip was used by the armed forces to carry out special manoeuvres. For that reason no one found it strange when, at the end of October 1991, squads of soldiers arrived to cut the low brush from the plain with machetes and clear the strip of obstacles.

A week later, on the morning of 7th November that same year, 1991, the army, the federal police and a Cessna light aircraft of Colombian origin became embroiled in a bloody scandal that only just managed to evade the tight grip of government censorship: members of the 13th Infantry Battalion opened fire on a group of federal agents before said agents could apprehend the crew of the Colombian plane, which had been spotted from the Nicaraguan coast by the US Customs Service. The Cessna, allegedly manned by Colombian traffickers, landed on the Viper plain at 6.50 a.m., followed by the feds' King Air. The crew, a man and a woman, abandoned a cargo of 355 kilos of cocaine in sacks and disappeared into the undergrowth, while the soldiers of the 13th Infantry Battalion, positioned in two columns along the landing strip, opened fire on the federal agents until they were "neutralized".

Of this incident, I recall two photos that appeared in the local paper *Notiver*. In one of them, seven men were lying in a row on the grass, face down. They were the agents who had been riddled with bullets by the army. Five of them were wearing dark clothes and the other two were dressed as farm workers, and although they had black overcoats, soiled with earth and straw, none of them was wearing shoes. The second photograph showed an individual sitting on the ground, the barrel of a gun pointed at his face. The man, who wore the insignia of the PGR, the Attorney General's Office, on his chest, was looking directly at the lens. His lips, frozen mid-spasm, allowed a glimpse of a swollen tongue: he was the only federal agent to survive the massacre.

It was December—or perhaps January or February—by the time I saw those photos, printed in the pages of an old newspaper I had spread out on the floor to wrap up the dead leaves swept from the patio. And I say that it must have been those months because that's the only time of year when the tropical almond trees in the port are stripped of their foliage by the cold fronts. I remember kneeling on that patio, looking at the images and reading the crime section spread out across the cement floor with curiosity, but another ten years had to pass before I could make a connection between the two images, the photograph of the dead agents and the strange lights I saw in the sky that summer, and come to the conclusion that that unidentified craft wasn't carrying aliens but Colombian cocaine.

After the shooting at the Viper, the municipal government banned night-time visits to the beaches for some months, so we were unable to return to Playa del Muerto until the end of 1992, by which time the place had lost all its charm. New breakwaters had claimed ground from the sea and swarmed with hawkers and tourists. They had even removed the rough signage with skulls that warned of sudden pools, and in time, the name Playa del Muerto fell into disuse in favour of the much less morbid Playa Los Arcos.

I don't think I ever believed in anything again with such faith as I believed in UFOs. Not even the Tooth Fairy, Santa Claus or the Headless Man (whom my father told me appeared at Playón de Hornos every night searching the waters for his head, which had been ripped off by gunfire during the US invasion of '14), much less in the giant, man-eating, flying manta ray of the Fiji islands, and later, not even God would escape my scepticism. They were all a lie, inventions by grown-ups. All those wonderful beings were fruit of nothing more than parental imagination.

The current residents of the area say that when there's no moon, strange coloured lights still cross the night until they land on the plain. But I no longer have the heart to search for extraterrestrials. That chubby little intergalactic sentinel no longer exists, just as Playa del Muerto no longer exists, or the brave fools who drowned there.

Translation by Beth Fowler

HAWKER

EMILIANO MONGE

—I—

The hindquarters of the vehicle that has just dumped two more bodies fold into the depths of night, their flickering tail lights disappearing in the distance. Only then do the two old men who founded "The Inferno" turn and, grabbing Hawker's arms, begin to walk back towards their kingdom.

"They have to talk first," Hoarhead explains to the old man who does not understand how it can be that he is still alive.

"Have to call, have to say how many they're bringing and how much they're paying," adds Dyer, catching a brief glimpse of the immigrant who, just hours ago, had been reading the palms and telling the fortunes of the other immigrants whose corpses are now piled high.

"That's how they could come and go with no problems," explains Hoarhead, watching as Hawker and Dyer heave closed the twin wrought-iron gates that guard The Inferno, a rag-and-bone yard that, until the people of the zone renamed it, was called "The Three Brothers".

"Because they called a while ago… they always call in the morning," Dyer concludes, shooting home the bolt that locks the two gates. "Only them as have called can be allowed in here."

"What about the padlock?" Hawker asks, clutching at Dyer as he wheels around and turns his head to scan both sides of the street on which Three Brothers stands, implying: What if they come back?

"I'm the one always puts on the padlock," growls Hoarhead, shoving aside his triplet brother, the oldest of the men and women who came from the desolate lands, and the only one who, up in the mountains, had come unscathed through dust and fire.

"I already said I don't think they'll come back," Dyer says, turning back and dragging Hawker. "Least not for several days."

"And even if they do, you've no need to fear them no more," Hoarhead says, snapping the padlock and wheeling around in turn to drag Hawker along. "The bastards who killed these fuckers won't touch you… Because…"

"Because we bought you for a reason… You belong to us now and there ain't nothing they can do!"

"This here is your new home!" Hoarhead says, his arm sweeping around to indicate this place where furnace fires crackle and smoke dances between broken-down cars.

"Here you'll be safe at last," Dyer explains, and two brief spurts of flame erupt as if to underscore his words.

"But back to us…" snaps Hoarhead. "Forget about them, let's talk about this," pointing to the place where the bodies ravaged in the high mountains now lie in piles.

"You should go there now and see if you've under—"

"If you've understood what you'll be doing here."

The flames emerging from the furnaces set the night's shadows scuttering and mark out a path for the men as they trudge through The Inferno without another word. Silently, the two triplets that remain savour the knowledge that soon they will have an assistant, someone to do what their brother used to do, while Hawker thanks fate and resolves not to fail these two men who saved him just a few hours ago.

Prowling around the old men who, as they walk, cleave the stone-grey clouds of smoke, come the dogs who live in this place: when their masters walk abroad in their kingdom, the beasts are never more than a metre from their heels. High up, where the rising smoke melds into the darkness, a flock of storks is migrating to another world: the colour of their plumage, framed against clouds that appeared only a moment since, is more grey, less white.

A few metres from the place towards which they are heading, where the pile of broken bodies are bleeding out and the warm, snaking, ashy smoke from the furnaces becomes thick, sweltering and unbreathable, the two triplets who founded The Inferno and who grow older every day cover their faces with their hands and, beneath the sheltering palms, begin again to speak in tongues.

"I hope that you do not fail us," Hoarhead warns, turning to Hawker, and adds: "And that the smell does not bother you."

"I can tell that you will not fail us here," Dyer says as he, too, turns to face the oldest of the migrants who crossed the frontier to meet the hail of bullets in the mountains: "You'll get used to the stench, you'll see."

"I don't know whether I could get used to it," Hawker blurts, suddenly stopping to spit out the acrid liquid that churns in his gut and rises in his throat until it finds the minuscule church that is the soothsayer's mouth.

"Everyone gets used to it," Hoarhead declares, tugging Hawker by the arm and laughing at the way he arches his body.

"Most days you can't even smell it," Dyer agrees, tugging at the oldest of all living creatures who came from other countries and, pointing to the flames rising like huge sunflowers from one furnace, announces: "You'll start here with this fire."

"You'll see, you might even get to like it," Hoarhead insists, laughing suddenly; and, stopping next to the barrel his brother just mentioned, he turns towards the limbs severed by barrages of lead. "We threw up ourselves the first time."

"We have never smelt what humans smell like when they burn," Dyer says, laughing; and, turning to the mangled bodies, he quickens his step.

"Someone brought in a car that had been shot up, and inside was the mangled remains of a woman," Hoarhead explains, following after his triplet brother and pulling Hawker with him. "They wanted the car back, so we charged them for cleaning it and getting rid of the body."

"Later, they came back with another bullet-riddled car and this time there were lots of bodies inside," Dyer adds, coming to a halt next to a pile of corpses. "That was the day we turned this business around… now it really was a rag-and-bone yard."

"So you might say we diversified… these days we not only dismantle, we also dismember," Hoarhead says, laughing even louder. "You have to adapt. If you don't, then someone else does and you're fucked."

"That's true… we've not forgotten the past," Dyer says gravely and stops laughing. "We couldn't give up the old business altogether, because this place was set up by our parents… but these days flesh is as important as scrap iron."

"If they leave us the vehicle, they can have the bodies burnt for free," Hoarhead explains, bending over the pile of bloody, emaciated limbs, then picking up an arm and waving it in the air. "If they take away the clapped-out car, we charge them for the bodies… but w—"

"But we explained all that already," Dyer says. He too has picked up an arm and now pretends to lunge at this old man who, after they had all been captured, contrived a promising future for the other migrants.

"I lied to them all," babbles Hawker, but before he reaches the end of his sentence, the surviving triplets start to laugh again and interrupt.

"Ha ha ha!… Too much talk and not enough toil," Hoarhead growls between booming laughter.

"Best get back to work right now and stop wasting time," Dyer says, tossing the arm he has been waving back onto the pile. "You finished hacking this lot up a while ago and you still haven't tossed one onto the fire."

"So get a move on, there's a lot to deal with there, we'll be watching you… and don—"

"And don't go stopping next time people show up."

"If anyone else comes, we'll go to the gate," Hoarhead explains. "You don't move from this spot until you've finished your work."

"When you're finished, then you can come see us," Dyer agrees, turning and pointing to the shack where he and his brother live, then adds: "Not just when you've finished burning the bodies… when you've finished cleaning up the stakes."

"We'll be there waiting for you." Hoarhead in turn gestures to the shack and then heads in that direction.

"And just remember… we can see you from there," Dyer says and trudges off, following in his brother's footsteps.

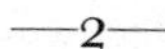

—2—

The echo of the door Hoarhead slams shut booms around the vast wrecking yard but it does not penetrate the ears of the oldest of those creatures who left their lands days ago; he raises the machete Dyer has just set down and as he does raises memories of the voices of those men and women who crossed the frontier with him: how could I do that to them?

All around Hawker the dogs slink, they growl while the fire crackles in the barrels: these sounds, however, do not reach his ears. Why the hell did I lie to them? the oldest man wonders and as he does raises the machete he is holding until it is at eye level. What good did it do me? Hawker mutters over and over as the edge of the blade cuts through his sightline, then he tosses the weapon onto the pile of jumbled corpses.

The sound of the machete striking the shaft of bone that rises from the bodies like the mast of a sunken ship sets the dogs' growls louder, but the sound does not reach the ears or the mind of the oldest of the migrants, who is studying the palms of his hands in the nervous, flickering glow of the flames. It will do you no good in the end… that's what it says in the lines of his palm, Hawker thinks and starts to laugh though he does not know why.

Why the fuck am I laughing? Hawker wonders between loud booming laughs only to be interrupted by the voice of Hoarhead, a whipcrack that booms across The Inferno, lashing the oldest of all the migrants and lashing at the baying hounds that yelp in surprise: "Get to work, you fucker… we watching you!" Hawker bows his head and shakes off the lurking thoughts and laughs the way a dog shakes itself dry: he cannot fail these men.

I can't afford for these bastards not to like me, Hawker mutters silently to himself, and as he does finally sets off to the pile of corpses and severed limbs. Just as he is about to raise the machete, Dyer's voice booms in the distance, the words not only urging him on but numbing the oldest of the migrants: "Get a move on! We want to see that work done!" At Dyer's roar, the barking of the hounds becomes a howl, and those same howls take Hawker back to the years when he was a soldier.

"We're not going to wait all night… And don't expect us to put up with you if you can't do your job," roar the brothers, but Hawker is no longer listening: of the years when he was a soldier, he is now reliving the period when he joined the paras, the years he spent wiping out whole populations, gutting pregnant women, hacking the young and the old to pieces: even then I knew the fire and the light would return.

I could see it clearly written on my palms... the past is always waiting up ahead, Hawker thinks, and as he does so, he finds himself laughing again and it is the sound of his own guttural laugh that rips the oldest of those who left their homelands from his daze and drags him back to The Inferno where the two brothers, watching from their window, are suddenly puzzled: something has changed in this man, who now picks up the machete from the ground and, raising it high, begins to hack and howl, driving away the baying dogs skulking around the corpses.

Hawker's roar serves only to madden the dogs: their howls rise to shrill yelps and, hearing this cacophony, the man who tried to repay the world for the chunks he snatched from fate pauses to forge a future for himself, pauses again and sees himself in the jungles of the ravaged lands. But before those squandered years return to overwhelm him, he hears a booming laugh he does not yet know is his own.

When Hawker finally realizes that it is his own laugh that has dragged him from the jungles, he also notices the brothers roaring and the restless hounds crowding him again. Taking another step, the oldest of all the men and women, he who forsook the ravaged lands, plants his feet between the piles of bodies, raises his machete above his head and furiously lets it fall.

One after another, with quick and expert slashes, Hawker hacks away arms, legs and skulls from the corpses; the dogs become frenzied and, watching from a distance, the brothers are surprised by how well he is doing, this man who no longer seems troubled by the stench or the smoke or the flames emerging from the barrels, these barrels that are spread all over The Inferno like the tattoos spread all over the skin of the man who now rips off his shirt and carries on hewing at the corpses.

When he has finally finished cutting up the bodies, Hawker tosses the machete aside and, renouncing the devil who led the brothers to the place where they found him, scoops up a pile of arms with both hands and stacks them on his shoulder. Eyes half-closed, mouths wide open, the two old men who founded The Inferno gape at the oldest among all of those who crossed many frontiers: they cannot understand what is happening in their kingdom, cannot understand the behaviour of this man whom they bought just a few short hours ago.

This man who even now is moving towards the barrel they pointed out to him, and as he moves, he is thinking about the bundle of arms on his shoulder and about the men and women who once owned these arms: how could I lie to them? Hawker then implores again, feeling a spasm shudder though his belly; as the glow and the flames die down, he stubbornly plunges himself in silence and once he sees the jungles of the ravaged lands ablaze, sees himself torching a village whose inhabitants are locked inside the houses.

Increasingly confused and alarmed, Hoarhead and Dyer watch as Hawker strides towards the barrel and notice that this man is talking to the sheaf of arms he is carrying on his shoulder: the brothers cannot know, they cannot imagine that not only is he talking to these lifeless hunks of flesh he has just caked to pieces, the oldest of all the migrants is addressing his own fate: the past is always waiting up ahead.

Stopping as he comes to the huge furnace, Hawker takes one of the arms from his shoulder, examines the hand attached, prising open the fingers which are clenched into a fist, and briefly studies the palm. Then laughs without realizing he is laughing and, licking the palm with his tongue, tosses it into the fire; as it falls into the flames, it emits a mute, silent cry that echoes around this world. "What the devil is he doing?" wonder the two old men, and they both scrabble towards the door of their shack. "He's raving mad!"

Having thrown all the arms he was carrying on his shoulder into the flames, Hawker picks up the can of petrol the brothers left next to the barrel and, sprinkling it on the flames, watches their savage flickering power rise just as in the jungles of the ravaged lands: those mighty flames once razed whole cities, towns and villages.

It's all here… my past, my present, my future, laughs the oldest of all those who came across the ravaged lands and laughs as he raises the petrol can above his head and as he does so, in the distance, he sees the two old men who founded The Inferno rushing towards him and roaring: "Completely fucking crazy!"

"What the devil are you doing?" Hoarhead roars and Dyer shouts: "What the The Inferno is wrong with you?" But the old man they are addressing does not hear their words: drenching himself in the petrol that streams down his body, he turns, moves towards the fire, and plunges both hands into the flames. "Crazy bastard… stop that right now, you lunatic bastard!" shriek the brothers as they pass the pile of corpses where the starveling hounds are finally sating their hunger.

Still laughing, Hawker moves closer to the barrel and, using his hands as torches, illuminates the landscape all around: clenching his jaws and blazing like a hunk of knotted pine, the oldest of all the migrants finally leaps headlong into the flames, deaf to the voices of the old men who founded The Inferno as they reach the furnace: "What the fuck is he doing?"

Translated by Frank Wynne
From the forthcoming novel *Las tierras arrasadas*

THE WHOLE BIG TRUTH

EDUARDO MONTAGNER

I don't know if that letter from Oliver triggered something within me, but the fact remains, a few days after I'd taken in his words (and the books and films), I went for it: I grabbed the contraband key, the copy I'd made from the original, which I'd temporarily extracted from Paolo's house a few days after my return to Belmondo. It was two in the morning. Outside, the tempest stirred up leaves, spirits. I slipped the key into the pocket of my worn-out trousers. I'd dressed in shabby clothes on purpose, because I could tell what ending the night held for me. I was excited but at the same time fearful: it was like I was on my way to a murder. And perhaps the feeling was not misplaced because, if there was to be a murder, it would be the killing of my own self at the hands of Paolo's ghost, as represented by his clothes, his wellington boots and his smell. It was a memorable night. I was slow to leave the house, but at the same time couldn't wait—the minutes were precious and Paolo would be up at around five. Since this was the first night I'd spend furtively with his rubber boots, I didn't know how much time the rendezvous would require. I looked at myself in a full-length mirror, and nodded in unfaltering approval. I forgot about myself and focused my absolute attention on them, on the act they invoked in their stillness. I stepped out, got steadily on the bike and let myself be consumed by the speed, the fear, the thrill and the wild night wind. When I stopped pedalling at the shut gates to Paolo's barn, I wrote myself off as a madman possessed, and nearly turned back. How could I be doing this? How would I sneak in to debase myself lying on the ground, next to a pair of stinky wellies and a bunch of clothes permeated with a dry, moribund sweat, and left to their own devices for a scant few hours? A car drove past, but I was able to hide from the headlights. It was now or never. I took out the key and opened up, painstakingly slow. I thought about Paolo's sleeping body, his innocence defiled by a miserable sleepwalker who was preparing a strike despite all uncertainties. I left the bicycle on the floor inside the barn. The cows were uttering sparse, inoffensive sounds. I shut the gates as warily as I'd opened them. Two steps in and Chispa and Canela, Paolo's dogs, barked at me with blind fury. I'm dead, I thought. Unhinged as I was, I'd completely forgotten about the dogs. But I quickly called them by their names and hunched down to pet them, and in doing this they recognized me, because according to them—given my regular visits—I was someone familiar by now. Canela was so excited she peed on me when I picked her up. I wiped my hand on my trousers and guided my steps towards the utility room, where I knew Paolo left his soul transformed into clothes and rubber boots during the brief periods he was off work. The dogs trotted ahead of me, willing to accompany me wherever I went, with no regard for my intentions and without questioning my motives. Perhaps this is why they say a dog is man's best friend: they keep you company no questions asked, no quibbles, no snitching. Once in, I clicked my torch on. I didn't want to switch on the lights in case Doña Antonieta or Paolo turned up. I spotted the wellies. My pulse quickened. Each one of my movements would be branded into my memory from then on. Canela and Chispa became sincere if nosey friends. I ushered them out of the room and shut the door on their snuffling. But it wouldn't be as easy as that: gregarious, the dogs started to whimper for my presence. I decided to let them in. After all, it was their house and I had to trust I'd be able to dodge their canine displays. It was the first time in my life I'd have the opportunity to spend time alone with those wellies, those unwashed clothes. It was, of course, a Friday. Because one inevitably gets dirty working in a barn, the most convenient thing to do is to wear the same outfit throughout the week. The only cleanliness that matters is that of the clothes you wear *after* work. I could rest assured, therefore, that the clothes I was about to take possession of were completely impregnated by a week's worth of work in the life of Paolo. That very afternoon I'd come to see him under the pretext of needing to ask something. Nothing important. I just wanted to see his rubber boots in action, because I'd decided to initiate my fetishist adventures that night under cover of darkness. It would be the first time. The first. I couldn't help myself any longer. I flashed my torch at the wellies: one, then the other. Paolo usually wore them without socks. I crouched down, but the dogs thought I wanted to be at their level and rushed at me with eager tongues so I might pet them. After a snub or two, they figured out they needed to leave me alone. Here we go. I took a whiff. Of the outer, I took a whiff. Paolo always washed his boots after work, so they weren't smeared with cow dung, but they still carried the smell of his daily surroundings. I couldn't help myself. I took one boot and again directed the circle of light onto it. I sniffed the inner. Rubber mingled with hour upon hour, day after day of Paolo stuck inside them. It was more than I could bear! The aromas: sacks of cattle feed, veterinary medicine, rubber and clothes mixed with cow dung, fodder and sweat, were my way of demystifying a young man as he slept—Paolo, his clear gaze resting on the mooing of the cows, a perfect gaze that could have advertised expensive clothing in glossy magazines, a model who preferred to dress unpretentiously, coarsely even, in the eyes of society. Oh! Unbearable beauty touching the thorniest heart of ugliness, only to bounce back now, like a reflex, as a beauty of enormity, no less! My erection pushed for freedom. I unzipped and let it out. Overcome by a wave of passion, I frantically grabbed Paolo's clothes, and lying stretched out with them thrown on me, biting the lip of one welly and clutching the other tight against my chest, I masturbated, for the first time the absolute owner of my member. The torch tumbled to the ground, shining about randomly. I don't think it took me even one minute to reach orgasm. The gush of semen wet my shirt, my belly. The echo of Paolo's voice in my mind, any one of his phrases emphasized with a virile gesture, his smile, the memory of his swaying penis, all produced in me a surge of guilt. My eyes looked up in amazement at the ceiling in the utility room. The torch lit the space dimly. With the rim of one welly still in my mouth and the sole of the other flat on my chest, I knew I was mad. That I had to cry even though I didn't want to; that my life was irreversibly lost. Right then I discovered how after a fetishist experience, any immediate act, no matter how inconsequential, brings about a great deal of sorrow. I had a feeling I was never going to find my way out of that mess: lying out on my back, Paolo's clothes spread over my body and his rubber boot clinging to me in a lifeless yet steadfast contact. I opened my mouth and the welly flopped dead on its pair. Both now rested on my chest, quietly scorning me for waking them in the off hours, and, as if this weren't enough, staining their purity. I sat up, slowly, although I wasn't able to find any answers. I didn't know how long it was going to take me to put everything back in its place. A cold dread of being caught mired my soul. How could I? Why did I not study the way Paolo had left his things? If I didn't put them back exactly as he'd done, within a few hours he might suspect the presence of a stranger in his home. I hobbled towards the torch and stooped to pick it up, feeling tremendously exhausted. Luckily, Paolo didn't fold his clothes, just flung them into a thoughtless pile. I attempted the same. I threw the trousers onto the sack of cattle feed I'd usurped them from, then the shirt on top. I glanced around for the cap: it was on the ground. I placed it on the pile. Then I stood the wellies one next to the other, though not before wiping away the evidence of some splashes of semen on the leg and instep of the right boot, which would soon be occupied by an innocent heterosexual body. Manolo—just about to emerge was the memory of Manolo, blemished and trampled on, but I was smart enough to block that mental suggestion, which otherwise would have disarmed me. Immediately after, I shone the torch on the wet patch on my belly, left behind by that extreme self-ejaculation. I felt vile, an Onan more solitary and deranged than the biblical one. I put my penis away, and pulled up the zipper. I wondered about the dogs and flashed the torch around looking for them; they were snuggled up in a corner. They glanced at me in disbelief, like they were disappointed in me. My muscles were worn out. I felt I'd never be able to turn around, head out, get home, sleep. I stood there for a while, motionless, defeated, shoulders slumped, my torch shining at the ground in a woebegone, useless effort. I had no desire to see anything any more. The encounter had been extremely beautiful, excellent, but I felt like those people who want to experience real sex, and when they do, it turns out to be not powerful enough to sustain such an amount of sublimity and vileness at once. I was one of those girls who lust after a gigantic phallus and end up crying in the shower because they got ripped apart. My lack of a vagina cried out, victim of rough handling. I suddenly felt like waking Paolo, telling him everything, letting circumstance envelop me, come what may. I'd tell him a Chilean painter had entranced me with false ideas and that only now had I realized it was all a huge mistake. Paolo would understand, and maybe so would Doña Antonieta. Ha! What stupid notions came into my head! Then it dawned on me. They were right there, at hand, they were mine! The rubber boots, which I lit up in a fresh attempt removed from fierce passion, revealed my happy reality. There they were, calling me again, beckoning like a spirit moves the Ouija! How could I think of this as fraud, as deception, if such acts were beyond them, if I didn't yet know anything about them? I approached the boots again, and cradled them in my arms. The smell hit me once more. My arms were trembling. I was the addict seized again by the fetish, the drug. But this time a divine instinct showed me the true path: I undressed completely and put his clothes on; I dressed up as Paolo. First the trousers, then the shirt and last the wellies: in reality, that was his kiss, his passionate kiss, his sexual act! I almost forgot the cap, but put it on, and with that I finally became him. I wished I had a mirror in front of me to witness the miracle. I had to carry on through to the ultimate consequences of this night, the first of my life. I sneaked out to the barn, having become Paolo through his work attire. I walked around the stalls, lay on the alfalfa which would feed the cows in a few hours. I climbed into the tractor, peed through the zipper of *his* trousers, wriggled my body at leisure in a nightly oasis of exciting, solitary, absolute adventure: all to demystify the body of Paolo through mine. I was happy, impossibly happy! I ended up masturbating again, but standing this time, amid the mooing of the cows, before the countless images of Paolo I held in my mental gallery, and I prolonged the pleasure until I could no longer stand it. When I ejaculated, I was about to let myself be swallowed up by guilt, but I shut the door on any bad feelings. I couldn't allow myself to become dispirited again—what else could I ask for? I walked to the utility room. I undressed, and kissing them, caressing them, sniffing them like those dogs who wouldn't leave me alone, I restored the clothes to their original position. I dressed and, retracing my stealthy movements, stepped out of that acrid and cold nocturnal world with the certainty that the events that had transpired had been only the beginning of a long chain of experiences still to be had. I meandered around the empty streets on my bicycle, trying to adjust to my brand-new existence. After an hour of thoughts and recollections, I got home and slid under the sheets without washing my hands. Minutes, hours or days afterwards, I was able to fall asleep, probably dreaming of that lingering scent. Of course, I told Oliver Ackland everything in a letter. I received no reply.

Translated by Juana Adcock
From the novel *Toda esa gran verdad*

HISTORY

ANTONIO ORTUÑO

1. It would be wrong for me to try to explain the profound motives that drove the invaders, because I don't know them. Although I like to speculate. For years I lived with my back to politics and newspapers, my head in the streets as if in a bucket of water. But, that said, I do know which films people want to watch, I know which toys kids buy. I know the kind of shirts you have to start producing in bulk for the poor because the rich are wearing them. I know everything that's sold and most of what's bought, but the faces and names of those who governed us, those who govern us, escape me.

2. I understand that drug trafficking, the black market in organs, the kidnap and murder of foreigners, this country's current fashion for anarchy and the mass migration of thousands of pariahs were too much for the enemy to resist, so they broke in and grabbed control of whatever they could while no one was watching the door.

3. It's not easy to explain to the citizens of any country that an army must be sent to impose calm in a neighbouring territory. The anthology of these pretexts is called World History.

3.1. I'm just a guy who works at a market stall selling *fancy goods* (nothing fancy whatsoever about these goods), but I studied two terms of History at university. Compared to the guys on the next-door stalls (one of them says hello to me every day with his hands full of stolen jewellery) I'm practically a scholar. I read. Applaud me. Thank you.

3.2. My country likes to think it lives at the margins of the planet's History. Our books are full of anything but our own long, disastrous History.

3.2.1. Our History is a never-ending stream of invasions, some bloody, some comical. Why should our luck have improved? Only one hundred years went by without us being invaded—the century had made dull statues of anyone who might warn us of the malice of foreigners—and certain people took it for granted that it would never happen again, that our borders would remain proud, impenetrable.

4. We were invaded for the first time so many centuries ago that there wasn't even a country waiting for the invaders. From the moment the nation was born we were subjected to the will of the conquerors: our country is the scrap of land the conquerors saved in their fight against others like them, others perhaps more depraved still.

4.1. The conquerors were white, my mother used to say, like the men in our family. They must have been equally inept, too. In any case, they ended up mixing with the native population and with slaves and forming this unhealthy race that I see in the street, white and mestizo and black, to which I belong, although my mother maintains we look like the conquerors.

4.2. A foreigner has never taken me for one of them. There must be some poverty in the way I carry myself, in my clothes, which alerts them to my true nature.

4.3. For years people at the market called me *Güero*, the same nickname as my father, because I shared his light-coloured eyes. He was a butcher who had taken advantage of his refined looks to throw himself at all the women in the place: dark-skinned, podgy or pale.

4.4. My mother spent her life shut up at home, pretending to suffer all kinds of respiratory problems. It seems she spent a good many peaceful years that way, complaining about the weather and the maid's bad manners, relieved of her conjugal responsibilities. My father used to get home so tired from lying with market girls that he never laid a hand on her again.

5. The greatest foreign invasion of our History ended with the loss of half our national territory. The next was simply a clash that left a few fatalities on each side: a mob had eaten a foreign baker's rolls and he asked his government for help, so they sent a punitive expedition. A third imposed a government for a few years and made this ruinous country an empire (on paper).

5.1. The people must have thought this beggared such belief that they rebelled en masse.

5.2. We can deal with going hungry in a simple republic, but from an empire we expect earthly salvation rather than the perfection of poverty. (OK: only I think that, and deep down I miss the Empire, its pomp and essential stupidity.)

5.3. The rebels worked hard to overthrow the invaders, shot the Emperor and founded an awkward, languid, corrupt republic, but at least a coherent one.

5.4. Who ever thought to call this swamp of ours an empire, *his* empire.

6. One of the most interesting consequences of this third foreign incursion was that the invading soldiers, who were blonde and had large moustaches, fathered hundreds of children in the country—so the story goes. I don't know whether it's possible they had time or strength enough to set about raping so many women but, ever since they left, every blonde child born has been attributed to the irregular intercourse of foreign soldiers with native women.

6.1. Such cases, if there were any, were in all probability few and far between, but it was fun to allude to them, and those bearing the brunt took such offence—after all, they were being called bastards, a particularly weighty word among the insults of the time—that the version became History.

6.2. It's also probable that my mother married my father because she imagined he was descended from some long-lost colonel of the invasion.

7. Every time we've had a civil war, even an attempted one, someone has rushed to invade us. In our last revolution, for example, three different expeditions entered the country and captured whole provinces, meeting no resistance whatsoever or only symbolic opposition.

8. The school I went to was named after one of the heroes who tried to resist one of those expeditions and was killed in the process. It was, naturally, an ugly state school. My father had enough money to send me to a school full of girls with blonde

plaits, but he refused to grant my mother's wish. I was sent to the local primary.

8.1. In the third grade, a classmate went into school with an illustrated magazine that revealed the mystery of coitus, to which I'd never previously given a moment's thought. The guilty boy's father had to attend a meeting with our teacher and a child psychologist sent especially by the local inspector. It had all been a terrible mistake, said the man, his son had taken the magazine from home without permission. The teacher and the psychologist sat in shocked silence. They decided to give the child a verbal warning and forget the issue.

9. My father, I later learnt, was friends with that astonishing man who calmly accepted having a magazine rack full of pornography: he ran a cream and cheese stall next to our butcher's. He was a bald, talkative individual. His only noteworthy feature was that every Friday he used to drink a whole bottle of banana liquor while listening to the radio.

9.1. He had a short, dark-skinned daughter with an immense pair of breasts. She was my first girlfriend, the first I touched with any certainty of what I was doing.

9.2. One Friday, while her father was imbibing his liquor and humming his songs, she took me to the stall's storeroom, where the first floor had been set up as an office. The cream-seller wouldn't give a copy of the key even to God, but my girlfriend got hold of it secretly: she had decided to take advantage of the first floor to consummate what we had started and interrupted so many times in dark corners.

9.3. Mirrors on all the walls and a red bed: the place was so dodgy it inspired little enthusiasm in us. We opened a drawer and found it full of bottles of lubricant. The leather harnesses were in a second drawer. My girlfriend went to get a glass of water and came back distraught, holding a gold contraption. It was vibrating.

9.3.1. In a final drawer we found photos of her father being sodomized (with the gold contraption) by a woman neither of us knew. We went to consummate our relationship elsewhere.

9.3.2. Years later, when the cream-seller had died and my girlfriend and I were no longer speaking—she cheated on me with a municipal inspector and I on her with a girl who sold household appliances—I learnt that the first floor of the storeroom was intact and still in use.

9.3.3. As it happened, the box of the gold vibrator was on the desk, in full view, in that cross between office and dungeon. The contraption was foreign and called "the Pleasure Invader".

10. Some people claimed there was no way we could be invaded again. That was not so: we have, in fact, been invaded again.

11. What I think, as soon as I find out the first foreign soldier has crossed the northern border, is that men will fantasize about him or his colleagues raping their wives and girlfriends and sisters and neighbours and even them at gunpoint.

12. I decide to turn to the papers in search of news. I go to bars. I buy rounds, not caring if my fellow drinkers are unstoppable bores, dried up or devoted to mutism. I have to listen to some

idiot declaring that his ancestors were blonde, "country types" and descended from invaders.

12.1. Someone, an obese young teacher with plenty of whiskey in his veins and scholarly airs, sends me to read Shakespeare. I have the sangfroid to go into a library, request the dog-eared volume and find the quote.

> By faith and honour,
> Our madams mock at us, and plainly say
> Our mettle is bred out, and they will give
> Their bodies to the lust of English youth
> To new-store France with bastard warriors.

So says the Dauphin. That is what all the men in this country fear and desire. They want blonde children, even if they aren't their own.

12.2. I corroborate my theory. What is my theory? That my compatriots are excited by the possibility of foreigners stealing their women. They have no way of knowing for now whether the fantasy will shrink their testicles or if, on the other hand, it will cause them infernal palpitations.

12.3. I go out into the street. I offer small sums of money to schoolgirls who appear to have attained mastery of organic chemistry by force of fellatio; I offer to help foul-mouthed, haughty matrons with their shopping bags; I offer cigarettes in cafes to women in their thirties who want a man who'll take them to the cinema. I discover that most women aren't interested in foreigners, they simply keep thinking about their boyfriends, husbands, friends. Perhaps, like the females of certain tribes of savages, they feel they deserve nothing more than a man of their own stock. Or perhaps they are sincerely indifferent to ambition. A nuance: they all like blonde boys.

13. The foreign soldiers are tall, pale and stupid. But their ferocity renders their stupidity irrelevant. They are quick to advance and shoot. Meanwhile, I read in a magazine (I have begun to read them) that they're sensitive souls who send photos home every week, tremble with fear in their tents at night and dream anaemically about local girls spreading their arms, smiling, leading them to a hasty bed and making them moan.

13.1. Others send their friends photos of nude native girls, with plaits and avid mouths and vulvas like black cats.

13.2. The foreigners say they're going to re-establish order in the country. On their television programmes, soldiers swear that what they want in life is love and happiness. This means they're willing to shoot at anything that moves in order to safeguard their future comfort.

13.3. Or perhaps, like Achilles, they learn to read love in the dying gazes of the girls they kill. (I've been back to the library and I'm not sorry to admit it. I'll leave feeling ashamed of the people who listen to the radio and drink banana liquor.)

13.4. The first operations of the invasion are unexpectedly quick. Our army deserts the border en masse, after three disastrous skirmishes.

13.5. When people block the path of the conscripts sent to replace the traitors, it doesn't cross their minds that in a few centuries those terrified individuals might become popular heroes.

13.6. We'll never really know whether some of them, the most aggressive, are members of existing bands of guerrillas or if some holy spirit transmutes their souls on the way north, but the units of conscripts elude the advance of enemy columns, ferociously attack a border post (they hang the guards by their thumbs) and enter foreign territory.

13.7. Popular imagination assures us that they form a guerrilla army in the invading country and succeed in attacking enemy settlements. I suspect, having heard it from the father of a conscript in a cantina, that most of them end up doing other things: they are gardeners, plumbers, electricians. And if they do keep their bellicose instinct, it is only to become criminals.

13.8. The country, then, is left defenceless. Foreign soldiers form small contingents to control every moderately important city. Our president hands over powers of government to their commander-in-chief less than a month after the start of the invasion.

14. The occupation had been predicted by leftist thinkers, so an adherent tells me, seventy-five years ago. Those who handed down this ruling have died, but their descendants rushed to claim the glory of their predecessors' foresight. What abnegation, to predict what would happen, without fail, for seven and a half decades, and to have always been ignored.

15. My father never tried to get involved in politics: he stuck to cutting meat in his stall and voting for the losing candidates in every election called.

16. The invaders are here. The tank, gigantic and green, fills the street. The next-door stallholder runs and shouts for me to follow him. Someone turns off the market's lights. A doors slams and then darkness. Fear exacerbates my clumsiness and I clutch the metal handrail. The fear of falling. The fear of being left behind. There's a tank outside the door and we hear the creaks of the cannon adopting its firing position. It's lining up the front of the building in its sights.

17. The kid who helps me at the stall didn't come. Not even on the day of the Apocalypse is he capable of turning up when asked. Stallholders and shoppers, united for once, all flee. As we slip through gates and passageways I imagine that one of our colleagues, one of the girls who sells juice, perhaps, will have already been arrested, undressed by pale and indistinct hands and submitted to the vices of the soldiers. Blonde hair and red jaws.

17.1. Would they rape her even if she was blonde? One of the juice girls was blonde. I remember that.

18. We climb up to the roof of a neighbouring building and hide among the clothes drying there. At the end of an alleyway formed by sheets and underwear there are steps leading down to the next street. If we're lucky, we won't meet another tank waiting on that side. If we're not, they'll arrest us and maybe kill us. Although I haven't been able to stop thinking that because I'm white they should respect me. The stallholder I'm with isn't white. Will I leave him? Will I call out to the invaders and say: "As you can see, my friend isn't one of us"?

19. People say that when the foreigners are nearby it always smells of the same thing: their bleached uniforms. Even their shit must smell of bleach.

19.1. The invaders are tall, fit and cleaner than us. But they won't catch us. We run down the metal steps. It's no time for discretion and our footsteps ring out. There are no tanks. Hope springs up at the back of a dry throat.

19.2. The stallholder crosses the street in three long strides and launches himself into a conveniently dark alley. I follow him, breathless, moving my feet because there's no way to stop when you're scared you'll be riddled with bullets.

19.3. The juice girl must be naked in the hands of some artilleryman, at the back of a greengrocer's stall, her skirts around her neck.

19.4. It occurs to me that if I could run to my father's house, this would be a good moment. But I'll suffocate first, I'll fall down dead without them having to shoot me. I can already feel the deadly pain blossoming between my ribs.

19.5. "Stop looking back," grunts the stallholder, two metres ahead of me. My shoelaces are untied and any sensible person would give me a moment to do them up before carrying on. I'm crying. I can't help it, just as I can't help biting the cuts in my mouth over and over until they reopen.

19.6. A cloud of glass and dust tells me the tank has blown up the front of the market. A second later, the noise of the blast reaches us and knocks us down.

19.7. I imagine that the invaders will appear with their precision rifles at any moment, that I'll start hearing shots whistle past my head and seeing small craters form around my feet. But no one appears and we get lost in the alley and I don't stop even though I'm white, I don't stop until the stallholder stumbles and we find another building to hide in. There are dozens of rubbish bags pulled open in the entrance, like stone lions guarding the way.

20. We hear the buzz of the helicopters. Tired, gasping for breath like old men, we go upstairs. We knock on a door, any old one. Nobody answers. A strong smell of bleach infects the air.

It must be them, they're coming.

Translated by Lucy Greaves

From the short-story collection *Agua corriente*

THE LITURGY OF THE BODY

EDUARDO RABASA

Para Alejandro Ortega, gran amigo, mejor persona

Abigail and I were in the habit of leaving erotic fiction in the vicinity of a girls' school run by nuns. We stuck stories on walls nearby and to phone poles in the neighbourhood, as if it were subversive material, or we just scattered them on the ground, hoping the girls would pick them up while they were waiting for their mothers or chauffeurs. There was something powerful about the contrast between their long, grey, plaid skirts, their white knee socks, their hair smoothed back into ponytails so tight they looked like they might suffocate their skulls, and the efforts they made to suppress their reactions to reading our filth.

To increase their anxiety we played with their minds in a variety of ways: for weeks on end we distributed the flyers each morning before dawn, so the girls would see them early in the morning, and some of them would come running out to read them the moment classes ended. Then we'd go on hiatus—to the relief of the nuns and their futile attempts to tear down the trash we had pasted to the walls—and later we'd counter-attack with stories so pornographic that they'd unleash a sort of mass hysteria in the school halls. Amid the cries of their mothers and the hyperventilation of the nuns, the girls broke into nervous laughter or grasped their skirts with tight fists, as if to prevent their knees from trembling. The lucky ones who returned home alone were able to search for the papers we had strewn about, folding them carefully and putting them in their backpacks. We enjoyed contemplating what they might do with them later.

I don't want to make light of my participation after the fact, but if I'm honest, it was all Abigail's idea. I think it was the tedium of daily life that prompted her. After a few years of living together, we had captured the perfection of joy without pleasure. Both in bed and outside it, we were getting along well enough to maintain what Abigail referred to as our project of a life together. I've never liked to argue, least of all with her. Plus, I don't know anyone who has the ability to bend things to her will like she can.

The truth is that from the moment that I shut myself in a room to write those stories intended to get teens all hot and bothered, Abigail underwent a transformation that was destined to last until we had fulfilled our own fantasy. It was a departure from the cosy somnolence in which we spent our days together. But things are never so simple for Abigail: ever since I met her she's needed complex fantasies rooted in reason and logic to feel uninhibited. And I needed to have blind allegiance to the vagaries of her logic. The fact is that she was motivated by a belief that we were liberating these tender minds from the cages of sanctimony they had been trapped in. Each time remorse threatened to bring an end to our little war against the tyranny of the nuns, Abigail would launch into her old rhetoric as if entranced: about how these schools teach girls that the Devil lives in their clitoris; that they're assembly lines producing young women incapable of orgasm, angry at the world; that the nuns are just as deviant as the priests, but their methods of psychological warfare are more subtle, which is why more cases of their abuse haven't come to light; and a long list of etceteras justifying our own little sin, without a doubt perverted in its own right.

As I said before: I'm at least as guilty for the series of events leading to the accident. In the first place, I had a fiendishly good time writing the stories. On top of that, I got carried away thinking that I was becoming an incredible writer. Abigail frequently reminded me how she had sacrificed her creative impulses because one of us had to earn a living, and her work as a manager at a renewable energy multinational allowed us to live in relative comfort. In return, I would one day provide our entry into a world less ordinary. In the meantime, since I hadn't managed to fix the dripping tap in the bathroom sink, which tortured us nightly, I ought to dedicate myself to subverting the work the nuns were doing, right under our noses. I should add that reading these erotic stories aloud was the only remedy for Abigail's periodic attacks of hysteria, triggered by her feelings of guilt about an endless string of subjects, ranging from Somali children to the extinction of the dodo.

As if part and parcel of the same state of mind, she would move from crying uncontrollably to devouring me with fervour that seemed like she was faking it. Abigail seemed to leave her own body in order to demonstrate the levels of intensity she was capable of reaching. On these occasions I felt more intimidated than excited, because how can you fulfil the needs of a body erupting with frenzied desire? What happens if you fail? Luckily, I understood that on these occasions I represented little more than a kind of animate dildo, so I just closed my eyes and enjoyed, as best I could, the *mise en scène* of Abigail screwing herself with my help.

The trouble started when someone decided to compete with us, pasting flyers on top of ours along the walls of the school. Apparently it was some new-age shaman who called herself The Neplusultra. It was an affront for her to invade our territory, suffocating our anarchic eroticism with her calls to discover a mystical ecstasy which, she promised, "no mind prisoner to the flesh" could experience, other than by an age-old technique of which she was the only living custodian. Abigail argued that I ought to be the one to confront her, because at the time she was engaged in a critical rollout for her company, in addition to which The Neplusultra might be less favourably disposed to our request to go fuck herself if it came from a member of the same sex. To save a little time, while Abigail waxed lyrical on this topic from the perspective of the Theory of Subaltern Studies and Diacritical Post-feminism, in my mind I rehearsed what I would say to The Neplusultra on the phone call Abigail had enjoined me to make.

I don't know whether it was my nerves, but that night the dripping faucet in our bathroom sink was more irksome than usual. As a veiled punishment for my ongoing failure to repair it, Abigail had decided a while back that we wouldn't spend a single penny on getting a plumber, because if I was home all day, every day, the least I could do was to keep things running smoothly. This was on top of her conviction that if I was going to become a writer, I had better develop a high tolerance for frustration. The incessant dripping should have driven me to remedy the problem, or at least put my mind into a state of suspension, in which I'd be impervious to the sound of those damn drops, which never ceased sliding down the drain. She, on the other hand, slept with earplugs because she needed to go to work in the morning.

The next day, as soon as Abigail had closed the door, I mustered all my courage and dialled the number on The Neplusultra's flyers. After three rings, a gravelly voice completely threw me off the speech I had been rehearsing throughout my long, sleepless night:

"Good day, Nestor, I've been awaiting your call."

"Who is this? How do you know my name is Nestor?"

"You know the answer to that question better than I," The Neplusultra shot back in her slow and deliberate voice. "Why don't you come to the sanctuary and we'll talk things over in person? Those of us travelling the same road eventually end up finding each other."

Without knowing what I was doing I wrote down her address, said goodbye very politely, and undertook my journey to The Neplusultra's residence. I tried to reach Abigail to let her know, but I couldn't get in touch with her. Perhaps it was better that way. I didn't want to worry her with the details of the call. I'd tell her all about it once I had put The Neplusultra in her place.

On my way there the traffic annoyed me much more than usual. Until that fateful day, the one we'll rue forever, my relationship to Abigail's car had been a remote one; to be honest, I didn't leave the house that often. Even so, my usual stoicism about the frenzied honking was doused with a mixture of fear, curiosity and, above all, an inexplicable premonition that it would be best for me to turn around and leave that bloody deranged woman in peace. In these situations I often resorted to the technique of mentally counting the endless drops in our bathroom sink. When I reached a number that was difficult to keep track of, I arrived at the building marked 415 Natalicio Street. I got out of the car and rang the bell of apartment 201 for the first time. I trembled at the sound of the mechanism that allowed me to open the gate, and I proceeded ahead, determined to put an end to The Neplusultra's offences.

Once again I was unprepared for what came next. The apartment door was ajar, a clear invitation to let myself in. Once inside, I was overwhelmed to find myself in what can only be called a museum of the vagina.

The Neplusultra had made her home into an indiscriminate ode to the vagina. There were large paintings in the realist tradition, cubist vaginas, vaginas that melted like Dali's famous clocks, copies of revolutionary murals in which the vagina was both hammer and sickle. At the other end of the ideological spectrum, a lascivious Uncle Sam pointed at an open vagina while pronouncing his usual, "I want you for the US army." There were also sculptures and figurines in a variety of styles, and I even bumped into a female pubis made of screws, keys, nuts and other discarded bits of metal. The list went on: clocks, salt-shakers, tablecloths, cushions, teacups, carpets: the vagina was omnipresent in The Neplusultra's sanctuary. When I hesitated to sit down in a chair made to look like a woman's open legs, my host made her appearance, calculated to achieve a decidedly dramatic effect.

The Neplusultra was the physical embodiment of the vaginocracy that was her home, yet there was nothing the least bit vulgar about her, quite the contrary. Despite the fact she was no longer a young woman, The Neplusultra retained the vestiges of a majestic beauty for which the passage of time is insignificant, a mere accident unworthy of consideration. Wrapped in a fine tunic of different colours, she gravitated towards me, without shifting her gaze away from me for a single instant. There was something hypnotic about her eyes, as if you were standing beneath a Gesell dome, contemplating nothingness indefinitely. I extended my hand cordially, and she invited me into one of the two bedrooms of the apartment, the one she called the vault, where she practised the ecstatic ritual of her supposed thousand-year-old technique.

I passed through the curtain of strings hung with imitation precious stones and sat down in one of two chairs facing each other. The Neplusultra sat in the other. For some period of time, I honestly couldn't say how long, she remained seated, contemplating me impassively, with that look of molten glass, to which there was no alternative but to surrender. When she finally closed her eyes for an instant, I took the opportunity to take in my surroundings, expecting to find more ingenious vaginal representations, but apparently the vault was a place where said organ was forbidden: the walls were covered with enigmatic phrases like "God's true gift is grammar" or "The true task of every ruler is to correct names". There were even more cryptic ones, in the vein of: "Words and things are words and things," and even: "The abyss which separates meaning from that which is meant cannot be severed by the razor's edge."

It's possible that The Neplusultra sensed my imminent departure, because she again fixed me with that look while she began to speak in the same gravelly tone she had used during our brief telephone call:

"Nestor, I know very well what you're thinking. You think I'm a lunatic, and you're not even sure if I'm a harmless one. Relax, you don't have anything to fear. At any moment you may refuse what I'm offering you and return to the grey prison in which you have spent your existence. In any case, as you have perhaps realized, the language with which I prefer to express myself differs from the adulterated version we have inherited for communicating. So, what you want most in the world is to become an important writer, or am I mistaken?"

"Who are you? How do you know these things?"

"That doesn't matter, Nestor. What matters is what I can offer you. Would you like to know the secret of the greatest poets since ancient times? Contrary to appearances, they were not just simple writers. At least not in the watered-down sense of the word as we use it today. Regardless of the language in which they expressed themselves, they all spoke the same primeval one, and their works are nothing more than translations adapted to their time and place. Can you really not guess what this language threatened with extinction is?"

"I don't have the faintest idea, Mrs Neplusultra."

"The answer is simpler than you think. They all mastered—to perfection—the purest language available to us humans: the language of the body."

Drip, drip, drip, drip. It was hopeless, I was up against a creature who was too much for me, in every sense of the expression. Not even the drips could save me now.

The Neplusultra's words flowed with the same inevitability as the drips, except that instead of exploding spectacularly against the sink, her words seemed to gather around themselves, acquiring such precise meaning that it was as if they had been created expressly for The Neplusultra to speak them to me, at that very moment, in her vault. My memory of what she said after that is, by definition, imprecise, despite the fact that on my later encounters with The Neplusultra—all prior to the night when I crashed the car into a retaining wall while I masturbated Abigail with my free hand—the shaman never expressed herself verbally other than was strictly necessary. In effect, her mother tongue was the language of the body. And in light of this, neither Abigail nor I was remotely prepared for what would come next.

During that first meeting, The Neplusultra explained that for some time she had been following our plans for the erotic subversion of the students at the nuns' school. Sometimes she spied on us when we went to distribute our stories around the school's environs in the middle of the night, and as proof she showed me a fairly exhaustive collection. After reading and contemplating our erotic fiction, she concluded that we were basically on the same wavelength, despite the fact she thought our methods were mistaken. In her words, we had "the right intention but the wrong tools". I didn't have the courage to admit that I was just a puppet putting Abigail's theories into practice, but I'm certain that The Neplusultra knew.

We were on the right path, she continued. Those nuns made it their business to crush any hope those girls had of enjoying their own bodies, but, contrary to our beliefs, it wasn't due to the clichés of repression, guilt and sin leading to eternal damnation.

In fact, there was proof that all religious mythology about womankind as a vehicle for the Devil—symbolized by partaking of the forbidden fruit, and the endless representations of the feminine as a source of calamity and disaster—only served to foment the exact behaviour it was intended to prohibit. Had I not heard the famous dictum, passed down from generation to generation of respectable female members of Opus Dei, that the duty of every wife towards her husband is to be a lady at the table and a whore in bed? That summed it all up. The real problem, according to The Neplusultra, was rooted in the nature of language. Or in language and the body, to be more precise. The destruction of the body through language, if I would permit her one last clarification of her philosophy.

At that moment the drips falling in our bathroom sink, Abigail herself, our juvenile and perverted games, these were all a distant noise somewhere in the far reaches of my mind. The Neplusultra had begun my process of conversion before revealing even the basics of her technique to me.

Intensifying the glassiness of her gaze, she prepared me for the final blow before proceeding to her physical demonstration. Our real enemy, she specified, was the liturgy. The liturgy—that damned method of brainwashing us into thinking in formulas and incantations, as if all of life were nothing more than one interminable mass.

"And that's the way it is, my dear Nestor," The Neplusultra concluded. "The liturgy as a mode of thought gradually stifles the expression of our body language, until our bodies become completely mute and give in to decomposition. If you think about it for a moment you'll understand that layers of fat and other kinds of physical disintegration are above all the disintegration of language. You'll also realize that thinking in incantations ends up embodying even transgression itself. Can't you see that today rebellion is part of the same structure it aims to destroy? That's where you got it right. The nuns you chose as your opponents are the most extreme example of what is occurring at all levels of so-called education." After a pause intended to ensure I would not forget her words, The Neplusultra modulated her voice to charge it with meaning, beyond the slightest of doubts. "You must always remember that it's not the hand that massages the body, it's the body that massages the hand. Ay, Nestor, little by little you will come to understand that the pleasure of giving far exceeds the illusory pleasure of receiving. Once you learn that, you'll have what you need to become the writer you wish to be."

Immediately, The Neplusultra raised her tunic to her thighs and took me gently by the hand, which she placed on her knee. My eyes, which were like saucers, relinquished themselves to the liquid emptiness of hers, and we remained like that for a few moments. I'm at a loss for words to describe what I experienced in that first moment of contact. At some point, I realized it was time for me to leave. And that soon I would be back in the vault for our next session. I hurried out, afraid the vaginas that lurked in her living room might bite me, jumped in the car and headed home as fast as I could. The drops in the sink materialized in my head with a vengeance. It seemed as if they were trying to prevent me from considering whether The Neplusultra was a true shaman, possessed of ancient wisdom, or a shameless fraud whose designs on me I was totally disregarding.

I had never before felt such a desire to possess Abigail with no holds barred. Our sexual routine was based on the premise that my desire was a mere extension of hers. The few occasions when I took the initiative usually resulted in excuses about how tired she was from work, her headaches, and the other clichés that composed our libidinal economy, managed by my girlfriend. All the way home, I pondered the possible consequences of being rejected in the state I was in. The drips had become a waterfall, which no one, not even the best plumber, would be able to repair. I couldn't take any risks. And that's when I made the decision that would lead directly to the accident.

As soon as I was home, I searched doggedly for a TV show that would give Abigail one of her hysterical attacks. At that point I would materialize with one of my stories in hand, I would begin to read to her, and as per usual Abigail would suddenly go from being grief-stricken to horny. For my part, I would sate the desire that was burning me up, while at the same time testing out my budding knowledge. I wanted to touch her, kiss her, bite her, pull her hair, but all without touching or kissing or biting or pulling. For her breasts to massage my tongue, despite the illusion that it was the other way round. As The Neplusultra had explained, though the difference appeared to be a simple matter of perspective, it was in fact monumental.

My plan worked perfectly, although not without a few hitches. Abigail arrived two hours later than usual because of a meeting that had totally wiped her out. While I was awaiting her, preparing for her arrival, I spent a long time watching a parade of human suffering, sanitized and produced for television. After viewing parts of documentaries, news shows, reality shows, mean-spirited game shows—all the things that I thought would make Abigail fall to pieces if she saw them—it was I who temporarily lost the will to live. When I heard the keys in the lock, a Palestinian was wailing while he held the scorched body of his child in his arms. I ran to the bathroom, hoping Abigail would see this, and a moment later I heard the lengthening gasps which always preceded her breakdowns. On this occasion, I had chosen a particularly graphic story, the kind that sometimes drove the nuns to conduct exorcisms along the school walls, sprinkling them with holy water to purify them. Abigail interrupted me before I even got to the most obscene part. Never before had we come together with such violent tenderness.

I began to visit The Neplusultra of a morning. I think that all along Abigail suspected something, but she was quite strict with herself when it came to emotions she considered old-fashioned, which intelligent people should eschew: jealousy was one of them; she associated such emotions with the objectification of things, a manifestation of possessiveness that infringed upon human dignity. In our particular case, the problem was solved in a preventive manner: my self-esteem was so low that it would never have occurred to me to look at anyone else. And really, who would be interested in a lapdog, enslaved by his forward-thinking girlfriend, whose primary occupation was writing repetitive stories that sometimes didn't even excite schoolgirls?

My sessions with The Neplusultra began to alter this landscape. With each new step in the secrets of her technique, I mastered the language of the body a little more. Gradually, I began to hear a soft, suppressed whisper coming from my own body. My meetings with The Neplusultra weren't the least bit sexual, in the traditional sense of the word. Even so, I decided to keep them secret from Abigail, who had accepted my feeble explanation that the charlatan wouldn't be bothering us again. To make amends, I imposed a strict rule upon myself: each time I visited The Neplusultra I would precipitate one of Abigail's breakdowns, which would end in wild sex. And thanks to my growing ability to communicate with her body, the sex was getting wilder and wilder. When we'd finish, Abigail would carefully inspect her bruises, scratches, bite marks and all the other traces on her body of a process she didn't begin to understand, and which she wouldn't have dreamt of halting. And now that I find myself prostrate in a hospital bed, my face disfigured, perhaps beyond recognition, and without any knowledge of Abigail other than the fact that the doctors were truly surprised we didn't both perish in the accident, now that our depraved games are nothing more than a distant memory of another life, one that's no longer ours, I understand that those marks on her body prefigured what would eventually become of us.

Abigail's transformation had an ambiguous opacity, as if she were made from frosty ice. The rigidity of her logic began to show cracks that I wasn't able to interpret correctly, if only because I was blown away by the force of her silence. Her outbursts of uncontrollable grief became more frequent. Her tolerance was lowered to the point that a documentary about the difficult lives of ants was all it took to send her to pieces. Conversely, I was producing erotic fiction with power and precision, which surprised even myself. It was rumoured that the nuns had hired a detective to find out who was guilty of creating the flyers that were disrupting the life of the school. The Neplusultra had been right: as my instruction in the language of the body progressed, my literary ability grew.

Abigail couldn't even manage to put on two socks the same colour. Our deranged screwing was amazing. Meanwhile, The Neplusultra told me that soon she would reveal the secret, after which our meetings would immediately cease. At night the sound of the dripping sink had become unbearable. It felt like those goddamn drops were drilling into my skull, like sharp needles made of water, and my earplugs were no use. Abigail was in no state to object to my using them, or to anything else for that matter.

Shortly thereafter, on one of my secret trips to the apartment at 415 Natalicio Street, I realized as I stepped across the threshold of The Neplusultra's sanctuary that this was the last time I would find myself in the museum of the vagina. I realize it's possible this is a false memory; nevertheless I had the distinct feeling those vaginas surrounded me expectantly, as if they wanted me to choose between them and myself, and that this choice would produce a domino effect of unforeseen circumstances. Before the drips could interrupt and distract me, The Neplusultra appeared in a wave of nostalgia. Even her welcoming gestures were imbued with an absurd attitude of finality. It was true that throughout our meetings I had made impressive progress. She had taught me all the techniques she knew, and her obscure warning from our first meeting had become clear: the difference between touching and being touched had lost all distinction. That's why Abigail had come to the edge of the abyss. That's why the nuns had resorted to more radical methods to stop the flyers appearing. The Neplusultra's thousand-year-old techniques threatened the very nature of identity, without which the differences that separate and classify us would disintegrate. Standing in The Neplusultra's sanctuary, awaiting initiation into the final mystery that would terminate my education, I understood that the hierarchies that define us are nothing more than fears that have fossilized into mores and conventions. Fear of the likelihood we will spend our lives buried by the brittle magma of unwritten rules and vanity. Fear of our bodies, or what we're denying them the opportunity to express. Fear that makes life a living death, while we await true death itself. Fear of…

"Come, Nestor. You're ready," The Neplusultra said patiently while she ushered me for the last time into her vault.

She removed her tunic and lay down naked, face up, on the massage table. Before daintily opening her legs she handed me a bottle labelled Foria, which contained a kind of greenish oil. I put some on my fingers and began to massage the outer parts of The Neplusultra's vagina, carefully avoiding premature contact with her clitoris. I massaged her with the tips of my fingers, waiting for our breathing to become perfectly synchronized. The Neplusultra emitted a few faint moans of approval, confirming

I was on the right path. Without thinking, I began to massage her more vigorously, using all the skills I had learnt under her tutelage, making sure that the mysterious oil would disappear without a trace. When I finally brushed her clitoris, she arched in anticipation of what would come next. It was true: the difference between my fingers and her vagina had lost all distinction. So we continued, increasing the pace until, a few moments later, she began to shake and emit blinding howls that lasted for what seemed like an eternity. The Neplusultra's orgasm went beyond the limits of her body and of time, until both of us had joyfully accepted the disruption of inexorable calm. There was nothing left to say. I put the bottle in my backpack and permitted myself one last step into her blurry field of vision. I hurried to leave the sanctuary with full knowledge that I would never set foot there again.

That night, when Abigail got home, our roles had changed: her hysterical fit seemed a little affected to me. And for the first time, I didn't comply with her wishes. I hid out in my study and wrote the most erotic and most perfect story I was capable of producing. It was so good that I didn't want to defile it by using it as a pretence to violently screw my girlfriend. And the goddamn nuns weren't worthy of it either, it was beyond their comprehension. I had completed a perfect translation from the language of the body to our everyday language. I put it in my backpack and renounced my pretension of becoming a famous writer once and for all. I slept like a rock, as though the dripping sink had become inaudible. I knew it was still dripping, but I had found an acoustic frequency where I couldn't hear it.

Things returned to normal over the next few months. Abigail's rigid adherence to logic regained its strength, and once again I blindly submitted to her; the interlude that had lasted for the duration of my relationship with The Neplusultra had come to a definitive end. Abigail's breakdowns occurred less frequently. I continued writing the stories that we stuck to the walls of the nuns' school, because I still hadn't told Abigail that my contribution to the plans for our life together was changing. Maybe I'd open a massage parlour. I wasn't sure. And it didn't matter much either. I was busy trying to listen to my body.

Until the denouement. Early one morning, like so many others, while I was apathetically hanging the zillionth story to make teens horny, while Abigail watched anxiously from the car, I was ambushed by the ruffians the nuns had hired to catch us. When I had finished hanging the first story they landed a debilitating blow on my back, and I was dragged inside the school, defenceless. My apprehension had been carefully planned: the mother superior was awaiting me in her bare office. Clearly they had been following our movements for weeks, until the boss nun had decided to pull the string that would activate the trap.

The office where I was to be interrogated was obviously inspired by a nun's cell. The light from a street lamp filtered through the iron bars on the window, illuminating half the mother superior's face with a macabre symmetry. When she realized I was inclined to confess everything, she said, in a tone of forbearance,

"My child, before deciding what to do with you, I would like to find room in my heart to forgive you. Please, tell me what drove you to do something so heinous? What did you gain by corrupting the minds in the care of this house of Our Lord?"

"Listen, Mother," I said sincerely, "a few months ago I would have told you our intention was to liberate these young women from the tyranny of your dogmas, that we wanted to show them that you were indoctrinating them, and other such pseudo-conceptual nonsense. But I don't care about all that crap any more. The only reason I haven't stopped doing it is because I'm a pathetic lackey. I have learnt too late that the sacred exists, beyond all representation and appearance. So do what you want with me, the truth is I don't give a fuck."

The shadow of a smile appeared on her face, but her chin remained resolute.

"If I understand you correctly, my child, you're telling me that you're a sheep who has strayed from the flock but has finally seen the light of Our Lord?"

"Yes, I have been shown the way to give a tremendous amount of light. And I can make you sing music as heavenly as the trumpets of the archangels. If you'll allow me to demonstrate, lie down on your desk and relax. I promise you, you won't be sorry."

I closed my eyes in anticipation of her caning me, or her calling her henchmen to rough me up and hand me over to the police. It was one thing to write erotic fiction anonymously; it was another to insult a mother superior to her face.

Dumbfounded, I watched as the nun stood up, and, exposing a body worn down by time, she got up on her desk and lay down. She folded her hands on her chest in prayer, as if she were putting herself in God's hands while she let the Devil experiment with her. She was willing to do whatever it took to experience the path to ecstasy I had just described to her.

I took the Foria out of my backpack and focused to put myself into a trance. I harnessed all of The Neplusultra's tutelage and concentrated on communicating with this small body bowed by deprivation, protected by a carapace in the form of a nun's habit. With careful determination, I proceeded to use each of the methods that had been imparted to me. At the critical moment when our breathing synchronized I threw myself into the abyss without any parachute other than blind faith in something I couldn't even name. I did briefly consider what the punishment might be for attempting to rape a nun in her own office at dawn.

Even the dripping inside my head had stopped, petrified by the consequences of what might happen.

The nun's orgasm surpassed all expectations. Despite the fact that in the realm of ideas we were and would continue to be mortal enemies, our bodies had communed in this unrecreatable vortex. The Neplusultra had warned me: the pleasure of giving far exceeds the pleasure of receiving. Even if it was with the nun against whom Abigail and I had been waging such a fruitless war for so long.

Before the mother superior caught her breath, became outraged at what had just occurred, and called her henchmen with cries for help, I quickly put my things away and asked if I could leave. Lying there, shivering with goosebumps, the nun blessed me and said goodbye with a few terse words:

"Go with God, my child. Now we are at peace."

Once I had made it safely past the mother superior and her henchmen, I realized I faced another obstacle: Abigail. I walked out of the school and found her sitting in the car, the engine still running, like a bank robber waiting for her accomplice to jump in the car and speed off with the loot. As per usual, in a situation of real danger she had been able to maintain admirable calm. Nevertheless, when she noticed my inexplicable serenity, she immediately began gasping like she did before her hysterical attacks. I decided it was not a good moment to lie.

I started driving without knowing where I was going and began to tell her in as much detail as I could about my double life, which had so recently ended. With each twist in my story her sobs became deeper. She was shaking her head, as if she were rejecting my words, the entirety of my being, even her own, and the stupid game which had blown up in our faces. Her usual rationalizations weren't capable of overcoming the creature that they themselves had created. When I finished telling her about the nun's orgasm, Abigail broke into wild howling that seemed like a poisoned arrow had pierced her, tracing circles that seemed to hurt her more each time. My pleas to calm down only seemed to make her worse. We were on a highway so I couldn't pull over. Suddenly I remembered the perfect story I had written, the one I hadn't used, was stashed in my backpack. Steering as best I could, I took it out, along with the Foria. I was holding the steering wheel with one hand, and in the other I was holding the only two things that were capable of halting what was on the verge of becoming a psychotic episode.

I began reading the story and with my free hand I began caressing every inch of her convulsing body. This remedy had its usual effect, and like everything else on this damn night, seemed to be amplified. Between my words and my thousand-year-old technique, Abigail burst into screams that threatened to break the car windows. But that was hardly necessary. The moment she removed her trousers and her underpants, getting completely naked, the windows seemed like they would melt in the ignis fatuus of our mutual insanity. With the first drop of Foria on her expectant clitoris, Abigail exploded into an orgasm that made the sum of all previous orgasms pale in comparison, including The Neplusultra's, the mother superior's and the orgasm of any other woman that was not Abigail, writhing in a car speeding through the night, just a few seconds from colliding head-on with the retaining barrier on a curve.

I came to covered in blood, bewildered by the shouting paramedics who were trying to put a catheter in my penis. I wanted to scream, to ask about Abigail, but I couldn't form any words. On the edge of death, I could only think in the language of the body.

And yet, I didn't die. And I don't think she did either. I'm still in too delicate a condition to receive a shock, but all indications are that I'll make it. They won't let me look in a mirror. My left eye is useless, and my nose is about half of what it used to be. I hope with all my soul that Abigail's better off than I am. But not that much better. We need to remain more or less on the same wavelength. Otherwise it will be impossible to adjust our project of a life together to our new circumstances.

Translated by Samantha Schnee

SINGING FOR THE DEAD

ANTONIO RAMOS REVILLAS

—FIRST STANZA—

My father would sing for the dead.

Imagining him beside the corpses turned my childhood into a nightmare. I could see him before an audience of unhappy, agonized men and women who wept copiously when they should have applauded him. But it was not the mourners who drove me to my wildest fantasies, but those corpses lying there beside them: all so really, weirdly and filthily dead. No sooner had I closed my eyes than the tempestuous lyrics of every verse of those ballads engulfed me in the darkness just as I was desperate to get to sleep. Even the tunes evoked the babbling of infants deceased in their first year of life; the rattling sighs of the old on the point of death; the last scream of a woman being murdered. My father's songs brought back to life an outpouring of lamentations, a crush of corpses hammering on the door of my room, so that I too might bid them farewell in song, not that I found myself in any sense able to sing a song to death. *Forget your spite, love me a little, / nothing awaits us all in the end, but in this life of ours / not even nothing can separate us from our love.*

At times the funeral dirges turn bitter and violent. Then I used to put my hands over my ears, hide my head under the sheet, switch on my battery-powered radio and seek out chat shows or songs by pop bands. I tried to tune the reception in to a programme lively enough to afford me some shelter, enfold me in its harmonies and succeed in putting to flight the voices I was hearing in my mind. The voices of the dead were full of fury and confusion. Often, before falling asleep, the last sound I heard was that of the static that follows the end of daily transmissions.

From time to time my father attempted to teach me his profession. He said it had a particular *raison d'être*, all the more so since no one took it up any more. He spoke with satisfaction of our family, the Rodases, professional funeral singers. He studied the palms of my hands and said that when they grew to full size, my fingers would be firm and long, perfectly agile for plucking guitar cords. All I could muster by way of response was a blush of embarrassment.

Occasionally, I would ask myself about the songs with a degree of real curiosity. Which one was the saddest? How had he learnt to play them? Why did he do it? But I never questioned him on anything. One evening when there were no wakes to attend, Papa chatted with Mama about how well the stall selling sports outfits she had on Arteaga Street in the city centre was doing. She moaned about how expensive the shiny fabric for making soccer kits had become, especially if you used shiny fabrics like Umbro, or stretchy ones, ones with logo types, whatever has most recently been dreamt up by Marce, who prints the numbers and designs onto the shirts, while he cusses his favourite football team for having just lost against the worst one in the league. Normal life, I called it. And if anyone were to ask me I'd have told them I was quite content with this normal life of mine. The public tends to give too much importance to people who lead extreme lives. I prefer to say they don't know what they're talking about.

It was my father's insistence that I learn the songs and accompany him which finally led me to despise that whole other way of life, to an extent that even now I can't properly understand. We were watching a television programme in the living room when a guy with an accordion came on the screen. Papa whistled and commented: "One of these days, when you sing with me—and you will—I'll buy you an accordion so you can learn how to play, and you'll appreciate what it is to have an instrument as good as that." This was exactly the way he put it. He had already decided I would become a singer, and that I would accompany him; my life was in his hands, no argument. I got to my feet and it took all my courage to stare him down, without saying a word. Whatever was he thinking of, that I would become a mariachi singer for the dead, as the neighbours on our street and all around the block were in the habit of calling him? Did he see me as another him? It was at that instant I broke with the fearful child I was, in order to become the kind of person who despised "all that".

I went to my room, telling myself that I would have nothing more to do with funerals, holy oils or black weddings celebrated between the living and the dead, or any form of darkness deeper than shadows, or funeral candles with wobbling flames, and made my decision to flee death and embrace life, even though I hadn't the least idea what this meant. At such an age, when nothing amounts to more than good intentions, I swore to myself that life would treat me well, excellently well, if I could only avoid these nocturnal attributes: a song of ill omen, raps on the door in the dead of night, continual ruptures in routine that would fill my family and me with shame: me, the son of Salvador Rodas, singer for the dead.

Sometimes I would go to my father's shop in the city centre. On the way, I enjoyed seeing people doing the sort of things that living people do, listening to the cars and lorries hooting their horns, the calls of manioc-vendors or music emerging from the record shops bathed in afternoon sunlight, pointlessly desiring no more than to cover themselves in the shade of their awnings against the biting light from the heat of the day.

In the end it proved impossible to flee my fears. Little as I wanted to, bit by bit I came to see everyone around me as dead: the girl working on the shop counter and the bus conductor, a boy waving his arm out of a car window. I pondered on the form of death awaiting the ambulant newspaper-seller, the little girl who had just crossed the avenue and the seamstresses who worked for Papa; but when I thought about my parents' death, my mouth went dry. I also wondered what my own cause of death would be, if I would be aware of its coming, whether I might at least have time to bid my grandmother Sol farewell. Or anyone else for that matter, and then I wondered if anyone would remember even the year of my death.

So it was I determined to seize life to the utmost. I ran and jumped until I reached the point of exhaustion, I ate enormously and drank Coca-Cola in huge gulps until the bubbles tickled my throat, and caused me to belch. I got on my bike, rode it all around the neighbourhood, played football, keeping score and yelling at each goal. I didn't want to hear death so much as mentioned: there was enough of it around at home, I only had to go up my father's room to come face to face with the guitar he played when he sang for the dead.

The guitar was a deep cherry red, with a transfer of a cock on one side: it could have been any old guitar, as good for livening up a wedding, serving to while away tedious moments, alleviating boredom with polkas and ragtime, *hurangos*, a whole mixture of folk songs and dances from the north-east of Mexican. Once, at a family reunion with my maternal aunts and cousins—for my father was born an only child—I tried to have him play something light-hearted but he refused to let me pressurize him. "This guitar is only for the dead, nobody else," he replied.

And the dead laid claim to him. Every so often, people from the high sierra would turn up at the house, old men or ashen women, looking for my father to play at a wake for them. They tapped on the door, I would open up and, on observing the distress on their faces, I would taste such an acrid lump rise in my throat that I could hardly swallow. It was not in response to them, of course not, but because they had barely got the words out—"Is Don Salvador at home?"—when Papa would emerge from some dark corner of the kitchen, or from the snug of his room in order to attend to them.

He always left everything behind him. His coffee half-drunk, his tortilla still neatly folded, there on the corner of his plate. The mourners waited beside the medlar tree while Papa went upstairs to change his outfit. When he came down again, he looked like another person: kitted out all in white, shirt and trousers alike, his cravat tied in a typically northern fashion. His blacked shoes and the cherry-coloured guitar contrasted strongly against so much whiteness. Then he picked up his guitar strap. Before slinging it over his shoulder he tuned the strings and gave a timid riff holding out the promise of a touching lament, fit to fill eyes with tears, condemn the whole world to mourning, to howls accompanied by snot and wails.

Preparations for his departure had become a ritual that no longer held any surprises. Nonetheless, neighbours regarded him with curiosity. It didn't count that my dad was sponsor of the football teams the neighbours equipped every three months to compete in the plains, nobody knew him as the man who kitted out the team, but as the singer for the dead. Some whispered when they saw me, I imagined they were referring to me as "the mariachi's little son, you know, the singer for the dead". I knew full well they also referred to Papa as "that old crackpot". Sometimes I'd hear the other children talking about the mariachi for the dead, only to break into guffaws. Others used to approach me, to ask: "Hey you, how come your father goes and sings to corpses?" but no sooner had they satisfied their curiosity than they went off silently, bored, and began shooting me ugly looks, as if I were infectious. Then the rest would look at me and at once the jeers would begin.

I was good to begin with. I wouldn't put up with jeers, or any of the rest of it. I threw my whole self into contradicting what anyone asked. Those were some days: fights, blood, shouts, wounds, so that at the end only one simple question remained, one last question deep inside the guitar, in the most humid part of the coffin: why did my father sing for the dead? Why didn't he do something else? The songs made me scared, woke me from my dreams, and each time I tried to defend him from the jeers of the other children things only got worse for me. But he had it all clear in his mind. Every song was like a wedding celebration with a dead spouse, tying ribbons around bare bones, crowning inert skulls with flowers, like the song has it: *the hideous maws of death covered with kisses*. My father was the madman who sang to death and celebrated its loves.

I had never heard him sing. It was Camarena, a kid on the block, who sparked my curiosity one afternoon when we were wandering aimlessly about the neighbourhood, with its vacant lots and burnt-out bars covered in graffiti. We roamed the streets to watch nothing more exciting than scrapyard workers strip down a car, or trailer-drivers playing dominoes in the shade of a corrugated iron lean-to.

"Wouldn't it be cool to hear your old man's songs?" Camarena's interest seemed genuine enough. I noticed that on the front of his shirt he bore the distinctive caricature of Don Gato.

I didn't answer him, but remembered all those nights when I visualized the funeral parlours as noisy bars where customers flung coins down on the floor, and Papa sang or drank cups of coffee with a shot of mescal and women cried as if they were smiling.

"I don't think so," I told him at the end.

Just at that moment, I recalled a time when at school they gave us homework on writing a description of a day in our parents' lives. Next day we were invited to read our set work out aloud. Camarena read to us about his father's job just outside the school: he sold the kind of white turnip they call *jícama*, toasted and sliced with creamy sauce, and album prints. Ernesto bored us with his father's life story as an accountant in a paint factory, and went so far as to bring us samples in marble grey, sandy beige, roof-tile red, canary yellow, and oyster white, facing down the mocking laughter of the class. From that day forth he was known as "Oyster Ernesto".

I anxiously awaited my turn. When the schoolmistress called out my name, I got to my feet, stared fixedly at the blackboard, where she was drawing up the list of our fathers' occupations, inhaled deeply and said, without a moment's hesitation:

"My father makes football kits, his shop is on the corner of Arteaga Street and…"

I hadn't finished my sentence when from the back of the room a child called out: "It's not true, Pablo is Don Salvador's son, the singer for the dead…"

The classroom fell silent. The teacher shushed the boy, the neighbour with whom I'd fought a couple of weeks earlier, and looked at me pityingly, as if I were guilty of something. I felt as if the rest of my classmates were also staring at me with disgust, surprise, even curiosity, while they all withdrew, as far as they could away from me, as if the son of a singer was bound to stink, as if I stank as much as one of those dead cats that moulder away under the soil.

The schoolmistress quietened down the mutterings around the room, but I felt as if I were trailing a dirty, yellowy fog around me. The next one up was Julia. The plague I was carrying didn't diminish. Julia hurriedly explained her father's profession then gave me a strange look and sat down again. The expressions on the rest of the children's faces slithered around my shoulders. At break time some of them approached me to ask all about what it meant to be a singer for the dead. Was it really possible? What did he sing for them? I didn't know what to reply. I stammered when they asked me to sing a verse, even a line.

"I don't know anything about that stuff," I told them, feeling myself more than ever the son of a mariachi singing for the dead, not Salvador Rodas. The kids ended up keeping their distance, and me by growing still more annoyed with my dad. His task belonged on the ranches and now we belonged to the city.

That was how come I'd never actually heard him sing. There was a brief period, when I'd optimistically tried to accept my father's vocation, when I believed he had a band of singers for the dead, with a trumpeter, a violinist, a funeral accordionist and a guitar player. They even managed to get hold of a bus, like some of those other northern groups that went out on tour in their coaches converted to contain television sets, bunks and showers.

His band, Los Fantasmales—The Phantoms—de Salvador Rodas performed hits from their latest recording, *Patience and Serenity*, at whatever funeral they happened on along the way, wherever a murder or a suicide or a knifing or a goring by a bull or a natural death had taken place.

All the same, reality was not like that.

When Camarena asked me how, finally it would all turn out, I realized I needed to see him with my own eyes, and learn what he was truly about: it was now high time to put paid to assumptions.

"Would you help me to follow him?" I asked him with such confidence I surprised even myself.

Camarena didn't hesitate.

"We'll have to find some money in case we need to follow him in a bus or a taxi."

"Not a problem," I assured him. "If necessary, I'll pinch it from my dad, or you can from sales on your father's stand."

The weeks I spied on my father were the best of my childhood. I had decided to confront reality and it felt terrific. Camarena and I pulled together some money selling pineapple and prints on his father's stall; I saved up my pocket money, and even managed to run a couple of errands for my granny, Sol. I felt clever, sharp, as speedy as any of the graffiti artists in the neighbourhood I often saw running in flight from the police, or any other enemy. However, there was one thing I hadn't taken into account: the dead. The dead had now disappeared. Not a single grieving relation had arrived at our door for weeks past. Papa was working in the shop, Mama took care of the house; while I, bored and troubled, put up with Camarena who asked me every afternoon if there were a fresh death anywhere on the horizon. It would have all gone to hell had not an old couple turned up at the house one afternoon.

"You have come for the singer, have you?"

The couple looked at one another and one replied:

"We're looking for Mr Singer, and have come all the way from—"

I didn't so much as give them time to tell me the name of their godforsaken village, before setting off at a run to call Mama to come down and assist them in taking down the date of the funeral, the name of the deceased and the address where the wake was to be held. Mama called Papa at work and I could tell from the look on her face that he would lose no time in arriving to change his clothes and set out for the village. Camarena and I went outside to wait, already furnished with money and curiosity. When he got to the house, guitar over his shoulder, we got going.

We followed him a block behind, intermittently concealing ourselves between parked cars by crouching down, adrenalin coursing. One block before the avenue, we altered our tactics and ran on ahead to get there before him. My forehead was throbbing with the effort, and I gulped for air. Papa jumped into a taxi, and we took the next one.

I stammered as I told the driver to follow the car in front. He was a fat and sunburnt guy, who insisted we showed him our money before he put his foot down. Then he took another look at us as if he thought there was no way of getting rid of us, and set off.

We left our neighbourhood far behind us, and we stared straight ahead, heads together peering between the front seats. Our sweat was making the back seat in his Tsuru as sticky as chewing gum. We passed over crossroads scattered with old men and women with children in their arms, who sold mangos, sunglasses and bottles of water. We passed disused factories with dead chimneys, leaving far behind train tracks and supermarkets, a couple of commercial centres, always closely tailing the taxi in which my dad was travelling, always just behind him until the driver, by now suspicious, pulled up at the roadside:

"Show me your cash. Who knows if you've got enough there to pay me?"

We froze. There wasn't enough money for the fare. The man put us down, muttering under his breath, and accelerated away with a squeal of tyres. We found ourselves alone, many miles from home. We turned back, bitterly regretting that we obviously hadn't collected as much as we'd thought. On the return journey, Camarena made fun of the trouble I would find myself in.

"It's all your fault," I told him when we got as far as the train track, "you idiot taco-seller."

Then Camarena turned serious, and summoned all his fury to tell me:

"Damn son of a mariachi."

No sooner had he said this than I felt a surge of the same courage I experienced when Papa came out to sing. We hurled ourselves into punching each other. Passing cars started hooting at us. A woman came up to separate us but failed. In the end a bus driver on Route 82 pulled up and got out to separate us, under the sardonic stares of his passengers. Camarena didn't stop calling me names until the driver hauled him onto the bus. I was left behind.

Beaten, I walked the rest of the way home. I had never felt so distant, or so alone, surrounded on every street by strange characters I didn't know. In an empty lot beside the avenue, a foul smell reached my nostrils: it was a dead cat. Someone had thrown lime over it but it had gone yellow and the smell escaped despite their efforts. I have never forgotten that smell or that afternoon. When night came I was still far away from our house. Graffiti artists were smoking in the wastelands as cars droned on their way.

The first familiar house I reached was Sol's, intending to establish that I had been with her, but I found my mother there. I was forced to confess everything. Mama scolded me like never before. However, next day I was made aware of something far worse: Papa had now learnt that I was interested in him. So now he would think that I was also interested in his work. And so there was no reason to be surprised when one morning, while my lunchbox was being prepared to take to school, he approached and said:

"You will be coming with me to the next death."

Translated by Amanda Hopkinson

MADAME JAZMINE, OR NEWS OF THE DECAPITATION

EDUARDO RUIZ SOSA

To whom does it belong, this body we love so much?…
Your body will perhaps be a question with no answer.

SALVADOR ELIZONDO

We each carry within us the potentiality of our own death, which—wrote Juan Pablo Orígenes on his way to the border—is exactly as it should be if we are to preserve a minimum of justice. Suicide should be the only possible crime; euthanasia, the one act of complicity.

I told Gil Paz how we had wandered the rain-wet streets that night. It was a night without hope, and without hope, there is no mystery—I think it must have been Strogowski who said that, because he was there too. The drizzle suddenly became a downpour, as if we were miles away in distant tropics, as if we were dreaming and being carried back to where jungle and desert meet on a frontier formed by torrential rainstorms, hurricanes, droughts full of dust and bones, and where dried-up rivers seem the very embodiment of the whole world's thirst, and just at that moment, we happened upon a door lit by a bright-yellow sign bearing a name scrawled in red neon. Once inside and plunged once more into darkness, we found a small bar with a counter, a huge mirror, some seats apparently salvaged from an abandoned theatre (Strogowski, his glass eye misted up, said they resembled the seats in the far-off Teatro de Apolo, which had burnt down years ago) and, in the back, a disparate collection of chairs and tables. Further inside, albeit only by a few steps, were the kitchen, a few customers and the echo of unfamiliar music. And almost nothing else. It was only when we sat down and had a good look around that we noticed—on shelves, on walls, on every available surface, on improvised ledges cut out of the wall, on sharp corbels like the tops of tiny cliffs, on niches carved out of the old plaster—a strange motley array of dolls' heads. Only heads: old and dirty, separated and doubtless very far from their bodies, heads of different sizes, some with hair, others with their mane of hair torn off: everywhere disembodied heads, with eyes wide open or with no eyes at all, like a cemetery of childhood and of all that is irrecoverable: a shrine to decapitation.

Then the Magus Strogowski told us the story: Madame Jazmine, after whom the bar was named, had worked as a prostitute in the Barrio del Raval in the early part of the twentieth century. Legend has it that her body always smelt of flowers, that she was captivatingly beautiful, began working as a prostitute when she was only fifteen and, some years later, became the madam of a brothel; she had green eyes and a dark complexion; she was from Cádiz or possibly from some still more southern part of the Mediterranean; she was haunted by dreams of Scheherazade (possibly a prelude to her fate); she began consulting the Tarot cards because she lived in constant fear of what the future might hold; she slept alone in a bedroom on the top floor, and she had loved three men: a poet, a pharmacist and an avant-garde painter, in that order and almost equally. When we heard this, I think we were all reminded of the story we had read somewhere of the prostitute-cum-witch, Alba Urrutia, who vanished one day without trace, and who bore such a striking resemblance to Ximena Ríos, the famous singer, who also disappeared weeks after the Arroyo de los Perros burst its banks.

The avant-garde artist was younger than Madame Jazmine and came from a wealthy family, and out of their romance was born a child, a boy, who never knew his father and grew up among the women of the brothel as if he were the son of all of them, as if each exercised over him the maternal rights denied them by their profession, but, above all, the boy grew up in the domain of Madame Jazmine like a resentful prince waiting to recover an unpayable debt. It would not take him long to find a way of collecting an inheritance promised to him by his mother in the form of a secret that would never be revealed. Eager to take revenge on his unknown father, he began trafficking opium and hashish and lost all his money at the gaming tables; he tried to make Madame Jazmine's brothel his personal harem; he tried to get into trafficking morphine by robbing pharmacies and small dispensaries, but he failed to prosper in that either. With each new failure, his resentment grew like a wasp's nest, like a cosmic cancer, like a stone of Sisyphus that grew and grew in the innermost workings of his loathing.

It was summer when Madame Jazmine's son disappeared. She woke up shortly before dawn and sighed a deep, deep sigh. She could read in the fast-fading stars, as only mothers can, the message that her son would break her heart.

Absence lasts for ever, Gil Paz once said, but the unknowns surrounding an absence can have an end if you discover the reasons for someone's departure, journey or disappearance; the chief weapon of all regimes (both political and criminal) is that eternal combination of absence and ignorance: not knowing where the disappeared have gone is both weapon and wound; there can be no shrine to their memory until their bodies turn up (perhaps because we deny that they really are dead and grant them a kind of suspended life that would cease were we to erect a monument to them), and then the very thing that drives us on to look for them instils in us a terrible anxiety that leads us to believe they will come back of their own accord, that we must wait for them, that we cannot leave the house because they forgot to take their keys when they left; and because, if the unknown persists, if there are no answers as to why they disappeared, the absentees can always be publicly humiliated by accusations of surrender, desertion, cowardice and criminal complicity; Gil Paz would say: that's what They think, the ones who take them away, the ones who snatch our loved ones from us.

For the two or three days that the absence of Madame Jazmine's son lasted, it was said that he had run off with a young girl who had just started working at the brothel; it was said that he was hiding away in a house his mother owned on the coast, because his creditors were after him; that he was in a clinic, recovering from his addiction to tranquillizers; that he had finally claimed his inheritance from his unknown father and gone abroad; it was said that there was no reason to worry, that sometimes he went on binges lasting days or even weeks, and that, at some point, he would resurface. So many things were said and there were so many possible answers that, in the end, all and none of them seemed possible, but Madame Jazmine said nothing. One morning, on the third day, her son's decapitated body was found just outside her house, presumably left there during the night.

Little was known about the causes or the details of the murder, only that the naked body was found separated from its head, and although, according to the police report, certain distinctive birthmarks served to identify the corpse, some insisted that what made the body instantly recognizable was the strong smell of jasmine, a scent he only inherited from his mother on his death. The body was lying prone, almost immediately outside the front door, a rotting jasmine flower, arms outstretched, legs together, as if he had fallen face forward and failed to reach out to break his fall, then dropped asleep in the uncomfortable pose of a horizontal Christ; but the head, with its thick hair and its eyes, along with all the words spoken before that final moment, along with the ideas and the ears that would have heard his own cries, that head never reappeared. People blamed the burgeoning local mafias, who were looking to set an example; others said that some enemy of Madame Jazmine had wanted to exact revenge by taking her son's life; that his death was mixed up with some matter involving trade unions and workers' organizations in which he had played the role of informer; it was even said that when the painter's illegitimate offspring came too close to discovering who his father was, the artist's family had decided to get rid of him and erase the one possible identifying mark—his face. Madame Jazmine had always told her son that he was the very image of his father, that he could be his father's twin, that he had his father's nose, eyes, voice and laugh.

Finally, driven mad by the death of her son and by the manner of his death, by having seen his body with her own eyes and having to bury him like that, incomplete, without the head that would never turn up, his mother began to wander the streets of the city and, every evening until long into the night, she would, they say, sit on a bench in the Ramblas, until her weeping became so loud that, in the end, a couple of policemen would come and take her home because she was frightening the tourists, as she sat cradling a headless doll in her arms, asking anyone who passed if they had seen a disembodied head lying around somewhere: a head with these eyes, this smile, with wide-spaced teeth, or something like that, or so people say. All cities have their living ghosts, said Gil Paz.

Ever since the head of John the Baptist was given as a gift to Salome; or that of Holofernes beheaded by Judith; or of Agostino Tassi decapitated by Artemisia Gentileschi in that nightmarish painting from the seventeenth century; even the head of Sir Thomas More that would fall before Anne Boleyn's did; or the head of Goliath after his fight with David; the head of Charlotte Corday after the death of Marat, and that of

Robespierre biting the air, and that of Marie Antoinette, who apologized to her executioner for treading on his toe, or that of Mary Stuart, who could not see the waiting crowd baying themselves hoarse; even the heads of the sultan's three thousand wives or the head of Lavoisier, which, after it was cut off, continued to blink for a whole twenty seconds, offering proof to his students of how long consciousness lasts once the head is separated from the body, and each of those heads, each with its own name, is cut off once again in order to appear in the photographs printed in encyclopaedias of famous people, there they all are, like Mr Taylor's shrunken heads, detached from their bodies, in the place which, all these years later, is known as Madame Jazmine's Bar. Then, while the rain continued to pour down, and while he repeatedly adjusted the glass eye in his left socket, Strogowski told us about the caged heads that used to be hung from trees as a warning to rebels; heads like caged birds; and although it hardly seemed logical, someone else said that the Spanish expression meaning to be scatterbrained, *tener pájaros en la cabeza*—literally, to have birds inside one's head—had its origins in those punishments, to demonstrate that rebellion was sheer madness and would lead to birds taking up residence in those heads hanging from branches or from aerial roots. During the war of independence, said another, the insurgents captured in battle were decapitated and their heads displayed in cages or on pikes on the top of watchtowers, on the walls of forts, on bridges and by the roadside. Today, said Strogowski, looking at Madame Jazmine's collection of heads, we continue to cradle a headless body in our arms; we call it our country. And the head has still not turned up.

I am merely a corpse with no name, Gil Paz said to me. Then he began to talk: A decapitated animal continues briefly to live, racing madly across the desert, scorching its feet without actually feeling the heat, spilling its blood on the sand and the stones, while its head, lying on the ground, blinks to see its body running off, only to topple over just a few metres away, exhausted by that impossible act of rebellion. Death asks a question with no answer. Disappearance offers us the wound of the speculative, of the possible, the possibility of what we once deemed impossible. Absence creates a debt with time. Amputation and decapitation cancel out the idea of an endless search, said Gil Paz, no one will look for the head, too afraid to see its final expression, its last look of grief and pain.

One day, after a long time away, I returned to the tropics, where many of the things I love most still live, and in the countryside I found, roasting in the summer heat, an army of headless bodies: they came and went from the TV news programmes to the front pages of the newspapers, from the mouths of the rumour-mongers to the ears of the morbidly curious; they trotted about in fields, by the banks of streams, the sides of roads, embalmed in colourful blankets, conserved in earthenware jars brimming with corrosive acids, infernally sulphuric and poisonously hydrocyanic; they walked among us like members of a sect, reminders of a continual threat that might suddenly fall upon every house. And yet, impossible though it may seem, that kind of decapitation was a double decapitation, because the perpetrators, themselves condemned men, had first been robbed of consciousness, ideas, identity, name and all the other things stored inside the brain; they were robbed of memory, which is situated in the hippocampus, of will, by the destruction of the frontal lobe; and by damage inflicted on the corpus callosum, they lost any connection between the left and right side of the brain, thus establishing the necessary confusion of mind conducive to crime; the ability to dream disappeared along with the ability to distinguish between sleep and wakefulness, which makes everything seem unreal, and in that unreal state anyone can commit any kind of atrocity; the heart was removed from the amygdalae and love became impossible; in the end, all that remained intact was the most primitive part of the brain, the reptilian brain: fear, rage, hunger, aggression, anger: the millenarian crocodile that serves to kill and be killed; when it ceases to be useful, then comes the second decapitation, and it's off with the reptile's head, as St George did with the dragon, Perseus with Medusa, Hercules with the Hydra, St Michael with the serpent, as well as St Martha of Bethany, the sister of Lazarus, the one raised from the dead, and St Margaret who was shut up with the Devil in a tower, and Siegfried and Beowulf in those legends from the snowy northern peaks. First, they create the monster, then they cut off its head. That's what I found in the tropics: a cemetery of headless bodies, or, as in Madame Jazmine's Bar, a display of disembodied heads.

It was then that I met Gil Paz in La Ceiba and told him about our trip, about Madame Jazmine's Bar, about the headless dolls, about Strogowski and his glass eye, and he talked to me about The Country, the decapitees, the unforgiving heat, the prolonged absence of the Magus Strogowski. And while I walked the streets of the tropics, that imaginary line around the throat, I was thinking about Madame Jazmine's Bar, about the dolls' heads that filled it, about the name of the bar, written, like the name of The Country, in blood-red neon letters, and I thought about the words of Gil Paz, who was saying that, in an earlier age, the criminal beast would have been satisfied simply with making someone disappear, and with the seed of disquiet that the unknown sows in the hearts of those looking for the disappeared person. But fear nowadays is a more complicated affair, it can no longer be summed up in a few words, it's no longer a concealed body, it's more precise than that: absence is no longer enough, he said, the gnawing anxiety of doubt is no longer a useful wound because it leads to anger, and anger is a vital engine, a driving force: and what violence seeks now is stasis through image, paralysis of the will by offering consequence rather than uncertainty, a definitive ending, rather than the possibility of some future return: that makes a response impossible because a response requires, as a first condition, the ability to come to terms with what is going on, and who can possibly come to terms with such violence, said Gil Paz, and who has the strength to raise an angry voice? For the time being, we are all sitting in the street, on the edge of the precipice, cradling in our arms a headless body: now we know what happens to the disappeared.

We reconstruct the disappeared through memory, said Gil Paz, their strength lies in our search, our weakness in their unending suffering: the disappeared never die; the disappeared are always dying. You cannot recover the disappeared, but you don't entirely lose them either; the search is what defines this alternative form of travel. Once the threat has been carried out, it becomes a fact; freedom or imprisonment are no longer options, because the killers have achieved their desired result: death, violence, humiliation. To remember someone inevitably means that he or she is not here with us: memory is proof of absence, disappearance, distance, for to remember the disappeared person is tantamount to looking for them; to remember a murder victim, on the other hand, is to remember their death and, in such cases—said Gil Paz, imagining himself pointing at the dolls' heads in Madame Jazmine's Bar, which was tantamount to pointing at the heads of all this Country's disappeared—in such cases, he said, to remember the dead person is to remember the indissoluble violence of their death. In the case of someone who has disappeared, there is still the possibility of change, whereas in the case of someone who has been murdered, there is only stasis.

In The Country, as in Madame Jazmine's Bar, there is an altar of heads gazing at us from roads, from bridges—where they hang like dark, ripe figs—from maize fields and scrubland, from foaming rivers, thick with fish, warmed by steaming blood, from flagpoles, their flags fluttering in the breeze like hair, from the mirror of the seas, from the bay, where they float like buoys marking the outer limit, from the tops of trees, like fruit dripping with a juice and a pulp that water the earth. The heads are watching us, but that is not their function; their function is to remind us not to avert our gaze. They are the ones saying, with their fishy, putrid mouths, Look at me and remember the future.

Statistics, said Gil Paz, are the modern-day equivalent of what used to be called prophecy: in statistics lie the prediction of our possible futures. To come up with a statistic, you have to eliminate all the peculiarities of each individual case, to remove its individuality; give it a standard format that puts it on an equal footing with an appropriate and previously established scheme, so that its essence is erased from the faceless multitude of headless corpses. One death is erased by another death. One hundred deaths erase sixty thousand deaths. The memory, however, of the gaze of those who have been stolen from us can never be erased, said Gil Paz: don't forget, he said again, the gaze is something that is never lost. Then, as if gripped by a troubling thought, he asked me what happened that night at Madame Jazmine's Bar, what happened afterwards. I told him that, when no one was looking, Strogowski stole a couple of those doll's heads—a present, he explained, for a collector friend of his—he took a few photographs of the place, considered ordering another beer, calculated how much money he still had in his pocket, and then we set off again once the rain had stopped; a few days later, we said goodbye and I haven't seen him since. When he stood up,

Gil Paz took a few coins out of his pocket and, with them, a doll's head, which he held by its few grubby locks of hair, an old head almost identical to the heads in the bar. He put it on the table; he looked at me, as if looking at me through the eyes of someone else, of someone lost, someone hopelessly alone and silent, and then he left. The disembodied head sat opposite me on the table, fixing me with a lopsided gaze, its left eye socket empty.

Translated by Margaret Jull Costa

THREE HUNDRED CATS

DANIEL SALDAÑA PARÍS

I arrived home at night-time, late, too late, much later than I'd anticipated, dragging my suitcase laboriously up the stairs, up to the second floor, all the while struggling with my handbag, which kept slipping off my shoulder, hampering my movement. The noise of the keys in my hand must have woken the dog in the apartment opposite, because it started to bark in that shrill tone and that prestissimo tempo that has inspired me to fantasies of canine torture on certain Sunday mornings when I wake up wrecked with a hangover, all my intentions to sleep till noon frustrated.

At the door to my apartment, manoeuvring my handbag and my luggage, I dropped the keys with the clumsiness that's always been typical of me: I'm not cut out to be a burglar, and my timid forays into sports in high school always ended up with a collection of shocking bruises on my legs. The dog's barking, behind me, intensified a moment and then fell into a silence that only presaged a new, more feverish assault soon after. When I crouched down to retrieve the keys, all set to enter my home at last—after a three-month absence—I was alarmed at the dust I could see under the door, which is constructed with a defect and isn't completely flush to the floor. This dirtiness would only serve to complicate further my already complicated arrival.

I didn't retrieve the keys at once: I stayed where I was on the floor, as though praying to Mecca, just looking. I had never spied on my apartment before. I had never thought that I could look into my own life through a crack and find the remains of my daily existence, or, as in this case, of my absence. I could glimpse a heap of noxious-looking fluff, the size of a bottle top. And crowning this unpleasant sculpture, I was able to make out, there rose up a fingernail, perfectly visible, a few centimetres from the lower crack through which I was peering. On top of the little pile of dust, that nail, looking as though it had been placed there on purpose.

I retrieved the keys and opened the door carefully, expecting to find the whole apartment in a similar state to the part I'd spied through the crack. I imagined the whole place full of dust: the shelves, the furniture, the appalling rug my mother gave me when I moved into my own place. All dusty, covered in the habitual crap with which the city baptizes all things.

Still in the dark, recognizing by the hazy light that was coming in through the window the shiny edges of some of the furniture, I was tempted by the idea of calling Berta, the woman who cleaned once a week, to complain about her negligence—but it was too late, after twelve, and my tyranny had its limits. To my surprise, when I turned on the light, I could see that the monstrous little clump of dust, a sculptural kind of thing, with that nail on top of it, was the only perceptible trace of dirt there was. This confirmation calmed me—I wouldn't have to hoover or sweep the moment I was done unpacking—but also, at the same time, it sowed a seed of doubt that would come to be more disturbing than the widespread—and, all in all, quite explicable—dirtiness I'd imagined on the other side of the door, before coming into the apartment: how had that heap of dust got there, orphaned like that, on the very day Berta had cleaned in anticipation of my arrival, just like I'd told her to? Whose was the nail that rounded off the heap of dust like a disgusting sort of headdress? Berta's, perhaps? I set aside any attempts to solve these unknowns and, with the help of a dustpan and brush, removed the nail and the dust, throwing the composite mixture into the kitchen rubbish bin, where it would remain until the following Tuesday, when Berta would be taking the waste down to the building's communal dumpster.

Although my arrival had been marked by the discovery of the dust and the nail, I was very quickly able to get past the disagreeable—albeit domestic and, deep down, trivial—episode, and settled myself into the living room, barefoot at last after the uncomfortable journey, with a cold beer in my hand—I'd asked Berta to buy me a six-pack in the store opposite, anticipating the most pressing requirements of my return; in other circumstances I would have opened a bottle of wine, a drink that gives me more real pleasure, but something in the tiredness and slovenliness that follows my travelling always demands this ordinary, cold drink, which I tend not to have in other circumstances. I moved the enormous, exceptionally cumbersome suitcase in front of me and opened it, swearing at it under my breath for the *n*th time that day. I took out my toilet bag, buried under the clothes, and set to removing my make-up, once I'd turned on the TV so that the murmur of the national news, so unheeded in recent months, might bring me back to the grey reality of Mexico. (As I removed my make-up, I could see in the little mirror how the innate bags under my eyes became visible once again and watch as the features of tiredness that resulted from the flight overtook my face, like a photograph appearing in developing solution.)

Three months had been enough, if not to make me forget, then at least to reconcile myself, or that was what I thought, to the events that had triggered my departure, my untimely retreat to my aunt's house in Madrid, a city I thought I liked but which ended up boring me not long after I'd settled there—thereby establishing that my lack of tolerance travels with me wherever I go. After only a fortnight living in the dark, closed-up apartment, on the Calle del Pez, in Malasaña, I stopped going out almost entirely, and with rock-solid discipline turned down every invitation extended by my aunt, and naturally also by the potential suitors she'd found among the ranks of her friends' sons, every one of them unemployed. The coarseness of the Madrileños was more than merely a prejudice, it was a conclusion I quickly reached for myself and which I didn't want to refute with research that might destroy my slow process of emotional recovery, the only thing that mattered to me.

My mother had died and, in a further trauma, her inheritance—which was not substantial, but certainly potentially useful for someone with my lifestyle—had been handed over, as stipulated, to an animal shelter, for cats in particular, in a wretched little town in the state of Mexico. (I put up with my mother's rudenesses, her real delusions, for thirty-three years—as long as Christ tolerated life before roughly sacrificing himself—in order finally to enable a happy existence, albeit in overcrowded conditions, for some three hundred cats. Thanks a lot. I owe that particular little joke to Facebook, that system of hypnosis where Remedios, my mum, spent the final years of her life commenting with the sparsest syntax on hundreds, possibly thousands of photos of cats wearing piteous expressions.)

I could have survived my mother's death, like almost anybody else, without any substantial alteration to my habits and fundamental beliefs, but sod's law, which governs this part of the tropics, had brutally dealt me, at precisely the same time, a romantic break-up, and this demolished my already battered mental stability. In my naivety—fuelled by soppy films in which the lead character discovers the meaning of life while she's travelling around Tuscany—I believed that a happy trip round Europe, or a three-month stay in an idealized Madrid, would save me from falling into self-destructive behaviour, like making cuts on the inside of my thighs before going out to work, so I surrendered to my romantic impulses and asked for a bit of leave from work, which my boss granted me once I had set out my case—with all the usual exaggerations.

As I've already said, the trilling of bucolic birds that circled about all my plans for a European retreat never began to sound, perhaps asphyxiated by the noise of that irritating summertime song that could be heard in every Madrid cafe. Hiding away in the coolest room in my aunt's house, I busied myself arranging and un-arranging an album of photographs of my early childhood, discovered by chance among some cookbooks. A series of photos showed a trip around southern Mexico with my mother and my aunt. Remedios was driving a rickety Datsun that seemed to be propelled entirely by her smile. My aunt, who was more serious, was smoking in all the photos, while I, a very little girl at the time, looked wonderingly towards nowhere in particular as though trying to recognize unfamiliar territory.

I arranged the photographs in order that they would tell, depending on the version, many different stories. The story of a family, with same-sex parents, which ends up dissolving into the calm waters of the Caribbean Sea. The story of some Californian fugitives who kidnap this little kid and escape to Mexico. The story, finally, which seemed to be the most accurate: a woman and her sister taking the girl on her first holiday, in a perfect world from which all men appeared to have been expelled, transformed into pale sand.

But now I was back and not wearing any make-up sitting in the living-room armchair, while a TV presenter, a woman with impossible cheekbones, was unquestioningly repeating a government report about some massacre—perpetrated with gratuitous cruelty by another arm of the very same government that was now broadcasting, via the television, a report of feigned neutrality, as though with a double dose of cynicism. The first beer was dwindling dramatically and I was making an effort to float wearily as far as the kitchen, ready to open a second, when I remembered the nail and the little heap of dust at the bottom of the bin for inorganic waste—where I had tossed them in a mistake that could be attributed to the revulsion that the grey mess had provoked in me: my brain didn't want to accept that, according to the biblical parable, this lump of dust was made, after all, from the same fallible stuff as my own tired flesh. I don't consider myself a fussy woman, but I will acknowledge that dust, or rather those constructions of hair, mites, fluff and debris, have always prompted a tremendous recoiling in me. Despite everything, and even knowing full well that I was exposing myself to an attack of revulsion, I skirted past the fridge (my primary objective) and peered into the bin with a stupid, sick fascination. There was the lump, and the nail, all alone at the bottom of the plastic bag, just as they had been on the flagstone floor, just inside the front door.

For the actions that followed I can find no cause not involving a passing lapse in my mental faculties… I pinched the fragment of nail from out of the dust, with almost autistic determination, and removed it from the bin, holding it between my thumb and index finger, then bringing it up to the kitchen light for further scrutiny. It was a little nail, as though of a child or a woman with small hands (in my family we all have pianists' hands, though only my mother pursued this showy profession with any kind of success). It had some filth stuck to it, the nail, which reminded me of many childhood afternoons spent making models out of plasticine, while the clumsy exercises of Remedios's students, at the piano, flooded the living room, and even the house, to my annoyance.

Rather than cleanly sliced by some cutting implement, the nail looked as though it had been nervously bitten off, which made me think it might have been Berta, who is always in a state of anxiety over the health of her children—which has repercussions on her own, as she lives for them. But there were not enough factors to suppose that Berta, usually so meticulous—having been warned about my neuroses—would have allowed to elude her, and right beside the door, a bit of residue as dreadful as that. I put the nail away in the right pocket of my denim skirt—a pocket that was more or less cosmetic because neither a cellphone nor keys would fit in it—and returned to the living room. Now the TV was showing the news of a huge march protesting against the government, which the presenter was playing down with an expression of contempt.

I thought about the three hundred unfortunate cats who, notwithstanding Remedios's final wish, would live in a dreadful place until their death by asphyxiation (I don't know why I thought that was how they were going to die, asphyxiated, and—even more distressingly—all three hundred at once). My mother's piano, which occupied and still occupies too much space in that minute room, seemed to be smiling, as though mocking the fact that it was the only inheritance that had come to me—more as a final reproach for never having learnt to play it than as a sweet reminder of my departed mother.

I turned off the TV at around two in the morning—the newsreader was reporting a disturbance in the Zócalo square: for a few moments I dwelt on the word "cudgel", the sound of which seemed to me, at that moment, not quite correct, because it made you think of something soft, as though the policemen were brandishing sticks made of silicone against the people—and I sat in a silence, opposite the set, wishing it were Tuesday morning, when I would hear the problems that Berta always spills out, unashamed and unhurried, while she does the dishes.

I took the nail out of my skirt pocket again and looked at it on my open palm. Tiredness was making the back of my neck tense up, but I didn't want to go to sleep yet, I didn't want to go back to the bed where I'd spent so many nights suffering from insomnia, clenching my teeth.

It seemed closer, the nail, almost mine, like a forgotten talisman from some distant age. In a great burst of folly, the likes of which had never overtaken me before, I brought it to my mouth and bit it slightly, to check that it was real—and as far as I could tell, it was; then, with a dry retch, I regretted having bitten it. I was sad that Gonzalo wasn't living with me to make a joke of it; I could imagine his darkly funny remarks: that maybe it was the nail of a kid who slept overnight in the wardrobe, for example, or the nail of some neighbour who spent his nights playing with his own shit (all conversations with Gonzalo ended in scatological jokes: he was a very unsophisticated kind of guy).

I'm telling you, I can't explain everything I did that night, although eager to excuse myself I now put it down to my tiredness. As it was, I walked over to the piano and inserted the nail at the end of an octave between the B key and the C. Then I pressed down on the latter note, the start of everything that begins with strength and intent. I thought the structured, major tone of that C would calm my nerves, that it would remind me of those afternoons when Remedios and I used to play at trying to guess the note.

But as the key lowered, behind the solid C, I could make out the faint sound of scratching.

Translated by Daniel Hahn

BY AIR, LAND AND SEA

XIMENA SÁNCHEZ ECHENIQUE

The dictatorship has brought about the depopulation of Mexico. Fleeing from rapine and tyranny, our fellow citizens have been forced to cross the frontiers of the Fatherland. Such evil wrongdoing must be righted, and this will be done by the government that offers expatriate Mexicans the opportunity to return to their native soil and work peacefully, collaborating with everyone to make this nation prosperous and great.

Extract from the Liberal
Party Programme and Manifesto
to the Nation, St Louis, Missouri, 1st July 1906

Adiós flag, *adiós* watermelon, *adiós* moon, *adiós* rose, *adiós* star, *adiós* siren, *adiós* devil, *adiós* death, *adiós* sun. As you stroke the boxes on the lotto card, you realize you won't be the one speaking from now on, that things will speak. For the first time your hands feel nostalgic for fruit, nostalgic for bodies, are at a loss and start to cling to whatever they touch. You and your family aboard a steamer on the Atlantic have been banished from the New Republic. Unaware, as they move forward, that they are leaving a world behind, your grandchildren stretch out on the deck and resume their game between heaps of white beans.

"We have lost," says Grandfather from his leather easy chair.

"We lost." You give the card back and hold your arms out to pick your playing partner up off the ground. As you bend down, feeling your eighty years, your wife gripes at you.

"Let him be," says your son sympathetically, while your daughter-in-law disagrees: "Ay, Granddaddy, you look like a donkey." Your four-year-old granddaughter is on your knee playing with her china doll.

"Watch," the girl mumbles, "her eyes open and close at sea."

"That's true," you add, "I once saw a doll drown in a puppet theatre, a mechanism made the boards go up and down like waves, but I never did find out whether the kerfuffle came from the sea or the puppeteer."

"Lo-t-to," shouts the oldest of your grandchildren in what's still a childish voice. The rest of the little sailors, equipped with slingshot, marbles and tops, immediately throw down their cards for their nanas to pick up. In the turmoil, your granddaughter drops her doll and bawls when she hears it break.

Among the big trunks in the baggage hold are lapdogs, Angora cats, macaws, canaries, green parakeets, locusts in chilli and a dozen turkeys soaked in beer waiting to be cooked in *mole* sauce. Fortunately the turbine's voice drones on and silences every other. It's midday, the time when you and the gentlemen will gather around the captain. In straw boaters or panamas, the gentlemen are talking about the weather, the route to follow, the time it will take to reach the island. Under their respective parasols, the ladies are playing cards. Two maids, in caps and uniforms, offer them tea and vol-au-vents on a silver tray. In straw hat and stole, your wife is shuffling the cards, while your daughter-in-law, in a skin-tight dress, fans herself. The daughter of one of your former civil servants waves to you from the ship's rail. Perhaps the girl absented herself from the group on the excuse that she has a headache.

You can still see the port of Villa Rica fading into the distant mist. German steamers, French brigs, American merchant ships, vessels carrying the logo of the country's navy, half-sunken launches used for cargo and as shelters or lighters, and, beyond the fleet, on the other side of the old town, Mr Pearson's store where you and your family had to wait four days before setting sail. Fragile and beautiful, her back to you, the girl peers out towards the port. The Atlantic gusts unravel her ringlets. Back there, you can see the cathedral belfry, the turreted fort and the whitewashed walls that make the cluster of houses gleam.

As she grips the rail with one hand and her long skirt with the other, she alone knows that there is now no return. And the silk slides so slowly between her fingers the movement goes unnoticed, except when the material escapes her entirely and she has to lift it up to ensure it doesn't touch the floor and then the pleats concertina into a series of ridges that collapse without trace, only to re-form the moment the girl intervenes.

Tears, palpitations, vertigo.

In response to a signal from her father, one of your military attachés, the girl walks over to you. Her hoarse voice, at odds with her elegant features, begins to declaim the sad lines by a young poet from Zacatecas who will cause a stir in a few years. Of course, you don't realize the girl read the poem in a provincial magazine, of the sort you tend not to browse.

> Fuensanta:
> Give me all the tears of the sea.
> My eyes are dry and I feel
> A desperate need to weep.
>
> I don't know if I'm sad for the spirits
> Of my faithful deceased
> Or because our withered hearts
> Will never meet on earth.
>
> Make me cry, sister,
> And may the Christian mercy
> Of your seamless cloak
> Wipe away the sobs I shed
> Over a bitter, futile life.
>
> Fuensanta:
> Do you know the sea?
> They say it is smaller,
> Nay shallower than sorrow.

I don't know why I cry:
Perhaps it's the sorrow I hide,
Perhaps it's my infinite thirst for love.

Sister:
Give me all the tears of the sea.

Much moved, the gentlemen applaud. The seagulls in the sky are more insistent than the handkerchiefs the crowd waved in your honour a few hours ago.

"I know I only need to poke my nose over if I decide to throw myself into the sea," you confess to the two or three trusted men around you, when you see the heaving water the liner churns in its wake.

"Of course. A Napoleonic nose like yours will recognize the vanquished city by its smell," says General Fernández's son, referring to your legendary disappearance aboard the *City of Havana.*

"True enough," you recall the extent of that boat, "like then, my enemies want me to have an uneasy conscience. Like a sick stomach."

"Take a dive! Take a dive!" you hear the members of the new cabinet shout within you.

"The idea was spawned by those born with the demeanour and manners of gentry, when I was sucking juice from sugar cane. *They* wore leather shoes while I ran barefoot along the paths in Tehuantepec. *They* bought English pistols while I turned a rusty barrel into a rifle and a pistol lock and a hunk of wood into a gun to go hunting with my brother. *They* learnt to speak Spanish without an Indian accent. Just watch," you start to wrinkle your nose the very moment Celso Acosta, your old police inspector, extracts a painting from a canvas bag, "how my nostrils flare out when I look at this portrait.

"What times they were," you tell the boys as you contemplate the picture: two rectangles of different shades of blue, one above the other, representing the sky and the sea.

And to think that thirty years after your escape on the *City of Havana*, then captained by Samuel Phillips, across these very same waters, on your return from New Orleans, that that proclamation of yours against the re-election of Don Sebastián, known as the Tuxtepec Plan, would describe your own regime so well:

> That the New Republic is ruled by a government that has abused the political system, scorning and violating morality and the law, corrupting society, pouring contempt on the authorities, and making it impossible to remedy so many evil acts peacefully; that the political suffrage has become a farce, because the president and his friends, through every reproachable means, ensure public posts are held by the men they call their "official candidates", and reject all independent citizens; that in this way and even governing without ministers, it makes the cruellest mockery of democracy, which is based on the separation of powers; that the public treasury is wastefully spent on idle pleasure and the government has never put before the Congress of the Union accounts for the funds it handles.

A cabinet of octogenarian seaweed welcomes you. They also avert their gazes so nobody asks how, when and where they came to meet you. You slowly float up the five metres separating you from the surface: fifty centimetres, seen from outside the canvas. Next to you lay the suit, shoes, wig and dark glasses of Ramírez de la Rosa, the man you had pretended to be. Stripped of your Cuban doctor's disguise, you pound the seabed for two minutes before shooting up like a splashing whale, and that's the worst strategy imaginable since, despite your reputation as a swimmer, you have moved from the shore rather than closer. You place the dagger vertical to the sea to estimate the distance between the two boats that are chasing you, very few centimetres from the shore in the painting.

"Our beaches are always warm and occupy ten thousand kilometres of shoreline," declares a woeful General Fernández, bringing you back to reality.

After crossing Parque México the car lights give your white skin a vegetable glow. The city birds are kicking up a fine racket. There you go, thinking about the voyage across the ocean you're about to set out on, between a group of cyclists and two lordly palm trees that were apparently sown at the beginning of time. The large clouds in the sky suggest it's about to rain.

"Good evening, young man, did you find what you wanted?" After barely ten minutes you go to the checkout of a 7-Eleven with two litres of beer and a two hundred-peso note.

"Red Marlboro please."

"Here you are." Olmec effigy traits contending with hair dyed blonde, the employee hands you a packet of cigarettes. You pick up a Pelón Pelo Rico syrup. You hesitate.

"Should I take for that as well?"

"Yes, please."

"Lilac? Like the colour lilac?" Lilac, her name written with a felt-tip on a name tag: she's used to dealing with smart boys like you, and smiles condescendingly, her teeth full of caries.

"Paper or plastic?"

"Better no bag." You hold out your hand like a hero, all for the good of the environment.

You walk back into the park, and its oval path, erected on the Jockey Club racetrack, so confusing for visitors, soon surrounds you completely. You know every inch of that park. You can perfectly place every bench, waterfall, stream and man-made pond. Your residential development, originally conceived around a racecourse, is one of the few where one can still walk wherever one wants. Of course, you don't own a horse, but a big dog that's been with you all this time, off its lead and sniffing all kinds of filth among the bushes.

It's raining.

When you reach the corner, a woman at the wheel stops to let you cross. Naturally, you keep straight on, on automatic, dodging drains and dog turds and oblivious to the girl in the Mini Cooper staring at you from behind her Ray-Bans.

You take a few more steps—two beers in one hand, the tamarind syrup in the other—and continue down the street until you come to the elegant art deco-style building where you live. You stick the key in the lock and walk into the large hall. Weimaraner and *Homo sapiens* run together up the winding staircase that separates heaven and earth.

"Surprise!" shout all your friends in unison.

Three days away from leaving for the "Old World" and your friends and closest relatives decide to give you a surprise. Your dog takes one look at the gathering and howls, while you look round to survey your sopping-wet clothes. You're wearing sports trousers, a sweatshirt and a Nautica polo shirt.

After you've said hello, you tell them all: "Please wait for a mo, I've got to change." Then you head to your room and slip on random gear. Your head's so wet you dry it on a towel. In one of the drawers in the bathroom, you come across the aeroplane ticket that will take you far from the New Republic:

NOMBRE DEL CLIENTE/CUSTOMER NAME:
PALACIOS/ALFREDO
SEGMENTO/SEGMENT HORA/FECHA
LV NEW REPUBLIC CITY 1:40 PM 31 MAY
AR OLD WORLD CITY 6:10 AM 1 JUNE

Like a real start-of-the-century man, you slip your arms into the new shirtsleeves and anticipate that the best is about to come. In your future, there won't be any heavy traffic, pollution, poor people, stray dogs, barred windows or parents who keep telling you their house isn't a hotel. You button up and put your trainers back on, before running into the kitchen and kissing your mother, who is cooking one of the stews. It's almost eight o'clock and the doorbell rings for the *n*th time. "My fam-il-y is re-a-ll-y so un-punc-tual," stammers your mother. Your godmother comes through the folding door behind a saucepan covered in aluminium foil, followed by your godfather and a bottle of tequila, your grandparents and slices of melon and your other two aunts with beans and the cake. "Everybody in the 'Old World' has got venereal disease," your godfather declares the moment he sits down at the table. "Ugh, nobody ever washes there!" remarks your grandmother to rub it in, switching on the cooker. "Take care, make sure nobody puts drugs in your drink," one of your aunts advises, rummaging in the fridge. "*Bon appétit*," adds the other, downing a savoury tortilla. In the end, when your royal ancestral council has finished debating your trip and its possible pitfalls, your desperate desire to throw them out the window has almost subsided. After all, you think, you won't be seeing them for one, two or three years. The adults stay in the kitchen while the youngsters move to the lounge and the terrace. "Hey, Negro," shouts your brother from your bedroom, "it's your girlfriend." "Hello." You pick up the phone as you search for a pencil or a pen or a felt-tip.

By eight-thirty there aren't enough chairs, so people start to stand among the standard lamps, rugs, glass cabinets, paintings and tables in all sizes, though they're not antiques, that welcome them. Back to the wall separating the lounge from the dining room, the waiter contracted by your father is preparing tequila cocktails, *micheladas* and Cuba libres, while dozens of hands are getting beer out of the cooler.

"Am I right, or am I wrong?" asks your younger cousin who's sitting on the stair landing, as she signals with three fingers the days left to you in the New Republic.

"Spot on," you nod tearfully before taking another gulp. You light a cigarette and inhale slowly while you observe the crowd. Practically everyone is there. Sons and daughters of the family who have never bothered to iron their clothes, make their beds, feed their dogs, cook their meals, keep the servants in line month after month or pay on the nail the bills for a style of life only wealthy gents can afford in the New Republic.

It's hard to credit that, like all other new republicans, you and your friends aspire to a better life.

You exhale the last drag apprehensively, since you've decided to stop smoking. They say cigarettes cost more in the Old World than they do in the New Republic.

"Hey, guy, you never dreamt anything like this, did you?" asks Suma, the girl from across the way.

"No way, it *was* awesome," you reply like for like, snuffing out your cigarette.

"Hey, just wait," the girl, who looks seriously starved, interrupts you and her boyfriend, "it was me told Negro to chase blondes," before stepping on the chair, taking a deep breath and crooning a ballad, even though the other guests listening seem rather out of it.

"Fantastic, my little pumpkin," you high-five a brawny, well-fed youth, with only wisps of fair hair and permanently ruddy cheeks. Agustín Larín, captain of your university's football team, asks for a pen so he can dedicate a novel to you.

At ten past nine the queue for tacos spills out over the terrace. Around sixty people chew, swallow and digest, while the flat's windows rattle.

"Guy, I can't think why. My father's off on a month's cruise with his new wife. My mother spends the whole day in the university on the excuse that we're grown-ups now. No kidding, bro. And now Negro is going to live in the Old World." "You bet I am. It's *the* thing to do." "Only an idiot would stay in the New Republic if he could clear off somewhere else." The conversations vary according to the group. The preppies are analysing the eagerness to escape that's floating in the air, one of your cousins' hairdos, the price of one packet against another. "Truth is she looks like a little potty," reckons Remi, the least shy of the group, as a piece of crackling falls off his plate. The university crowd are talking about work surveys about works surveys about work surveys. "Do you like the story of Little Red Riding Hood? (a) Always, (b) now and then, (c) sporadically or (d) never." Why the hell ask that question? You move, feeling uncomfortably as if you'd entered the conversation late.

You make a triumphant entry into the kitchen after your fourth tequila of the night. Once they've eaten, the preppies around the table start throwing peanuts in the air and catching them in their mouths. "Rea-dy, Ne-gro." After washing a pile of dirty plates, your sixteen-year-old sister asks you to introduce her to the people in your band so she can get them to play at her school.

"No way."

"I'm crazy about them. Won't be helping you in a while."

You feel sorry for the girl. You throw a peanut for old times' sake. "Beating it," you tell her.

When you go back on the terrace, you confess to everyone that you've gone "from happy to sozzled". "So fucking what!" When you pronounce these words that are so characteristic of your generation, your jaw sags and saliva trickles off your tongue. You weep two big teardrops. "I'm going to miss you lot so fucking much." You hang on to two of your cousins, the first people you see. You sing the lyrics of a ballad to cut your wrists for, then straighten up, your face covered in slobber. Nadia, your girlfriend for the last two years, comes over with her friends. "Just to let you know," when she speaks her voice makes your inner ear quiver, "that when you leave, we're finished." "*Ay, síí*," you breathe in her hair's fruity smell as your moist lips slip down her cheek. By way of a love token, you hand her the tamarind sweet you'd put in your trouser pocket. Then, she leans forward to suck the plastic tube and you get a close-up of the shadow in her cleavage.

To tell the truth, there are few women left in either world like your girlfriend. Really top-notch specimens who aren't thin, that being the main aspiration of most New Republicans. Nadia's body is, in effect, made of small flakes of flesh that pile up where it's best. Her breasts, a double avalanche: her hips, a double avalanche: her buttocks, a double avalanche. Naturally, Nadia has a face too. Wide, thick eyebrows, big green eyes, snub nose and lush lips usually tasting of cherry jelly. In a few months you'll come across her spitting image in an archaeological museum in the Old World, a small terracotta figure: a goddess of fertility, you read on the small label. As nothing has changed in your genes from the Late Palaeolithic, your Nadia makes you feel in sync with life.

"Don't be fucking silly, you idiot, how could you ask her to wait?" You hear the voice of Coco, your best friend, in the distance. You press the lift button with your nose. You walk along the corridor. You run down the huge staircase. You say goodnight to the concierge's overcoat and his pit bull licks your hands. "Hey, bro, should I ask her to marry me?" You finally leave the Basurto Building with those freehand-style picture windows and balconies to a shattering cry from above that makes your hair stand on end.

"Cigaarettes, buy more cigarettes," your sister bawls from her bedroom balcony.

"Cig-a-rettes," you bellow back, drunk out of your mind under a night sky fluorescent in the light streaming from the city. When you rummage for your wallet in your trouser pocket, you hit long dangling arms, arms that you elongate like you did when you were a kid on park climbing frames. Then you watch your two hands open and close by themselves, your wet trainers on the pink pavement where it's just been raining, and all around, the flash buildings, crumbling facades, pavement-cracking mulberry trees and willows, streets packed with cars, cables and light posts. In Parque México, once Parque San Martín, you hug the first tree you meet, and impelled by your own weight, you swing on it until the branch snaps. Your friends catch you before you crash to the ground.

And upstairs, while cigarettes are being stuffed into the *piñata*, you go over to Nadia and whisper something in her ear.

Translated by Peter Bush

From the novel *Por cielo, mar y tierra*

THE BLACK PIGLET OF LOVE STORIES

CARLOS VELÁZQUEZ

I had a little piggy who was free style. A little piggy to die for. Not Dalmatian or atonal. Who doesn't give frozen milk. A blacker-than-black piglet. *Pedigree.* My little piggy had *filin.* She was 60 per cent *gruvi*, 40 per cent *suing*, *chil out*, *dauntempo*, lots of cumbia and soul. A roly-poly tasty 80 kilograms of glamour. No shortage of vitamins. No shortage of preening in front of the mirror. No shortage of *pediquur*. All she was missing was someone to love. Her cuddly macho. That was why the advert in the *peiper* said:

WANTED:

HI-CLASS PORKER TO SATISFY SEXY LITTLE SOW

My little sow was called Leonor. Oh, Leonora, Leonora.

I was given her for my birthday. My *sista*, who has always sold pork scratchings, found her in a pigsty. She was looking for a boar that would fit the bill. A candidate for the Sunday barbecue. That was when she saw her. Such a pretty little piggy. She was a black suckling pig, her little body just made for rashers.

She thought she'd make a great pet for me.

Piggy was still small, but she already had quite a past.

According to the pig man, Leonor had escaped once. She wanted to become a composer.

A composer?

Yes, of country ballads. She herself told me so, in my dreams.

Old pothead, thought my sister. As she was telling me the story, I could imagine the announcement on the community TV channel: "Your assistance is needed to find Leonor the piglet. Her owner is an old hunk who's not all there."

She was lost for three weeks until I found her in the house of a man living all alone. I reckon Leonor was in love with him. She looks like a loose woman.

That old guy is off his head, I didn't bother buying the hog. I got out of there as soon as I could with little Leonor, my sister said.

My little piggy was a lovely pet. Perfect manners. Noble. Almost a person. But she went off the rails. She was a lost soul.

One week she fell ill. I made an appointment with the vet. He told me she was perfectly healthy, but not completely. She was suffering from depression. She also had symptoms of anorexia.

How depressed is she, doc?

Up to her trotters.

How can that be? I bathe her every day, put on lipstick, spray her with perfume.

I don't know. I can't give a diagnosis. We'll keep her under observation. She'll have to stay here two days.

That was the first night I dreamt of little Leonor. My pet piggy spoke to me in my sleep. With a human voice and sexual intent.

Manolo, Manolo, the reason I'm depressed is that I need a man, oh sorry, a pig. I need a lover. We sows can't live without sex.

My little piggy was a slave to her hormones. But she warned me, she didn't want to get pregnant. So when she got out of hospital I would have to find her a supply of femidoms.

In that same dream, Leonor recited the lyrics to Pink Floyd's 'Pigs (Three Different Ones)'.

Three days later, I got a reply to my advert. A pig man brought the most *charm* example in all his stock. As good-looking as the hero of a Venezuelan soap opera. I'd even have liked him to be called Kelvin William Ananké. Shame, but he was called Valente. He would have suited a name like Yumber or Gelson.

He's been in competitions, said his owner. He's won first prizes all over Mexico.

Leonor didn't see him as a great romance, but she did want him. She wanted him madly. She wanted to roll him in the mud. To bury him in her mess. Chew him like a corncob. Humiliate him with passion. *The bitch was so hot.*

Damned men, damn them, damn them. They're all swine. That's what I wrote one morning when I got up. Leonor was still talking to me in my dreams. *They're all sons of bitches. Crap. Liars. Cowards.*

This disdain, which at first I thought might turn my little Leonor into a ranchera singer like Paquita la del Barrio, was the beginning of a long story. A text that every night in my sleep began to acquire the dimensions of a novel. It wasn't just any old story. It was a killer. The portrait of a man who liked to be around builders, trailer trash, thugs. The main character suffered because of his drug-addicted, thieving, violent faggot friends. I didn't know what to make of it: TV soap opera, or diary? Then one morning, Leonor told me it was a sweet little novel about homosexual love.

Around the time I was working on the novel, Claudia paid me a visit. A school friend who had become a well-known poet.

Way to go, Manolo.

While I was warming up some burritos for her, Claudia read Leonor's poem.

Aren't you the sly one? I didn't know you were a closet poet.

I let her think I was the author. I asked her what she thought of it. According to her, I had a lot of potential as a poet. She asked if she could publish it in a magazine.

It's only a *jobi*, I told her.

I don't know why I said no. I'd been in love with her since high school. I'd do anything for her to get her into bed.

Perhaps I was put off by Leonor's dark side. She was a little socialite piggy. Whenever there were guests, she would adopt a different personality: she could be the hostess ready to dance the first dance with the prince, or the altruist keen to collect funds to protect albino owls. But that afternoon she didn't leave her room. Before Claudia arrived, she asked me to put a face mask on her because the light hurt her eyes. She was in bed. Her head ached. She wanted aspirin. Bring me a tea, she said, as if I were her butler.

Claudia left at eight that night.

I'm out of here, dear.

I looked in to see how Leonor was. This was something new: the little bitch, who always did her business in her pen, had dumped the lot on my collection of *TV Soaps*. My beloved magazines. They were unreadable, smeared with pig shit. It was two in the morning by the time I cleaned all the mess up. That was the first night little Leonor didn't speak to me in my sleep.

Valente came to visit Leonor every Thursday at four in the afternoon. My job was to make her room *so romantic*, with candles, rose petals. To open a bottle of Villarreal cider, light incense sticks, put silk sheets on the bed. Leonor's perversions grew more sophisticated daily. They included dildos, disguises, leather clothing and edible underwear. Once she even ordered me to film them while they were having sex.

In order not to have to think about the fact that my pet was enjoying a wild sex life while I had none, I bust a gut doing household chores. I became like Robotina, the Supersonics' servant. In other words, with no *breiks*.

One day when I offered some tamales with cornmeal to Romeo Valente's owner, he said to me:

You work harder than my wife.

My face reddened with shame. The plate I was holding in my right hand with three sweet tamales fell to the floor and smashed.

Let me help you.

No, it's no trouble. You might cut yourself.

No, please, I beg you. I'll do it.

Following that incident, the pig man's behaviour changed. Instead of dropping off his stud and leaving, he stayed to keep me company for several hours. He was intrigued by the fact that little Leonora did not get pregnant.

She will, I told him. She will.

In any spare time I had, I went over the novel. Leonor and I had decided to call it *If God Only Knew*. Although I didn't think of myself as a very literary person, I'd been very good at handwriting in primary school. Besides, when Leonor was very young, I used to read her stories before she went to sleep. Her favourite was 'The Day the Pig Fell into the Well' by John Cheever.

Two weeks later Claudia reappeared. Her excuse was that she was sure I had more poems hidden, and she wasn't going to rest until she had published them. She edited a magazine, and worked for an *indie* publishing house. Before she rang the bell I hid all my cookery recipes. I didn't want little Leonor to throw up on them or exchange them for toffee apples with the street vendor.

But my, oh my, to my great surprise the piglet came out to greet Claudia.

What a sweet little piggy! Look at her little nails, painted like that singer Brian Molko's.

Sly little Leonor, her behaviour was so chic. Claudia begged me to show her more poems.

It's true, I don't have any. That's the *one and only*. In fact, to show I'm not a jerk, you can take it. Publish it.

That night in my dreams Leonor insisted I show Claudia the novel. I fought against it. It would mean me losing my chance with her. If I showed Claudia *If God Only Knew* she'd think I was gay.

Then it would be *adiós, lover boy.* The argument lasted a fortnight. Leonor insulted me in my dreams.

You're a damn loser. It's our chance to get out of this pigsty. To live the high life.

What if the novel's a flop? What if it's no more than an impossible dream? I argued.

When had Leonor become so keen on success?

Claudia gave me five copies of the magazine. Leonor was no longer unpublished.

Thanks a lot. Care for a tamale?

Yes, with pleasure. Do you have one with meat?

No, I'm sorry, in this house we don't eat pork.

Oh, I'm sorry. I understand. Of course. A sweet one will be fine.

I heard the cry from the kitchen.

Oh, fantastic.

Claudia had found the manuscript of *If God Only Knew* on the coffee table in the living room. That slyboots Leonor. She had left it out for Claudia to discover.

What's this? Could it be a novel?

And so on and on. Then she said:

Can I take it to read? Why didn't you tell me you were a novelist? Is that how much you trust me?

The world is full of novels. What's the point of adding one more?

She undid the binding and began to read: "When I was eight I saw my father naked. I knew then that I liked men, that I would always like them." Oh, fuck it. That was the end of it. I'd just have to go on beating my meat. After reading that she was bound to be put off me for ever. Even so, I told her:

The reason I didn't show you it before was that I was afraid you'd think I was gay. I'm not.

Then I launched into a moving spiel about the characters. Just because the protagonist was gay didn't mean I was. It was a real sob story. I've no idea where I got all that guff; I've never read any literary theory.

When Claudia left I shut myself in my room. To weep. Like a female without her mate. What am I going to do? I asked myself. I'm almost forty and still not married. Everyone in the neighbourhood thought I was homosexual. Claudia was my last hope.

The door opened, and there she stood: Leonor. And although no sound came from her lips, I understood everything. I could hear everything she was saying. I didn't have to be asleep to understand. I could hear her clearly, as if she was talking to a young woman from a good family whom they were forbidding to marry a travelling salesman. *That man isn't good enough for you.* A young lady who isn't allowed to follow her heart's desire.

It's for your own good, Leonor assured me.

But it wasn't so much what she said that astounded me; it was the sight of her, her swinish humanity blocking the door. Her figure, and the fact that thanks to her our low-cost social housing had been turned into a sexual slum. One huge slaughterhouse where Valente was endlessly processed. A hog sacrificed on the altar of Leonor's erotic passion.

I soon devoted myself to imagining a more romantic scenario. A world where I ran away with Claudia. Or with any woman who truly loved me. Not caring if I were poor, a peasant or sang in buses. A wild woman with no moustache. And if possible with the face of the actress Pilar Montenegro. Ah, and one who didn't have a black sow for a pet. *If God Only Knew* was published with a print run of 3,000 copies. It sold out in six weeks. As it wasn't particularly romantic, on the cover was the slogan "Pink Fiction". The publisher's bright idea. The critics raved over it.

"The story of love in the world. On a par with *Confessions of a Fried-chicken Vendor.*" After that came the first-novel prize. Then the translation into English. Within a year we had reached the eighteenth impression.

We moved to a really nice apartment. Our neighbours were TV stars. Now less than ever was Leonor going to allow me to get married. Not to Claudia or to anyone.

Success hasn't changed me a bit, boasted Leonor.

It wasn't true. The quality of her snacks had improved.

She still had her lover, Don Valente. No little piggy ever forgets the macho who deflowered her. Yet she kept asking me for men, sorry, I mean pigs. She demanded hogs. Loads of pigs. She was insatiable. She couldn't stop. Whereas others collected coats, shoes, china, little Leonor devoured kilometre on kilometre of porkers' weeners.

I thought my little piggy's behaviour was empty, meaningless. Just another vice.

You're a hypocrite, she would tell me. Fucking is just like love. I don't need affection. I console myself with my wardrobe.

She was the ultimate diva.

I signed a contract with the publisher: 10 per cent for hardback, 8 per cent for paperback editions. Our second book, *Men Are Dead*, ended up consecrating Leonor as the Fernando Vallejo of gay romantic fiction. Inevitably, she was compared to that gay Chilean writer Pedro Lemebel and the Cuban Reinaldo Arenas.

The house had become one long fashion parade of her lovers. Carrying all the pigswill for them did my back in. And cleaning out all the mess from the pens. It was only on Thursdays that I could take off my rubber boots and put on loafers to receive Leonor's *number one*. Valente.

Little Leonor's performances with him were unbearable. They spent the afternoon together, but didn't make love. She would say she had a headache. Or her period. Or that she was bored. She kept him at trotter's length.

As ever, the pig's owner was part of the deal. The old pig man was quite crazy. To calm him down, I asked if he was married.

Yes, for fifteen years. But my marriage is a bore.

He asked me: Have you never felt something like a tingling on the back of your neck? As if you'd like someone to rub their snout there?

No, never. But go on talking, I said, getting up to serve him the stupid tamales.

A napkin fell to the floor, and I bent over to pick it up. I could sense he was staring at my buttocks. He said:

You know what, you're not bad.

I felt him grab me from behind, so I straightened up.

A bit of respect, dammit, I told him. You dirty old man.

I'm in love with you, he confessed.

I stopped him right there. I shrieked at him: You're to sit down and eat your tamales. Without a word. Without moving from your chair. And you're to eat them all. Make sure you don't leave any on your plate. That's right. Sit still. Just because I'm on my own doesn't mean you can take advantage.

I kept Fridays for Claudia. Movies were a must. I went with her to her poetry readings. Every now and then, we kissed.

Leonor used to spy on us. One day she saw us kissing and cuddling in the apartment. She didn't say a word. She shut herself in her room to shit on my teddy bear collection. The next morning, I argued with her in the early hours. She was against my romance with Claudia.

It's not good for our image for you to be seen in public with a woman. You write gay literature. You don't deserve me. I'm ashamed of you every time we go out into the street together. I'm in Dior, with something from Dolce

& Gabbana, and you look like a tramp. Do you know what's missing for us to be a real literary sensation? she would reproach me. *You need to become a fag. To dress like a fag. To walk like a fag. To behave like a fag. You need to marry a man. You write homosexual novels but you look like a stupid straight.*

From that day on, Leonor and I were constantly arguing. She insisted I should become a queer, let myself be fucked. The Thursday love trysts continued, but the pig man could only come in on condition that he stay on his side of the table and I on mine. Without looking at each other. Without touching each other. Without talking to each other. If he loved me, he had to love me in silence. Period.

Our third gay romance, *Queenie, Put Your Hand There*, sold 19,000 copies in six months. After negotiating with Claudia, we agreed I'd dress like a gay, without being one. It was simply for publicity. And it worked. The book cover showed me dolled up as a transvestite. Seeing me like that moved a huge number of readers, straight or queer, to buy the novel.

Holidays. We planned holidays: we deserved them. Leonor, Claudia and me.

I'm not going anywhere without my beloved, little Leonor told me.

Shit, I would have to tell the pig man we would be chilling out in Mazatlán for a week. Fingers crossed he wouldn't want to join us. I could already hear the old guy:

I'll behave, I'll be good. You know I want you. Don't be mean.

I'm sorry, sweetheart, I thought. Two pigs is enough.

The news fucked up our plans. Valente had suffered a spectacular, unbelievable accident. The piggy had got lost, far from the farm's piggeries (stables for pigs). His worried owner organized a rescue operation. After two days of fruitless search, the pig man climbed a tree to get a better view of the countryside. He was overjoyed when he saw Leonor's fiancé was right below him. But the branch gave way under him and fell right on top of Valente. The pig man was heavier than the pig. The poor beast died instantaneously.

Our trip was cancelled. Leonor sought solace in men, I'm sorry, in hogs. She slept with one after another. And another. And another. Some other sow would have turned to drink. But she said it was in poor taste for a woman like her to lose her poise. Even at moments like that she never forgot her education.

All men are swine, she said when all that unbridled sex brought no relief. Consolation.

She asked me to put the ad in the *peiper* again. I did.

WANTED:

HIGH-CLASS HOG TO SATISFY SEXY LITTLE SOW

We got shedloads of offers. None of them satisfied her. She never confessed as much, but I know she loved Valente. He hadn't known it either. In spite of all her snubs, she loved him. She regretted never having told him so. If only she had let herself get pregnant. Now at least she would have his child.

She went crazy. So crazy that one evening I returned to the apartment and found her like sausage meat on the pavement. She had thrown herself from the sixth-floor window. Her leap made the most beautiful postcard of a flying pig in history.

No funeral parlour wanted to have a wake for a pig. So we held Leonor's at home. Claudia and me. I bought a pink coffin. She was to lie in the plot next to my mother. My sainted mother. The old lady who always used to say to me:

Son, why don't you go out with Claudita? It's obvious she cares for you.

I never told her how I felt. We went through school and college together. At university, Claudia became an older lawyer's girlfriend, but they never got married. According to my mother, she was still waiting for me. Perhaps now it was time to fulfil my mother's desires. She never doubted who I was, and defended me from the busybody neighbours who were always asking her why I was so set against marriage.

He hasn't found the love of his life, she would tell them.

Well, he hasn't made much effort. He's not a bit, you know, is he?

It'll happen. It'll happen, she declared.

Leonor's death left me depressed. Oh, Leonora, Leonora. I missed her. Even if she treated me like her manservant. She deserved it. She had sophisticated tastes. I respected her memory. It was thanks to her that I had met up with Claudia again.

Without little Leonor, it was the end of me appearing like a street transvestite. And of my literary career. There was still one unpublished novel. Then nothing. I wouldn't be able to write one on my own. I had never been an author, and never would be. Leonor was the one with talent. Leonor was the artist. And nobody idolized her. I hated myself. I hated myself because I would receive the recognition she deserved, the day I died.

The funeral was one long procession of tamales. Sweet ones. With raisins and pineapple. Claudia and I were the only ones keeping vigil over the flowery wreaths. We weren't expecting anyone to come and offer their condolences. Then the doorbell rang. It was the pig man. He came in carrying a bouquet of roses. When I saw him, I collapsed. I don't know why I had been containing myself until that moment. Why I hadn't accepted that I was so upset. Accepted that Leonor was my life. That before she came, my existence had been garbage.

I collapsed. I couldn't bear it. The sight of the fat pig breeder with his stinking clothes, hairy chest and back, and disgusting moustache, reminded me that without Leonor's advice I would never find love.

The pig man took advantage to plant a kiss right on my mouth. A passionate kiss. A real truck-driver's passion. I said:

Fuck it! This isn't the moment.

And Claudia:

Not the moment for what? Are you two, you know?

I exploded at the pig man. I already told you I don't like you. I'll never go with a pig man.

And Claudia exploded at me.

What's this? You told me it was all a front, that you weren't gay. Why did you lie? Why? There was no need. You could have been honest.

The old man wouldn't shut up, but kept saying:

I love you. I love you.

Claudia picked up her bag. She left, but not before shouting that all men were swine. Wretched swine. We were all the same. All tubs of lard.

I was so angry I threw the pig man out. Deep down though, I wondered if that was what I really wanted. And yet I shouted at him exactly what Claudia had said to me: men are all swine. Sons of bitches. I don't want to see you again, ever, you wretch. Coward. Filth. Rotten. Rotten.

I lay there stretched out on the floor, crying in front of the coffin, dressed up like a queer. I was inconsolable, but unsure whether my tears were because of Leonor's death, having lost Claudia, or for chasing away my oh so darling, darling pig man.

Two months later, I went back to my low-cost social housing. To make ends meet, I started selling tamales at the weekend. All kinds of tamales, even ones with pork in them. I'd learnt that all pigs go to heaven. And that it was better for them to do so as quickly as possible, before they jumped from a sixth-floor window. I never wore men's clothes again.

I forgot Claudia. And I forgave my pig man. I had to forgive him. Besides, he was a good customer. Every evening he stuffed himself with tamales. Since he was still so horny, I accepted him as a boyfriend. One day he took me by the hand and asked me about "that". When we were going to do the deed.

Ah no, I said. I have to get married in white.

So he asked me:

You want to get married?

Yes, I said. The wedding is in December. When the pigs have been fattened.

Translated by Nick Caistor

From the novel *La marrana negra de la literatura rosa*

ON THE WILD SIDE

What I Remember and What I Don't

NADIA VILLAFUERTE

Sex is what connects me to life. I've known it since childhood. And I didn't have a childhood. That land that everyone talks about, it didn't exist for me. There are no photographs, I mean. There's a gap of six or seven years, empty as the space inside the left sleeve of my blouses. The nearest thing to it is the murmur of a beach, the smell of the black marshes. After that, a patio. I'm on a patio and my mother is saying: "Move." She won't let me bathe when I want, and manages to instil in me a poetics of trauma that will not desert me in the future: a puddle of mud, a swampy sentimental mirror from which I will observe everything.

I learn to keep quiet, as though there was an all-absorbent sponge beneath my tongue. "Scrub!" The word explodes when I, entranced by the hairs covering an Adam's apple shown in a magazine, refuse to help her.

Her presence picks you over with the glint of a forensic eye. An unctuous gaze, small ears pinned on like twin brooches. I discover—and it comes from somewhere deep—that I am ashamed to belong to that place. Deep down I want to believe that I am there by mistake: a changeling. Her orders are like an endless snorting, coughing, spitting. But she's good at teaching me submission, fear, and although at first I try to resist, sometimes I feel guilty for being quietly above it all, especially when she calls me in to eat, sits down beside me and asks, "Did you like the stew?" with a clumsiness that hides affection. It's hard for her to caress me, to live with me, I sense that she can't overcome her pity. Sometimes I catch her looking at my stump, some nights I sense her desire to squeeze it, like the strangers' shirts she washes. I want to say, "Don't force yourself"; I remain with lips sewn shut, holding back uncertainties. Now and again, not often, I feel good sitting near her: looking at her head wrapped in a kerchief, at her fluttering around the radio that stays on all night.

There's no sign of any father. And no squealing little brothers, chasing each other naked and covered in mud. Before I run away, my suspicions harden: that woman was unable to have children and stole me from some other home, afraid of being alone.

We live right on the shore. When we go to the sea wall I feel a jolt like *I was here a very long time ago*. Not just in the past, but in an ancient time. Watch, don't talk, obey. A time will come when I'll set foot on other shores, different and alike to mine: frontiers between the sea and the deceptively dry land.

The place is called Paredón, a wall of water to the horizon. There are no waves in Paredón. It's a dead, mutilated sea: no prosthesis exists for that. Nets and drunken fishermen, bicycles gnawed by the salt that corrodes everything, women on the lookout to kill time: people's daily tasks distract them from their feelings, they seem little inclined to kindness but so cheerful that they don't mind how being constantly together, one on top of the other, wears down their individuality. Here the days end in passageways mopped by women with chlorine-chapped hands. That sentry box and its rotted boards comes to my mind, and the parade of shops lit up through the scorching exhalation of forty-degree heat. What a racket people are making. The smell of the crowd reaches me. Sand creeps over the ground and attaches to the skin, velvety and amorphous, threatening to bury us all for no reason. I remember very well the accordionist with one brown eye and one dead white, without a pupil, just like a bean, who cheers me up when he says: "If you must believe in something, may it be the God who lets you fall into temptation and delivers you from evil."

My mother's skin is a blue-black that you'd think would rub off on you if you touched her; mine is a light black. She makes me stay out on the patio for hours. "Do you good," she says. The sun gets under my hair, my head turns into an unprotected sheet of metal. I'll preserve that heat, then pour it off, as if it was in the way.

I imagine another world behind walls and ships outlined against the motionless afternoons. I resist the thought of life as nothing more than this rabble of fishermen, the knife plunging into the flesh of one of them, the rusty laughter of the drunks in the cantinas. Later I'll discover that these things just get compounded. That the world is the same forest, and loneliness inside it is the same walk again and again.

I know Paredón to exhaustion, not that there's much to know: it hardly takes hours to cross it from the train station to the sea wall. Once when I get lost, on purpose, I come to a house with open windows where there's a couple: a young woman leans her hands on the mirror of a dressing table to receive the thrust of a man from behind. The man pushes hard against the girl, holding her by the hips. There's an indistinct rhythm to it all, something in me goes happily askew.

Another morning I run across them in the market: under the zinc vault, wreathed in smoke from the stoves, the same girl with wild eyes, the same man. "She's crazy," hisses my mother. "During the day she begs. She picks up fruit and vegetable scraps and takes them to her table. Who hasn't she slept with. How would she know who the father is." "And what do you know?" It annoys me to hear her talk like that when she's never even met her. "Well I've seen them and it's obvious, she's promiscuous." The word flares out like a murder. If anybody had asked me,

What do you want to be when you grow up? I'd have said, with pride: "I'm going to be promiscuous."

Days later I find her skipping on the beach, wearing an organdie dress that conceals her bump. She looks like a kite on the loose. That afternoon I follow her. She runs and then throws herself down in the dunes. I lie down beside her. "Don't hurt me," she says and adds, "I'm so fast you'll never catch me." Her dress seems like a thing from another era. A dress like that overdoes it: the elegance of certain objects is a reward or an insult in places like Paredón. Stroking the rosy stuff of the dress I hear her say, to my surprise: "This baby is my father's." I have never in my life been struck by so hard a gaze, and yet there's still a childish spark in it. She's conscious of being admired, and frank in a way that makes you want to know more, like a promise that brazenly accosts you. Her gypsy eyes attack, she says: "You'll laugh at me." "I won't." She is so young, and I feel equally old. Nothing stirs in us but a sterile sensuality. We seem to be bored before embarking on the feast. We seem to be murmuring in the fog: "We thought there was something else away from here, but there isn't, only this, the Pacific."

Margit, that's her name. She says she doesn't have a lot of feelings; and of those few, none is exactly good and even so she knows herself to be a beautiful soul. "Some people live in absolute sadness. Or else they try to attract attention though they know how tiresome it can be, until they find there's no way out. I can't understand that sort of thing. Whatever the pain, it's no cause for pity. I take risks and I live my life with joy. I'm pretty. I shine. I've come to accept the idea that in order to attract people, even when you're not really interested, there's a price to pay." As she talks, she taps her lips with the pasty she's sharing with me. We are two grown-up women building our graves while birds of carrion stand round our corpses. It's the best period: a friendship made of perfume flasks, the cramps of hormonal change, funeral processions of crabs, an orphan bicycle in a field, mattress springs on the pier. We crash onto the dunes and hear the sand sliding until it catches up with us. We see how a scab of earth lies stretched between the sky and the sea: time is silent and smooth, a microscopic sparkling that coats us. I'm on the run from then on, but lying flat; an escape without dangers or consequences. At times I look at Margit's corpse floating in the water. But I don't know how to do it: I view the sea with curiosity and dread.

One afternoon I knock on her door. I can't see anything at first, it's so dark in there, but my eyes quickly get accustomed. "Margit, it's Lía." I'm in a galley with objects floating palely in the middle, pots and pans, a cooker, a wardrobe, a shelf with two books on it, a bed. Someone moves: a brief burst of surprise in Margit who ushers me and says, "Come on, don't be afraid," and finally guides me, with clinical casualness, to the mirror. She never seems repelled by my stump, she doesn't ask why or how. Neither does her father. I am speaking of the rough-featured man with the aloof, respectful manner and mouth curved into a soft and foolish smile: the man who smoothly homes in from behind, croons, presses against me, pushing, and repeats the gentle movement that rends the flesh, the silence that breaks while the scission cannot be stopped, the impression of at last being free. The man who shows me that all the heat of the earth can shelter there. Who by giving me a new body makes me return home on hands and knees, crawling like a snake between flowers.

Strange as it may sound, it is them I honestly trust; it is they who bestow on me an act that is decidedly not appropriate, but that shortens the distance between what I lack and what I long for. Now the sea is inside me, flowing to my measure.

The smallness of the port is unhealthy. Thanks to sex I discover the dynamic of plenitude and emptiness, those parameters deployed by domestic militias; the act of seduction whereby the adversaries' camp is breached before they are broken down, slowly and unpredictably, from within; the logic of the method when after making love, you realize that violence is the only road left open. And in place of intrepidness, docility. I breathe exposure, the danger of it. In Paredón this is quite usual. The coasts have the same music: despite the tedium, people sing and wreak violence to a beat that is not, in its undertones, as moving or exciting as we tend to believe, only simple and natural.

I will never remember his name: he's Margit's dad, he is not old, he is a face and virile to extremes. The first man to love me, or to desire me (it's all the same). Today he has no features. The smile perhaps, the gaze devoid of pleasure and wrongdoing. Nor his height, nor the curve of his back, nor his colour.

I go to secondary school, but my mother warns I'll never get away no matter what. She expects my fate to be like hers, why should I have a different destiny? She's a servant. And servants reproduce their species. It's not just the trade, it's the attitude. Letting go of the ambitions that portray, oh so delicately, our insignificance.

"Lía?"

"What."

"You're supposed to say *mande*, at your orders."

"At your orders," I repeat. She forgets to point out that obedience does not mean subordination.

I go to Margit's house twice or three times a week. With too much free time, I retain my interest before the wall of mounting rapture yoked to abuse, love tied to contempt. I identify with these things. I have become a different person. They teach me that the sea fulfils its task of setting us ablaze ahead of time. Bit by bit we become tamer, like flowers wilting in a jar.

There's a shelf in Margit's house, as I mentioned. And on the shelf there is a dictionary, the second great discovery. In its columns I find traces of what I had supposed to be a peculiar mental deformation. Distances and objects sprout from simple definitions. *Hostel*: a building providing inexpensive accommodation to specific categories of person such as students, travellers, the homeless, etc. *Abduction*: the act of tying up a person and taking them away. Bombay, Beirut, Tel Aviv, Cairo, Kyoto… Serene explosions that keep me attentive and submissive, places that gradually project me beyond the confines of my surroundings and turn into a throng which suddenly, inadvertently, expulses me.

Margit's stomach swells: a pinprick and it could burst. Now her demeanour tenses. And over this period she becomes slightly dull. Our conversations wander over the terrain of memory, she tips into hysteria. Her canny-matron look fades gradually away. The father seldom appears, and when he does, it's to manifest that he has become terminally displeased since realizing that Margit and her eight-month-old foetus exist outside of him, beyond his domain.

At noon one day I come across her looking pale and holding a baby. "I didn't have time to get to the health centre. And now here's this sprog ready to clamp onto my breast like a Doberman for the next ten months. But I like it," she says. Margit smells of milk, and focuses intently on the baby's pink face as if reading the future: it already has her enfolded in sweet tyranny, it won't let her eat until it's eaten, or sleep till it's asleep. "You'll never have any peace," I tell her. And Margit replies happily: "We'll be leaving here soon."

They go away that same summer, Margit's narcotic voice bouncing off the wall, the curt, silent father, the child that has turned Margit soggy with tenderness though she denies it. The family has departed that could have said goodbye at any time with no need for a "thank you" or a cruel word. It makes for an amicable leave-taking, really, though this may not be quite accurate of me. Perhaps they did a flit deliberately, leaving behind them all the violence signified by an empty house.

Some afternoons I prowl that whitewashed cement block, but all I find on the floor is a stiffened pair of underpants, a forgotten sock, an empty bottle with no message. Other times I go to the beach and at once remember Margit with me, our legs clean save for where a ribbon of seaweed clung on like a sign marking the skin. The truth is, I miss her: Margit told stories and the characters in her stories always came to a bad end.

In the meantime my mother grows more withdrawn. The blade of the new moon might slice the evening like a silver earring half sunk in water, and she's likely to turn round and argue that the coast is still a filthy circular trap and besides will I leave her alone, she's got work to do. It may be that her rejection is more like lucidity, which I, of course, don't have. It may be that behind her apparent detachment from the world lies nothing more than hatred turned to habit.

"Why do you talk like that?"

"Like what?"

"Like that, so full of yourself…"

Instead of replying I curl my lip, laying all my arrogance before her.

Then:

"Who gave you that dress? You look like a showgirl!"

"You sewed it yourself, it was yours."

Perhaps it scares her to see how I've changed into someone else, so she scrutinizes me like a mathematical equation. I understand, and begin imagining the day when I'll say to her: "Go on, let it all out, I won't tell, nobody can take it like I can, and when you don't even exist any more because you've spat all over me so often, I'll still be here." It amuses me to act like an aristocrat, even if I'm only what I see inside: a teenager prone to brief fits of rage who will harbour her grudge for a while, until the moment comes to cast it out.

I'm fifteen, or sixteen (I never know when's my birthday, sometimes I make up a date just like that). On the sea wall, one year after the departure of Margit and her dad, Glenda appears. Midday, I'm walking home from school and all of a sudden a far-off blotch disturbs the horizon. A bulk whose colours fray apart in the light. Its golden spray of hair hangs over the wharf. Perhaps she's dead, I think. It's a woman. A pair of pumps and a handbag placed around a body that's like a vinyl blossom washed up by the surf. Thighs in tight leggings: clothes to cut the circulation. Smeared lipstick as if the mouth had flapped its wings to escape the face. Purple toenail polish, broad soles, the feet of someone unaccustomed to walking barefoot on hot tarmac.

I could stand there for ever admiring the contrasts of the clothing, the promise of death on the sands. But then she moves. And bit by bit rolls over until seeing me. Shades her eyes from the sun. I ask point-blank:

"Where are you from? You're not from here. And if you're not from here, it stands to reason you'll be going back to where you came from."

She hasn't recovered from her amazement when I add, marking a distance now by using the formal second person:

"Take me with you."

The words come fluently, with a self-assured kind of diffidence, as though they'd always been on the tip of my tongue, ready to leap.

"You crazy muff, just tell me where I am."

"Take me with you."

"I'm in no mood, hell's the matter with you, I don't getcha."

"Neither do I. Take me with you."

It's not a request any more, it's an order.

"You're off your rocker! Someone being mean to you? You kill someone? Pinch something?"

"I know a taxi driver who can take us, only you'd have to pay."

"Help me up for starters. Need to know if this here queen is still in one piece."

You've lost, I thought. Helping someone equates to making them your slave. I stare, challenging her. She stares back the same way. Her eyes are smudged with mascara. After a while she says:

"Stop drilling into me, and stand back, do. You look like you want to eat me."

"Just to the bus station. I'll stay there." It's the first time I've ever spoken *out of turn.* "But you might want to take me along and I'd work for you. I just want to get to the station."

"Where d'you suppose I'm from?"

"Who beat you up?"

You've lost, I insist, and return to the attack.

"You're a mule, my darls, a proper mule."

"Is that a yes or a no?"

"First let's get there, I need a bathroom to fix me make-up, don't you hate it when an overnighter leaves you with all open pores? Guilt raddles a girl quite enough as it is."

I take her to the taxi rank on condition she take me to the buses. We gust away down the road, too fast, no time to think it's happening, as if it could never be real except for what the landscape offers up, supreme and humble, in the frame of the rear-view mirrors.

The central station. Now I hear its unprecedented babble, the creak of shoes, hands crumpling tickets, loudspeaker announcements: *Passengers destined…* A muffled voice slips another era into the departure hall: 1942, a phonograph, though we're still held this side of things: a circular trap where nothing of any grandeur could ever have taken place.

It's the first time I've seen so many people, perpetual hurry, going or coming and yet waiting nonetheless. It's the first time of all possible things. Unbelievable, to me: one false step and I've trodden on a mine.

"Sure you want to tag along? Cos we're two days' ride away, fancy-pants. We're headed down the map and the lower down you get, the more the earth splits apart. How come you couldn't do it day before yesterday, come to the station on your own?"

"I haven't got any money."

"Pull the other one. You're a fibster. I can spot the kind who'll do anything out of low self-esteem."

I don't know what's going on in her mind, nor why she decides to do it, but I see her set off straight-backed, a statue fluttering its lashes over the tyranny imposed by those high heels. I see her halt before the ticket window and grace the clerk with a discreet puff of morning breath around the words "Make it two". Because unexpectedly that's what she does. She pays for the two tickets and returns with epic stateliness, maintaining her balance, and hands one to me. As if saying, you're going to fall over yourself: the receiver of help develops a twisted sense of duty and surrenders their own will bit by bit, or in one go. And I respond straight away that that's fine, I'll be her maid because I'd sooner be humbled than back off from my commitment to running away.

The fate for which I'm destined, though I don't know it myself, is what's driving me to escape. I tell her: above, the noiseless drift of clouds; below, the flow of fish; the air, fragrant with pitch; and a new and savage song inside. I tell her: not a coat to keep off the cold, nor a change of clothes, nor a comb, nor the perfume flask, nor the dictionary Margit gave me.

Anybody could have laughed: my mother, for instance. Disbelief: but it can also happen that a fact one believes impossible comes undone as lightly as anything.

"Come the time for you to pay me back and shake my snake," Glenda adds.

A speechless smile on my face, I'd betray anything for you, I want to say, on the verge of kissing her.

"You can put me down in your city, I'll look out for myself. Or if you prefer I'd be willing to carry out odd jobs, water the garden, pull up weeds."

"Ain't got a garden. And look here, would you mind talking normally? You're like some Barbie doll who's forgotten we're in the Third World."

"I do talk normally."

"You said *I'd be willing to carry out*, that's not normal."

"I like to speak correctly."

"Too damn correctly for my taste. Careful you don't make me regret it."

"You won't regret it, I promise you."

"I came by plane, and behold me now: on the bus. Fucking yobs!"

"What happened?"

"I had an accident. Just shut up will you, you're making me nervous, you're upsetting me, OK? Glenda, my name's Glenda, and now what do I look like, leafless as a virgin in the climactic moment, in this hideous landscape like something out of Chilean socialist realism."

She tells me about the place that is her homeland: a suit, the fragile imaginary of her high heels and the animal life. I don't quite understand it anyway. Her ornate accent and padded, husky voice are what I like. She's a woman who gropes at what's around her, the same as me, astray but alive.

My talk is incoherent by comparison: I'm fifteen or sixteen years old, and it's not that Paredón is an outpost of hell but that I'm fifteen or sixteen and servitude consists in going round on the same axis. Of course I could have taken myself to the bus station, but I wouldn't have been able to pay the fare. I talk about Margit, and Margit's father, about the disquiet I feel in Paredón with its watery lethargy, the blank water that anchors you down. The woman is probably taken aback by so much decrepitude in a young girl. Or else she hasn't recovered from the most laughable request anyone ever made to her. "Take me with you." "Jeez, I'm not fucked, I'm crazy," she said when she gave me my ticket.

Next comes the red tape of the border, clearing customs, the loaded part of the trip. By the pitch of her voice, by the way her garment bulges right at the crotch, I can tell this woman is different from any I've seen before; the blouse and the leggings might be feminine, but not this mascara-blotched face where the shadow of incipient bristles pushes through. It's borne out by the wisecracks of the soldiers and he (or she?) doesn't retort, preferring to get the interrogation over with. "Where do you come from? What are you doing here? Who's this person travelling with you? Why are you dressed up as if you'd stolen every flower on earth?" To which he or she replies, "That's my name, as indicated on my passport, and I came over for a fancy-dress party, what's wrong with that? So if everything's perfectly clear and nobody has a problem, I don't feel like removing my outfit, I know, don't tell me, a frightful imitation of Madonna: a South American Madonna, there you go."

A few metres away from us a short, dark guard stands near a sack, wrestling with a dog that barks too fiercely for its bony frame. The sambo runs and opens the sack and stuffs the animal inside. He ties it shut, places it on the ground and the dog begins to growl. The rookies are ready with their clubs, they rain blows while the maddened bundle dances, bounces, howls. "Now what?" Glenda fumbles for her glasses in her bag. "Let's get on, they're about to send me back." I tug at her blouse. I guess the terror shows in my face but I'm in luck because the soldier nods me through without knowing I'm escaping illegally while he's beating the animal. "Chuck this bag," is the last we hear.

I asked the woman to take me to the bus station and now we're travelling together "down the map", as she said, and I picture a precipice. At first we talk a lot, until worn out by the twenty-hour exodus we stretch out our legs, or admire the outcrops of the landscape, me thinking that none of this makes sense, or perhaps it does, deep down, and the sense it makes is devastating, and I'm only nervous after all. A long journey, the pretext for the rub of her leg against mine, but all the energy too of the one who will be my first exploiter, his girlish titter envelops me already, like a threat.

The place at which we arrive is called La Ceiba, and it's in Honduras. A buzzing multitude. The din of engines and klaxons reaches us thickly deformed. My mother is behind me: she deserves it. She'll start missing me soon, with the chagrin of someone losing their accomplice in a mutual debacle. She'll have no one to dump her spite on any more.

This is the last time I ever perceive a place with such clarity: the tinned food in the kitchen, the noise of the cistern, steak and stewed quince when we get in, a rug with two bright hearts on it, Glenda plumping heavily down on the sofa, her anxious-tourist look replaced by that of the harried housewife. And later, Glenda (her birth and professional name is Genaro, which I find funny), her circle of friends, male crossbreeds stifled by the drudgery of computers and diskettes, the crackle of other people's lives snaking like tinsel through the pretence of a knees-up. Glenda and her house full of gushing objects. Glenda and her wardrobe where a carnival explodes. Glenda's wall and a clock eternally stopped on the dot of five o'clock. Lemons like a scatter of yellow drops in the basin. The coast, a very different one to mine. Photos on the walls and a long etcetera like the ebb and flow of waves making things advance or retreat, float or sink. I'm inside an aquarium that is strange to me. And Glenda meanwhile, eating fruit: "It must be super to have a scar to show off." Coolly: "Go on then, don't just stand there, fetch me some ice for me eye bags; redeem the home by making coffee in the midst of mayhem."

Maybe the images aren't really what happened. Maybe on that first night far from home, the decadent furniture of a stranger who was good enough to take me in conveyed a glimpse of what lay ahead. But the only thing that's indestructible is the beginning. When a beginning occurs in such a way, it's impossible to forget.

Translated by Lorna Scott Fox
From the novel *Por el lado salvaje*

WRITERS' BIOGRAPHIES

JUAN PABLO ANAYA (Mexico City, 1980) works as a teacher; he is a ufologist by conviction and writes both fiction and nonfiction. He is a doctoral student in philosophy at UNAM and holds an MA in philosophy and literature from the University of Warwick. He was an intern at the Mexican Literature Foundation in 2009. He has published essays, articles, interviews and reviews in publications such as Casa del tiempo, Culture Machine, and the Letras Libres blog among others. His first book, *Kant y los extraterrestres* (Tierra Adentro, 2012), won the José Vasconcelos National Youth Essay Award in 2012.

GERARDO ARANA (Querétaro, 1987–2012) graduated with a degree in modern literature at the Autonomous University of Querétaro. He was a scholar both at the Querétaro Institute of Culture and Arts in their Young Artists programme in 2009, and on the Young Writers Course at the Foundation for Mexican Literature that same year. He was the publishing director of Herring Publishers, Mexico, and the author of *La máquina de hacer pájaros* (Herring Publishers, 2008), *Neónidas* (Herring Publishers, 2009), *El whisky del Barbero Espadachín* (Urano, 2010) and *Bulgaria Mexicali* (Herring Publishers, 2011). In 2014, his novel *Meth Z* was posthumously published by the Tierra Adentro Publishing Fund.

NICOLÁS CABRAL (Córdoba, Argentina, 1975; living in México since 1976) is a novelist, essayist and editor, who studied architecture at the University of Guanajuato. Since 1998 he has been the editor-in-chief of the arts magazine *La Tempestad*. He has written for numerous publications in Mexico, Argentina and Spain. His work has been included in anthologies such as *Nuevas voces de la narrativa mexicana* (Joaquín Mortiz, 2003), *De lengua me como un cuento: Antología latinoamericana* (Axial, 2009), *La escritura poliédrica: Ensayos sobre* Daniel Sada (Tierra Adentro, 2012) and *Contraensayo: Antología de ensayo mexicano actual* (UNAM, 2012). He recently published his first novel, *Catálogo de formas* (Periférica, 2014).

VERÓNICA GERBER BICECCI (Mexico City, 1981) is a visual artist who writes; she makes visual pieces that are texts and texts that are visual pieces. She studied visual arts at La Esmeralda art school, before completing a master's in art history at the National Autonomous University of Mexico (UNAM) and has exhibited her work individually and collectively at the University Museum of Contemporary Art (MUAC) and in El Eco Experimental Museum, among others. She is an editor at the Tumbona Ediciones cooperative and has written for magazines such as *Letras Libres*, *Granta* and *Make*.

In 2010 she published an essay collection, *Mudanza* (Auieo), narrating the transformation of five writers into visual artists, and in 2013 she won the third Aura Estrada International Literature Prize. *Empty Set*, her first novel, will be published in 2015.

PERGENTINO JOSÉ (Oaxaca, 1981) completed a master's in Latin American literature at the Austral University of Chile. He has been a fellow of the Mexican National Fund for Culture and Arts (FONCA) (2005), and has won scholarships at the Oaxaca State Fund for Culture and the Arts (2008) and the Ford Foundation (2011–13). He is the author of *Y supe qué responder* (SEP, 2006), which was published bilingually in both Zapotec and Spanish. In 2011, he won the CASA Literature Prize for Zapotec language in their poetry category, with his book *Flor de zarzamora.*

Among his most recent publications are a short-story collection entitled *Hormigas rojas* (Almadía, 2012) and a book of poems, *Lenguaje de pájaros,* which was published trilingually in Zapotec, Spanish and English.

LAIA JUFRESA (Mexico City, 1983) was a fellow of the FONCA Young Artists programme and of the Mexican Literature Foundation. Her work is featured in magazines such as *Letras libres*, *McSweeney's* and *Words Without Borders*. She is the author of the short stories collection *El esquinista* (Tierra Adentro, 2014) and the novel *Umami* (Literatura Random House, 2015). *Umami* will also be published worldwide in English by Oneworld Publications.

LUIS FELIPE LOMELÍ (Etzatlán, 1975) is an engineer, ecologist and PhD in Science and Culture. His first book, *Todos santos de California* (Tusquets/CONACULTA-INBA, 2002) won the Instituto Nacional de Bellas Artes Literature Award. The short story 'El cielo de Neuquén', included in his second book, *Ella sigue de viaje* (Tusquets, 2005), won the Edmundo Valadés Latin American Story Award. He is also the author of textbooks and essays on ecology and in 2014 he published his latest novel: *Indio borrado* (Tusquets, 2014). He has lived in the United States, Spain, Austria, Colombia, Germany, Taiwan, and South Africa (as a writer-in-residence invited by Nadine Gordimer). He is considered to be the author of the shortest story in the Spanish language, which has been translated into more than a dozen languages: 'The Emigrant: –Forget something? –If only!'

BRENDA LOZANO (Mexico City, 1981) is a novelist and essayist whose work has appeared in several anthologies. She studied Latin

American literature and is a fellow of the FONCA Young Artist programme, and has had various writing residencies abroad. She edits the Spanish-language fiction in translation section of MAKE literary magazine. *Todo nada* (Tusquets, 2009) is her first novel—which is currently being adapted for the cinema—and *Cuaderno ideal* (Alfaguara, 2014) her second. She lives in New York and is studying at NYU.

VALERIA LUISELLI (Mexico City, 1983) is the author of the essay collection *Papeles falsos* (Sexto Piso, 2010), named as one of the best books of the year by the newspaper *Reforma*, as well as the novels *Los ingrávidos* (Sexto Piso, 2011) and *La historia de mis dientes* (Sexto Piso, 2013). She has lived in Costa Rica, Korea, South Africa, India, Spain and the United States, and has written for numerous publications, including *El País*, the *New Yorker*, *Reforma*, *Etiqueta Negra* and *Granta*. She has been a lyricist for the New York Ballet, and in 2014 she was selected by the National Book Foundation as one of their five most outstanding authors of the year under thirty-five for the English translation of her novel *Los ingrávidos* (entitled *Faces in the Crowd*).

FERNANDA MELCHOR (Veracruz, 1982) studied journalism at the University of Veracruz and art history at the University of Puebla. She has been awarded prizes for her short stories, essays and articles by Mexico's National Human Rights Commission (CNDH), UNAM and the Rubén Pabello Journalism Foundation, respectively. In 2013 she published a book of articles entitled *Aquí no es Miami* (Almadía) and a novel, *Falsa liebre* (Almadía).

EMILIANO MONGE (Mexico City, 1978) is the author of the short-story collection *Arrastrar esa sombra* (Sexto Piso, 2008) and the novels *Morirse de memoria* (Sexto Piso, 2010) and *El cielo árido* (Penguin

Random House, 2012). His first two books were shortlisted for the Antonin Artaud Prize, while the third won both the Jaen Novel Award as well as the fifth annual "Otras Voces, Otros Ámbitos" Prize. On two occasions he has been awarded a fellowship on the FONCA Young Artists programme, and he is currently a member of the Sistema Nacional de Creadores de Arte (SNCA). In 2011, he was selected by the Guadalajara International Book Fair as one of Latin America's twenty-five "best-kept secrets".

EDUARDO MONTAGNER (Puebla, 1975) is a linguist and writer. He writes in a variant of Venetian spoken since 1882 in the community of Chipilo, for which he has designed an alphabet and writing system. In 2009 he was a FONCA scholar. He won the third and second place in the Concorso Letterario Internazionale in Lingua Veneta 'Mario Donadoni' (Bovolone, Verona, 2005–2006). He is the author of *En la postura de mi muerte* (Ilunar/BUAP, 1998), *Parlar par véneto, víver a Mésico* (Conaculta, 2005), *Al prim* (Conaculta/Secretaría de Cultura de Puebla, 2006), *Toda esa gran verdad* (Alfaguara 2006/Punto de Lectura 2008) and *Ancora fon ora* (Conaculta/Secretaría de Cultura de Puebla, 2010)—a book written in Venetian that consists of a novel, eight stories and twelve poems. His texts have been included in the anthologies *Veneti nel mondo* (2005–2006) and in *Grandes Hits: Nueva generación de narradores mexicanos* (Almadía, 2008). He translated together with Giampiero Bucci the selected prose of Andrea Zanzotto in *El (necesario) mentir* (Vaso Roto Ediciones, 2011). His latest novel will be published in 2015 by Alfaguara.

ANTONIO ORTUÑO (Jalisco, 1976) is the author of *El buscador de cabezas* (2006), named by the newspaper *Reforma* as the best Mexican debut novel of the year, and *Recursos humanos* (Anagrama, 2007), for which he was shortlisted for the Herralde Novel Prize.

He has written two books of short stories, *El jardín japonés* (Páginas de Espuma, 2007) and *La señora Rojo* (Páginas de Espuma, 2010). His most recent novels are *Ánima* (Penguin Random House, 2011) and *La fila india* (Océano, 2013). His work has been translated into French, Romanian and Italian.

EDUARDO RABASA (Mexico City, 1978) studied political science at UNAM, where he graduated with a thesis on the concept of power in the works of George Orwell. He is the author of the novel *La suma de los ceros* (Sur+ Ediciones, 2014), and he writes a weekly column for the newspaper *Milenio*. He has translated authors such as Morris Berman, George Orwell and Somerset Maugham into Spanish, and he is one of the founding members of the publishing house Sexto Piso, where he works as an editor.

ANTONIO RAMOS REVILLAS (Nuevo León, 1977) studied Spanish literature at the Autonomous University of Nuevo León. He has been the recipient of various fellowships, including at FONCA and at the Foundation for Mexican Literature. For his stories and articles he has received several awards, such as the Julio Torri National Story Prize for Youth, and the Salvador Gallardo Dávalos National Story Prize, among others. He is the author of *Todos los días atrás* (Conarte, 2005), *Dejaré esta calle* (Tierra Adentro, 2006), *Sola no puedo* (ICA, 2008), *Habitaciones calladas* (Conarte, 2008), *El cantante de muertos* (Almadía, 2011), *El barco maya* (Ediciones B, 2012), among other titles. His work has been translated into English, French and Polish.

EDUARDO RUIZ SOSA (Sinaloa, 1983) is a writer, industrial engineer and doctor of history of science from the Autonomous University of Barcelona. In 2007 he won the Inés Arredondo National Literature Prize for his book of short stories *La voluntad de marcharse* (Tierra Adentro, 2008). His work has been included in various anthologies, including *La letra en la mirada* (Ayuntamiento de Culiacán, 2009) and *Emergencias, doce cuentos iberoamericanos* (Candaya, 2013). In 2012, he won the Han Nefkens Creative Writing Fellowship.

He is the co-founder of the digital magazine *La Junta de Carter* and he recently published the novel *Anatomía de la memoria* (Candaya, 2014).

DANIEL SALDAÑA PARÍS (Mexico City, 1984) is the author of the book of poems *La máquina autobiográfica* (Bonobos Editores, 2012) and of the novel *En medio de extrañas víctimas* (Sexto Piso, 2013). He has been a FONCA Young Artists Fellow (2006–2007) and Resident Artist (2012) as well as having a fellowship at the Foundation for Mexican Literature. In 2012 he edited and wrote the prologue for the anthology *Doce en punto: Poesía chilena reciente* and *Un nuevo modo: Antología de narrativa mexicana actual*, both published by UNAM.

XIMENA SÁNCHEZ ECHENIQUE (Mexico City, 1979) studied Spanish literature at UNAM, staying there to complete a master's in Latin American literature. She has written for magazines such as *La Experiencia Literaria* and *Luna Córnea*. Her first novel, *Sobre todas las cosas* (UAEM, 2004), won the Ignacio Manuel Altamirano International Fiction Prize in 2003. She is the author of *El ombligo del dragón* (Tusquets, 2007) and *Por cielo, mar y tierra* (Tusquets, 2010).

CARLOS MANUEL VELÁZQUEZ (Coahuila, 1978) is the author of the short-story collections *Cuco Sánchez Blues* (La Fragua, 2004), *La Biblia Vaquera* (Tierra Adentro, 2008; Sexto Piso, 2011), named by the newspaper *Reforma* as one of the best books of 2009, and *La marrana negra de la literatura rosa* (Sexto Piso, 2010), as well as a book of articles *El karma de vivir al norte* (Sexto Piso, 2013). He has been a fellow of the FONCA Young Artists programme, as well as a scholar at the Coahuila National Fund for Culture and the Arts.

NADIA VILLAFUERTE (Chiapas, 1978) is a writer and journalist. In 2003, she was a FONCA Young Artists Fellow and from 2006 to 2008 a scholar at the Foundation for Mexican Literature. She is the author of the short-story collections *Barcos en Houston* (Coneculta-Chiapas, 2005), *Presidente, por favor* (Edaf, 2006) and *¿Te gusta el látex, cielo?* (Tierra Adentro, 2008), and the novel *Por el lado salvaje* (Ediciones B, 2012).

TRANSLATORS' BIOGRAPHIES

CATHERINE MANSFIELD is an MA-qualified translator and communications professional currently living between Bogotá and London. Her published translations include *China's Silent Army* by Juan Pablo Cardenal and Heriberto Araújo (Penguin, 2013) and *A History of the World for Rebels and Somnambulists* by Jesús del Campo (Telegram, 2008). She is also co-founder of a small translation agency called ZigZag Translations.

JAMES WOMACK was born in Cambridge in 1979. He has translated several books from Spanish, including works by Silvina Ocampo and Roberto Arlt. He is currently working on the English version of Sergio del Molino's *La hora violeta.* He lives in Madrid with his family, where he helps run Ediciones Nevsky, a publishing house that produces Spanish translations of Russian literature.

OLLIE BROCK is a translator and literary journalist. His articles have appeared in *Revista de Libros*, the *Times Literary Supplement*, the *New Statesman*, *Time* magazine and *In Other Words*, the journal of the British Centre for Literary Translation. He has co-translated works by authors including Isabel Allende. He lives and works at the London Buddhist Centre, where he co-edits the *London Buddhist*, a new magazine.

LORENZA GARCIA was born and brought up in England. She spent her early twenties living and working in Iceland and Spain. She graduated in 1998 from Goldsmiths College with first-class honours in Spanish and Latin American studies, before moving to France for seven years. Since 2007, she has translated twenty novels and works of non-fiction from French and Spanish, and has recently begun translating from Icelandic. She lives in London.

THOMAS BUNSTEAD's Spanish translations have appeared in *Granta* and *Vice*, and include work by Aixa de la Cruz (the story 'True Milk' was selected for Dalkey Archive's Best of European Fiction 2015), Eduardo Halfon, Yuri Herrera and Enrique Vila-Matas. A co-editor for the *Words Without Borders* Mexico feature (March 2015), Thomas's own writing has appeared in the *Times Literary Supplement*, the *Paris Review* blog, the *Independent on Sunday*, www.3ammagazine.com, > *kill author* and *Days of Roses*.

SOPHIE HUGHES is a literary translator and editor living in Mexico City. Her translations and reviews have appeared in numerous publications, including the *White Review*, *Asymptote*, the *Times Literary Supplement* and *Literary Review*. In 2015 she co-guest-edited a feature on contemporary Mexican literature for *Words Without Borders*. Her translation of Iván Repila's novel *The Boy Who Stole Attila's Horse* is also published by Pushkin Press.

ANNA MILSOM is a British literary translator with a background in visual arts. Before moving to Ecuador in 2012, she taught translation studies at London Metropolitan University for seven years. She has delivered papers on translation and research at international conferences and contributed to *The SAGE Handbook of Digital Dissertations and Theses*. Anna's doctorate focused on new ways of translating Lydia Cabrera's Afro-Cuban folk tales, and she has co-translated novels by Evelio Rosero and Enrique Vila-Matas.

ROSALIND HARVEY's translation of Juan Pablo Villalobos's debut novel *Down the Rabbit Hole* was shortlisted for the Guardian First Book Award and the Oxford-Weidenfeld Prize. Her co-translation of Enrique Vila-Matas's *Dublinesque* was shortlisted for the Independent Foreign Fiction Prize and has been longlisted for the International IMPAC Dublin Literary Award. Her latest translation is Villalobos's *Quesadillas*, with And Other Stories and Farrar, Straus & Giroux.

CHRISTINA MACSWEENEY has an MA in literary translation from the University of East Anglia. Her translations of Valeria Luiselli's novel *Faces in the Crowd* and collection of essays *Sidewalks* were published by Granta (2012/2013) and Coffee House Press (2014). A second novel by the same author, *The Story of My Teeth*, is forthcoming in 2015. She also contributes to a wide variety of literary magazines and websites. In 2013, her translation of a collection of essays by the Paraguayan art critic Ticio Escobar, *The Invention of Distance*, was published in a bilingual edition by the AICA/Fausto.

Originally from Inverness, BETH FOWLER read Hispanic studies at the University of Glasgow. She became a freelance translator in 2009, working from Spanish and Portuguese to English. After winning the Harvill Secker Young Translators' Prize in 2010, she began to move her focus from commercial to literary translation. Her first novel translation, *Open Door* by Argentinean author Iosi Havilio, was published in 2011. She lives near Glasgow with her husband and son.

FRANK WYNNE is a literary translator from French and Spanish. His work has earned him three major prizes for his translations from the French: the 2002 IMPAC Prize (for *Atomised* by Michel

Houellebecq), and the 2005 Independent Foreign Fiction Prize and 2008 Scott Moncrieff Prize. He has translated a number of Spanish and Latin American authors, among them Tomás Eloy Martínez, Tomás González and Arturo Pérez-Reverte. He was awarded the Valle Inclán Prize in 2012 for his translation of Miguel Figueras's *Kamchatka* and again in 2014 for Alonso Cueto's *The Blue Hour.*

JUANA ADCOCK is a poet and translator working in English and Spanish. Her work has appeared in publications such as *Magma Poetry*, *Gutter*, *Glasgow Review of Books*, *Asymptote* and *Words Without Borders*. Her first book, *Manca*, explores the anatomy of violence in Mexico and was named by *Reforma*'s distinguished critic Sergio González Rodríguez as one of the best poetry books published in 2014.

LUCY GREAVES translates from Spanish, Portuguese and French. She won the 2013 Harvill Secker Young Translators' Prize and in 2014 was translator in residence at the Free Word Centre in London. She has translated two novels, Eliane Brum's *One Two* and Mamen Sánchez's *The Altogether Unexpected Disappearance of Atticus Craftsman*, and her work has been published by the magazines *Granta* and *Words Without Borders*, among others.

SAMANTHA SCHNEE is the founding editor of *Words Without Borders*, which has published over two thousand works of literature translated from over one hundred languages into English in the past decade. Her translation of Carmen Boullosa's *Texas: The Great Theft* was published by Deep Vellum last year and was one of BBC Worldwide's "Top Ten Books to Read in December".

AMANDA HOPKINSON is a translator of some thirty books from Spanish (Elena Poniatowska, Ricardo Piglia); Portuguese (José Saramago, Paulo Coelho); and French (Dominique Manotti). A former director of the British Centre for Literary Translation at the University of East Anglia, she is now visiting professor in literary translation at City University, London. She is a long-standing trustee of *Modern Poetry in Translation* magazine and of English PEN, the human-rights organization for authors and journalists, academics and students; in 2004, she founded the PEN Writers in Translation committee.

MARGARET JULL COSTA has been a literary translator for nearly thirty years and has translated novels and short stories by such writers as Eça de Queiroz, Fernando Pessoa, José Saramago, Javier Marías and Bernardo Atxaga. In 2013 she was invited to become a Fellow of the Royal Society of Literature, and in 2014 was awarded an OBE for services to literature.

DANIEL HAHN is a writer, editor and translator, with forty-something books to his name, whose work has won him the Independent Foreign Fiction Prize and the Blue Peter Book Award. He has recently finished translating an Angolan novel and compiling the new *Oxford Companion to Children's Literature.*

PETER BUSH's recent translations include Mercè Rodoreda's *In Diamond Square* and Josep Pla's *The Gray Notebook*, which was awarded the 2014 Ramon Llull Prize. His translation of Pla's *Life Embitters* will be published in spring 2015 and Joan Sales's *Uncertain Glory* appeared in October 2014. He has written widely on the art of literary translation and co-edited (with Susan Bassnett) *The Translator as Writer.*

NICK CAISTOR is a British translator from Spanish, Brazilian Portuguese and French. He worked for many years on Latin America for the BBC World Service, and more recently was writer in residence at the University of East Anglia for the Royal Literary Fund. He has been awarded the Valle Inclán Prize for Spanish translation on three occasions.

A journalist, translator and editor, LORNA SCOTT FOX translates from French and Spanish. Her latest published translation is *Teresa, My Love*, by Julia Kristeva. She has written for several periodicals in Mexico, Spain, the US and the UK, including *La Jornada*, *El País*, the *London Review of Books*, the *Times Literary Supplement* and the *Nation*.

Pushkin Press

Pushkin Press was founded in 1997, and publishes novels, essays, memoirs, children's books—everything from timeless classics to the urgent and contemporary.

Our books represent exciting, high-quality writing from around the world: we publish some of the twentieth century's most widely acclaimed, brilliant authors such as Stefan Zweig, Marcel Aymé, Antal Szerb, Paul Morand and Yasushi Inoue, as well as compelling and award-winning contemporary writers, including Andrés Neuman, Edith Pearlman and Ryu Murakami.

Pushkin Press publishes the world's best stories, to be read and read again. Here are just some of the titles from our long and varied list. For more amazing stories, visit www.pushkinpress.com.

═══

THE SPECTRE OF ALEXANDER WOLF

GAITO GAZDANOV

'A mesmerising work of literature' Antony Beevor

BINOCULAR VISION

EDITH PEARLMAN

'A genius of the short story' Mark Lawson, *Guardian*

TRAVELLER OF THE CENTURY

ANDRÉS NEUMAN

'A beautiful, accomplished novel: as ambitious as it is generous, as moving as it is smart' Juan Gabriel Vásquez, *Guardian*

BEWARE OF PITY

STEFAN ZWEIG

'Zweig's fictional masterpiece' *Guardian*

THE WORLD OF YESTERDAY

STEFAN ZWEIG

'*The World of Yesterday* is one of the greatest memoirs of the twentieth century, as perfect in its evocation of the world Zweig loved, as it is in its portrayal of how that world was destroyed' David Hare

JOURNEY BY MOONLIGHT

ANTAL SZERB

'Just divine... makes you imagine the author has had private access to your own soul' Nicholas Lezard, *Guardian*

BONITA AVENUE

PETER BUWALDA

'One wild ride: a swirling helix of a family saga... a new writer as toe-curling as early Roth, as roomy as Franzen and as caustic as Houellebecq' *Sunday Telegraph*

THE PARROTS

FILIPPO BOLOGNA

'A five-star satire on literary vanity... a wonderful, surprising novel' *Metro*

I WAS JACK MORTIMER

ALEXANDER LERNET-HOLENIA

'Terrific... a truly clever, rather wonderful book that both plays with and defies genre' Eileen Battersby, *Irish Times*

SONG FOR AN APPROACHING STORM

PETER FRÖBERG IDLING

'Beautifully evocative... a must-read novel' *Daily Mail*

THE RABBIT BACK LITERATURE SOCIETY

PASI ILMARI JÄÄSKELÄINEN

'Wonderfully knotty... a very grown-up fantasy masquerading as quirky fable. Unexpected, thrilling and absurd' *Sunday Telegraph*

RED LOVE: THE STORY OF AN EAST GERMAN FAMILY

MAXIM LEO

'Beautiful and supremely touching... an unbearably poignant description of a world that no longer exists' *Sunday Telegraph*